Blood Stains of a Shotta

Lock Down Publications and Ca$h
Presents

Blood Stains of a Shotta

A Novel by *Jamaica*

Lock Down Publications
P.O. Box 870494
Mesquite, Tx 75187

Lock Down Publications
Like our page on Facebook: Lock Down Publications @ www.facebook.com/lockdownpublications.ldp
Cover design and layout by: **Dynasty Cover Me**
Book interior design by: **Shawn Walker**
Edited by: **Sunny Giovanni**

Stay Connected with Us!

Text **LOCKDOWN** to 22828 to stay up-to-date with new releases, sneak peaks, contests and more...

Thank you!

Submission Guideline.

Submit the first three chapters of your completed manuscript to ldpsubmissions@gmail.com, subject line: Your book's title. The manuscript must be in a .doc file and sent as an attachment. Document should be in Times New Roman, double spaced and in size 12 font. Also, provide your synopsis and full contact information. If sending multiple submissions, they must each be in a separate email.

Have a story but no way to send it electronically? You can still submit to LDP/Ca$h Presents. Send in the first three chapters, written or typed, of your completed manuscript to:

LDP: Submissions Dept
Po Box 870494
Mesquite, Tx 75187

DO NOT send original manuscript. Must be a duplicate.

Provide your synopsis and a cover letter containing your full contact information.

Thanks for considering LDP and Ca$h Presents.

Chapter 1
ROCKET

I was leaned against the wall at Starlet's Gentlemen's club, with my dark shades over my eyes, surveying my surroundings. Pussy, ass and titties were popping all around. Niggas was stuntin' hard, making the feddi pour down on the strippers on stage, and at their private tables.

My nigga, Trap, was seated in a booth a few feet away from where I was posted up. Two thick bitches were draped all over him. One straddled his waist while her friend grinded her pussy against the back of his head. My nigga smiled and turned up a bottle of Patron.

Future thumped from the speakers and weed smoke filled the air. A shapely redbone had her ass pressed up against my dick, making her booty cheeks jiggle. Ma was working it, but I was paying her little attention. My eyes and my thoughts were on this one bitch ass nigga and his crew across the room. I had been watching him inconspicuously for the past couple of hours.

My trigger finger itched as I eyed Shep and his boys, balling out of control. It was as if he didn't know he was marked for death.

A year ago, I had fronted this cornball muthafucka two bricks to take down to VA and get his weight up. As soon as Shep got that work from me, it was like he fell off of the fuckin' map, yo. Son changed his cell phone number and stopped coming back Up Top to visit his peeps.

I had made a couple of trips to Richmond, Virginia looking for him, but he was nowhere to be found. Now, all of a sudden, he was back in Brooklyn, in my front yard, like he thought I wouldn't peel his cap for getting ghost with my shit.

The alcohol and the pussy had those niggas too fucked up to realize their worst nightmare was right here in their presence.

I turned my head toward Trap and made eye contact. He nodded at me, acknowledging that he was still on point.

In front of me, lil' mama was throwing that ass against me. She probably thought she was arousing the kid, but she wasn't. She was nothing but a prop, a way for me to blend into the atmosphere without being noticed. Because when it came to pussy, the only one who was ever on my mind was my woman— Island Gurl Jae.

Shorty stood up and turned to face me. “Did you like that, Papi?” she asked, wrapping her arms around my neck.

“Yea, I loved that shit, yo.” I gave her a couple of more big faces and continued to play along, but my eyes quickly locked back in on Shep and them.

“Thanks, Daddy. Now let me give you a reason to remember me.” She reached down her top and pulled out a package.

When I heard her rip it open, I glanced down to see what it was. To my surprise, it was a Magnum. Baby girl removed the condom and placed it in her mouth, and then she dropped the empty wrapper down the front of my shirt.

As she began to sink to her knees, I reached down and grabbed her arm, pulling her back up. “What you doing, yo?”

“About to suck this big ass dick.” She grabbed a handful of my wood.

“Nah, ma, that’s not happening. I’m good.”

She looked at me like she couldn’t believe I was refusing some head. But before she could say anything, I glanced up and saw Shep on the move. I figured he was leaving because he was dapping up his boys.

Without hesitation, I walked off from shorty and went over to where Trap sat. Son was up out of his seat and at my side in a matter of seconds.

“I’m about to blaze that nigga, B,” he said excitedly.

I put a calming hand on his elbow. “Don’t move too fast or you’ll draw attention to us. You can bet his boys are watching.”

“Fuck those pussies. I’ll bury all of ‘em!”

I felt the same way. Fuck ‘em all! But there was no need to get into a gunfight with all of them at the club when we could easily follow Shep and slump him without the extra drama.

“Be easy, yo,” I whispered tersely.

My adrenaline pumped fast and hot, but I didn't let it rush my steps. I eased back and let Trap walk alone. I would catch up with him outside.

Maintaining a comfortable distance behind my prey, I watched him leave out of the club with one of the strippers that had been entertaining him. I didn't let that muthafucka out of my sight.

I caught up to Trap as he climbed into his truck. Moving swiftly to the passenger side, I hopped in. "Tail that bitch nigga!" I pointed to the G-wagon Shep got into. He was pulling out of the lot. "As soon as I see the right opportunity, we're crushing him!"

"Say dat." Trap reached under the seat and pulled out a Fo-Fifth.

"Know dat." I grabbed my own joint from underneath my seat and slammed a bullet into the chamber.

Trap pulled out of the lot and followed Shep. About three miles from the club, he pulled into a gas station which, essentially, had just become his final resting place.

"Let's do it!" I said, pulling my hoodie down over my brow. My mans did the same.

No other words were necessary. We hopped out of the truck at the same time and moved in sync with each other's steps. In a half-dozen long strides, I was at the rear of Shep's whip. He was climbing out of the car when I reached the driver's door.

I raised my banger so it was leveled with his chest. With the other hand, I pulled my hoodie up just enough for him to get a clear look at my face.

Recognition registered in his eyes immediately and his hand shot to his waist.

"Too late, bitch ass nigga. I caught you slippin'." I squeezed the trigger and my toolie spat revenge, hot and lethal.

Boc! Boc! Boc! Boc! Boc! Boc!

His back slammed against the side of the car and his chest leaked. As he slid down to the ground, I lowered my banger and placed it right up against his forehead. His eyes had already begun to glaze over, but I didn't give a fuck. I owed him an ugly execution for trying me like I was soft.

"When you fuck with me," I exclaimed, "you're fuckin' with a certified beast!"

I squeezed the trigger once more and knocked the leaves out of his cabbage. Bits and pieces of his skull splattered up on my face before he crumpled down on his side.

On the other side of the car, Trap showed baby girl no mercy. I heard his gun roaring with deadly rapidity. *Boc! Boc! Boc! Boc!*

Her screams turned to gurgles as she started choking on her own blood.

My mans leaned inside of the car and blasted two shots to her head. *Boc! Boc!*

"No witnesses," he confirmed as we dashed back to our vehicle and mashed out.

***

Surprisingly, Jae was asleep when I got home. Usually, she was a nervous wreck until I walked through the door.

My baby must be tired, I thought as I walked into the bathroom, placed my gun on the counter and stripped out of my blood-soaked gear. I couldn't wait to tell her how we caught that clown slipping tonight.

After months of searching all over for Shep, catching up with him was much easier than I had anticipated.

I smiled as I stepped in the shower and adjusted the water as hot as I could stand it.

Tonight's events played back in my mind. I tried to think if we had slipped up anywhere and left behind any evidence that would connect us to the murders.

I had lowered my hoodie a bit, so he would see my face just before I sent him to his grave. But just for a fraction of a second, and the only other witness, besides Trap, was left dead with Shep.

There was nothing to worry about. And I felt no remorse over what we did to the stripper chick, either. Somebody should've taught her that when she fucked with grimy niggas, she exposed herself to whatever beef came their way.

It was much too late for her to realize it now, but maybe a few of the other girls at the club would learn from her death.

As for Shep's boys, they were most likely still at the strip club, popping bottles and pushing up on big booty bitches. Whenever they got the news that their man was dead, they would probably conclude that he had died by my hands. It would be a cold lesson that they could be touched at anytime and anyplace, as well.

If they didn't know it before, they'll surely know it now—I'm not playing no bitch ass games. If y'all niggas wanna avenge ya' man's death, step to me and get wet the fuck up!

As I lathered up and rinsed the soap suds off of my body, I thought I heard my baby moving around in the bedroom. I hoped she would come join me in the shower and give a nigga some of that shit that always made me sleep with my thumb in my mouth. It would be the perfect nightcap after putting another nigga in the dirt. Best believe Shep wasn't the first fool I had sent to Jesus, and I doubted he would be the last.

Chapter 2
JAE

The sound of the shower running awakened me out of my sleep. As soon as my eyes opened, I sat up and inhaled my man's natural fragrance, which was faintly in the air.

"Ummmm." I licked my lips. I was so glad he was home because I wanted his touch badly, tonight.

My pum pum jumped at the thought of him spreading my thighs and feasting on my sweet cookie, not to mention the way he could command my body when he entered me and thrust deep inside.

Anxious to see Rocket's face, after a day of nothing but back and forth texts, I swung my feet over the edge of the bed and went into the bathroom, wearing nothing but a smile.

"Hey, babi," I spoke to his silhouette.

"Hey, beautiful. Why don't you join me?" he asked in a deep tone that caused my nipples to tingle.

"I might do that." I teased while bending down to pick up the clothes he had left strewn on the floor.

"You might?"

"Yuh 'eard mi, babi." I giggled, 'cause he loved when I talked in Patwha to him.

"Girl, don't play with me. Bring that ass in the shower, so I can make that pum pum purr."

"Ohhhh! I like when you boss me around." I was wide awake now.

I did a little happy dance, and then, as I tossed Rocket's dirty clothes in the hamper, a small wrapper fell out of his shirt. I bent down to see what it was and my breath got caught in my chest.

I felt my eyes water as I picked up the object to make sure my eyes weren't playing tricks on me. *Lowdown muthafucka!* My hair felt like it had caught on fire.

"Damn, baby, what's taking you so long?" he called out.

"Uh, don't worri pussyclath, I'm on my way!" I stormed over to the shower and snatched the curtain completely off of the rod.

"Yuh a give bun now, my youth?" I was heated, and when I got mad, my Jamaican accent would fly out.

"What?"

My accent was so heavy and fast, I knew he didn't understand a word, so I repeated that shit in English for his no-good ass. "You creeping now, nigga?"

"What?"

"You 'eard me!" I swung hard and landed a fist in his face.

"What the fuck, yo?" He took a step back, away from my flailing arms, but I refused to let him get away. After all of the shit I had been through with him, how could he cheat on me?

My heart was shattered.

"You fucked another bitch? Huh? Is that how you're doing it now?" I swung at his face with both fists. My hair was getting wet but I did not care. I kept on punching his deceitful ass. One of my punches landed squarely in his mouth and busted his lip. "I'm going to teach you that I'm not that bitch! I'll fuck you up, Rocket! I'm a loyal bitch, you don't do me like that!"

"Jae, what the fuck are you talking about?" He pinned my arms to my sides and pushed me out of the shower.

"Get the fuck off of me! You know what I'm talking about!" Hot, angry tears poured from my eyes as I struggled to break free of the stronghold he had on my arms.

All of that shit he talked about loyalty was nothing but noise. In the end, Rocket had turned out to be the very type of person he claimed to despise. The realization of that made me mad enough to spit in his face. It was only my respect for his gangsta that stopped me from doing it.

As if he could read my thoughts, Rocket looked at me and shook his head. "I'm gonna let you go. But if you hit me again, I'ma knock you on your ass." He released my arms and stood there like his threat meant something.

Fuck that shit! I'm not no punk bitch. You got me fucked up.

Whap!

I slapped the dog shit out of him.

"Did you put that bitch you fucked tonight on her ass? Huh, pussyhole!" I reached out to shove him on the chest and ran right into his lightning fast hand.

Whack!

The next thing I knew, I was on the floor and my ears were ringing. Out of the corner of my eye, I spotted Rocket's gun on the sink's counter. *This nigga is about to meet his maker tonight*, I said to myself, as I pounced up on my feet.

Chapter 3
ROCKET

"Why you make me do that shit, yo?" I ran my hand down my face and let out a long sigh. "Fa real, ma, you're bugging." My voice was heavy with regret.

Jae got up off of the floor and looked at me with murder in her eyes. "Yuh hit me. You fuckin' hit me!" Tears ran down her beautiful face.

"I'm sorry, baby. But you left a nigga no choice. You know I never, ever, wanted to put my hands on you, other than to love you." The sound of sincere pain echoed from my voice.

Fuck is wrong with me? I should've just let her punch me until her arms got tired. Yea, she busted my lip but that shit didn't really hurt. Not as bad as what I was feeling now.

You're a bastard for dat! I cussed myself. Jae had been nothin' but one hundred with me from Day 1. My rider when the car didn't have no wheels. I didn't know why she was accusing me of creeping—something I would never do to her— but still, I never should've hit her, regardless.

I looked up as she brushed by me and walked over to the sink. A moment later, when she turned around, she had my strap in her hand.

"Get yourself right with God, Rocket, and do that shit fast. Because you're about to dwell in His house." She leveled the gun at my eyes.

A nigga didn't blink, even though I knew baby girl had no qualms about pulling the trigger. "You gon' kill me over something that didn't happen?" I asked calmly.

"Save em bloodclath lies. Yuh a guh bring a dutty dick home and then got the fuckin' nerve to put your hands on me? I'll send you up out this bitch in a body bag," she threatened.

Although there was fire in her eyes, I knew it didn't outweigh the love she had in her heart for me. And the fact that she was talking, and not squeezing the trigger, was proof that she didn't really want to body me.

"Jae, put the strap down," I said softly.

"Fuck you, Rocket! Yuh a dead dog! Fi mi pum pum nuh enough?"

Her words had the impact of hot slugs to the chest. I literally felt my knees weaken. I stiffened my legs and scowled. "You keep saying that foul shit but you haven't told me what the fuck I did."

"You know what you did!" *Boc!* A bullet whizzed past my ear and struck the wall behind me. "You fucked one of those hoes in the streets."

"Man, you're bugging!" I hadn't fucked nobody but her since the day we hooked up.

"I'm bugging, huh? No, muthafucka, you're lying! I found this shit in your shirt!" She slung something at me with force. It hit me in the face and fell to the floor. "Explain that, Rocket!"

When I looked down and saw what it was, all I could do was chuckle. It was the empty condom wrapper that stripper bitch had dropped down my shirt. Somehow, it had managed to remain there through murder and everything else.

"Ain't that a bitch!" I was astonished.

"Ain't it, though. You're busted, nigga. Now I'm about to bust something in you." Jae adjusted her aim, lowering the gun down to my limp dick. "The next time that bitch see your shit, it's going to be a nub!"

"Hold up, baby! I can explain that shit, easily. I mean, I know how it looks, yo, but that's not what it is." I ran things down to Jae just like they happened. When I finished recounting the story, I grabbed my clothes out of the hamper and showed her Shep's blood stains all over my pants and shirt.

"You could've fucked somebody afterwards," she said.

"But deep in your heart you know I wouldn't do you like that, don't you?"

"I don't know, Rocket. I want to believe you but…" Jae started crying harder.

I gently slid the gun from her hand and lifted her chin so our eyes were locked onto each other's. "Baby, I would die before I would give another bitch what's yours." I placed the gun to my temple. "Tell me you don't believe me. Just say those words to me and I'll take my own life. I'm dead ass, yo. Because if you don't trust me, we don't have nothin'. And if we don't have nothin'," I paused, "fuck everything else."

I kept the gun pressed against the side of my head as I waited for her response. I wasn't bluffing. If I had lost my baby's trust, nothing else mattered, not even living.

Jae reached up and wiped away the single tear that ran down my face. "I believe you, babi. I should've known you wouldn't do me like that. Will you please forgive me?" She looked up at me with puppy dog eyes that were full of tears.

I lowered my arm and sat the banger back on the counter, and then I pulled Jae into a strong embrace and covered her mouth with mine. Her lips parted and our tongues met in a hungry encounter. I sucked on her tongue as I backed her up against the wall and guided her hand down to my hardening wood.

"You see how rocked up I am?" I whispered in her ear.

"Yessss!" she moaned.

"This muthafucka is for you, only."

"Make me know it." Her voice was laced with passion.

I kissed her neck and backed her into the bedroom while my hands explored her body, stopping at the center of her heat. I gently spread her folds and let my fingers squish in her wetness. Jae stroked my steel up and down and begged me to put it inside of her.

"Hell no! You were going to shoot me." My thumb circled her clit, bringing it out of its hood.

"I thought you had creeped."

"But you should've known better." I slid two fingers inside of her dripping, wet pussy and moved them in and out.

"Rocket, I'm sorry." Her hips moved in a circular motion and her breathing felt hot against my neck. "Please, put it in, baby. I need to feel you."

"Do you?" I reached down and rubbed the tip of my steel up and down her slippery slit.

"I do, Daddy," she cried.

“Promise me you’ll never question my faithfulness again.”

“I promise. Never.”

“Now beg me to fuck you.” I guided the head of my dick inside of her just a bit.

Jae hugged me tighter and tried to pull me all the way inside, but I pulled back. “Rocket, please fuck me! Please, babi, mi a beg yuh. Give me my dick. A bitch is going crazy.”

Hearing her plead for me to fuck her made my dick swell to full size. I pushed my hips forward and felt her inner muscles grip me. Still keeping her back pressed against the wall, I lifted one of her legs and wrapped it around my waist while I plowed in and out of her pussy, vigorously.

“Take this dick! Take it all.” I banged her brutally.

“Oooh yesss! Fuck me hard, Daddy! Beat it up!” Jae moaned.

I gripped her ass with both hands and slammed all of my dick into her gooey walls. Her pussy was so wet, her juices splashed all over my lower body. She dug her nails into my back and bit down on my shoulder to stifle her loud cries as I punished that pussy so good.

“You like this?” I breathed heavily.

“Yes.” Her breathing matched mine.

“Tell me how much you like it.”

“I love it, Daddy!”

“You want me to make that pussy cum?”

“Oh yes, Daddy. Make it cum.” Jae grinded harder against me. “Oooh wee! Give it to me, babi. Don’t stop! Don’t stop, nigga!”

“I ain’t gon’ stop. Fuck this dick back.” I lifted her up and placed her ass on the counter. “I’m about to tear this pussy up. Open your legs wide. Let me get up in your stomach.”

Baby girl followed my command, and before long, I was all up in her guts. She screamed my name and I growled out hers just as we exploded together.

Chapter 4
JAE

I slept like a newborn baby in my man's arms, and in the morning, at the crack of dawn, I slipped out of bed, showered and then rewarded him with breakfast in bed.

Once Rocket's belly was full, he fell back to sleep while I gathered up the clothes he'd worn last night and took them outside in the back and burned them. One thing for certain, I always had his back.

I didn't let Rocket sleep for long because we had to make a business run to Newark.

Later that evening, we returned home with a backpack full of money. I put the money away in the stash spot while Rocket made calls, checking on his drug spots.

"Is everything good, babi?" I asked when he was done with his last call.

"Yea, business is pumping but I just got off of the line with Ro, and I don't like what I'm hearing in that nigga's voice."

Ro was Rocket's brother. A couple of weeks ago, him and his bitch, Red, had gotten knocked with a brick in the trunk of their car while making a run to Queens. Rocket was heated because the rollers never would have found the drugs when they pulled Ro over if his dumb ass would've put the brick in the hidden compartment.

"Fuck he think I paid to have that shit built for? I warned him over and over again not to get careless!" Rocket steamed at the time.

Although he was mad as fuck, Rocket made sure his brother and Red were out of jail as soon as their bails were set. That's one of the many things I loved about him. He always took care of his people.

After posting their bail, Rocket gave them $10,000 apiece and told them to lay low for a while in case the feds were watching them.

Now, from the tone of Rocket's voice, it sounded like his brother was considering the unthinkable. I just hoped Ricardo, which was Ro's real name, wasn't talking real stupid.

"What is that nigga talking about; running or something?" I asked. I was praying it was that, as opposed to the ultimate betrayal. But when Rocket didn't respond I began to worry.

***

Standing in our living room, a half hour later, Ro confirmed my suspicions. "Man, those crackers are going to try to give me and my girl football numbers if we take this shit to trial," he whined like a bitch.

"You're not going to trial. Our lawyers will work out a plea agreement. He told me you'll probably do a dime. Red?" Rocket looked at Ro's lady who was seated beside him on the sofa. "You'll probably be out in seven or eight years."

Red started rubbing her hands together nervously. Something told me to burn that bitch right then, but I waited to follow Rocket's lead.

"Sup, yo? You taking the plea or not?" he asked Ro.

"A dime? Damn, why so long? This is my first case. I know niggas who been knocked two and three times, and they didn't serve ten goddam years." He was huffing and puffing like Rocket was to blame for his situation.

Because I knew my man, I was sure he was seeing exactly what I saw, but he remained calm. "This is part of the game. With the money comes the consequences. Sometimes you win, sometimes you lose. But you never fold." His eyes searched Ro's face and then Red's, and mine did the same.

Red was near tears. I studied her face to see if her tears indicated a level of weakness that could not be chanced.

Rocket seemed concerned about both of their thoroughness. Otherwise, he wouldn't have felt the need to school them on things they should've already known.

"You don't get to choose which part of the game you fuck with. You're either all the way in or all the way out. And when you get knocked, you do your time," he went on.

"That's easy for you to say. You're not the one facing the time," Ro said.

I saw Rocket's face ball up. "Nigga, you bitching about a lil' punk ass ten joints?"

"It ain't just about that. It's about my girl. I'm not trying to see her locked up," said Ro.

"Fuck is you saying, yo! Red been eating off of the same plate as all of us. She gotta face the music like everybody else that gets popped."

"What if it was Jae? Would you be singing this same song?"

I couldn't hold my tongue a moment longer. "He wouldn't have to sing it because I would sing it for him. It's a hundred or nothing with a bitch like me. Burn that shit in your memory," I cut in.

"Son, I can't believe you're standing here talking reckless like this! You know the code. Snitching is never an option." Rocket turned from Ro and looked at me. "Loyalty over everything, even love and family!"

"In that muthafuckin' order!" I seconded his statement. Only a maggot ass bitch would expect her man to turn rat in order to save her from doing a bid.

Ro stood up from the sofa and begun pacing the floor. After a minute or so, he stopped in the middle of the living room and shoved his hands down in his pockets. "Yo, son, I hear that slick shit you're talking, but it ain't like I'ma give you up. We can give them Cuba. Fuck that nigga. We don't owe him shit!"

Me and Rocket rose out of our chairs at the same time. I grabbed my bag off of the table and reached inside of it for my heat. Rocket damn near knocked the table over as he stepped to his brother. Face to face, Rocket stood three inches taller but Ro outweighed him by at least 40 pounds. But there was no doubt which one of them was the baddest.

"Nigga, how the fuck you gonna stand here and tell me you about to turn rat and think I'm supposed to be cool with it!" Rocket was breathing flames.

"You don't have to be cool with it. I'm telling you 'cause you my blood!"

"Ya' blood?" Rocket snatched his .45 from his waist and pointed at his Ro's heart. "Nigga, we share half of a bloodline, and even that don't give you a pass to snitch!"

"We have different fathers, bitch! Same mother, same blood. Family over everything!" Ro tried to push the gun away from his chest, but the grip that Rocket had on the .45 was like a vise.

They wrestled over the banger for a few seconds. I kept one eye on the men and the other on Red as I pulled my gun out and got it ready to spit.

If that fool knew what's best for him, he'd better back down, I thought as I positioned myself to blow a hole in the back of Ro's head if he managed to take the gun from my man.

Just as I raised my arm, leveling my 9-millimeter, Rocket wrestled the gun from his brother's grip and shoved it under his chin. "Nigga, I ought to murk you right here!" Sweat dripped from his brow and his breath was heavy.

"Do what you do! If you got more love for your plug than you got for your fam, go ahead and squeeze," said Ro.

I was stunned when I didn't hear Rocket's tool clap. Normally, a nigga talking shit when my man had that hammer cocked turned into breaking news on local TV.

Seeing his brother's hesitation, Ro stepped back, turned around and headed for the front door. Rocket still had the weapon pointed at his back but I knew my dondada better than anyone. He would never pull the trigger if it wasn't face to face.

Red pounced up from the couch, scurried past us and followed Ro out of the door. As soon as it closed behind her, I looked at Rocket.

"I should've smashed him and his fat bitch." He shook his head from side to side in disbelief.

"We a guh ride pon deh bloodclath informa are not!"

"You know we are! The only reason I didn't kill that nigga tonight is because I don't know if he's already cooperating. He could've been wired and the po's could've been outside listening on a radio. Fuck! I might've said too much already." He walked over to the window and parted the blinds.

I joined him and together we looked up and down the block. Nothing seemed out of order. When no one bum rushed our house screaming "You're under arrest," we concluded that the rat hadn't flipped, yet. Still, he had to die. Blood or not, Rocket would never spare a snitch.

Chapter 5
RO

As me and my girl sped away from Rocket's house, I knew that even if I changed my mind about snitching, he would never trust me again. So, really, it was time to do what I had to do.

The seed had been planted in my mind the day I got arrested. One of the Narcs that interviewed me said, "Your plug is your get out of jail free card. If you want to save you and your lady, that's your ticket."

He gave me his card to contact him if I decided to cooperate. I had it at home, tucked inside a pair of sneakers. As soon as I made a few moves with the money I had stashed, I was going to give him a call. In the meantime, I would have to outrun Rocket because I knew he was coming for me, sooner than later.

Me and Red got a room at a Best Western motel in the Bronx. I figured Rocket wouldn't expect us to hide out there since I had beef with a couple of kids in the Boogie Down. The beef was minor, though, and it wasn't like we would be walking up and down the streets of Brownsville in broad daylight.

"You're going to have to stay in the room when I step out to handle business. Don't leave out for nothing, and if you see any suspicious cars in the lot, call 911. You already know how Rocket do it. He's going to have every shooter on his team gunning for us. And don't underestimate his bitch." I cautioned Red.

"Baby, are we going to have to go in the Witness Protection program?" Red's voice quivered.

I turned around from the mirror, where I was cutting off my braids with a pair of scissors I had bought from a store a couple of blocks away. Hearing the fear in her voice almost caused me to rethink my decision. I walked over and sat down on the bed beside her and wrapped my arms around her shoulders.

"We're not going in Witness Protection. Once I do what I gotta do, they're gonna snatch Rocket up. With him gone from the streets, Trap and the others will be running around without a clue. But if any of them come at us, I'ma make 'em regret it."

"Baby, I'm scared," she whimpered.

My compassion quickly turned to agitation. "Well, what do you want to do? Would you rather go to prison? You ready to leave your kids out here without their mother?" *Bitch, I'm doing this for you.*

"No, baby, I don't want to go to prison. I'm sorry," she apologized.

"A'ight. Now wipe those tears. Everything will be fine, yo. Like everything else we have faced: This too shall pass."

We had been through mad drama in the five years we'd been together. Everything from infidelities on both of our parts, to struggling to make ends meet when Rocket stopped fucking with me a while back because I had fucked up some product. The truth was I had tried to do that nigga dirty back then. I had put a jack boy named Knight on that ass but somehow, he had ended up floating in the Hudson River before he got the chance to rob Rocket.

To this day, I believed that Rocket had killed Knight but he couldn't know that I had been trying to set him up; otherwise, he would not have fucked with me again. But sometimes I found myself wondering if he had allowed me back on the team just to keep his enemies close. One of his favorite sayings was, "Niggas aren't too quick to bite the hand that feed them, but they won't hesitate to bite the hand that stops."

Well, this time I wasn't going to bite his hand. I was gonna bite off his whole muthafuckin' head since he was more concerned about his plug and a goddam street code than he was about his own blood.

Fuck letting mine go to prison. I held Red in a reassuring embrace. When her body stopped trembling, I got up and finished chopping off my braids. Tomorrow I would go get a fresh cut. But right now, I had to venture out in the streets and collect a few debts.

By the time I made it back to the room, it was past midnight. Red was up waiting for me. As soon as I stepped through the door, she ran into my arms and squeezed me tight.

"Ro, I was so worried," she said.

"About what? I told you everything is going to be okay." I tossed a bag of money on the dresser and then handed her a bag of Yo Burgers I had picked up on the way back.

Although she hadn't eaten all day, Red didn't really have an appetite. She ate only a quarter of one burger and a few fries. My appetite, on the other hand, was ferocious. I wolfed down three burgers, two orders of fries and drank two Michelob's.

When we went to bed, my sexual appetite was just as turned up. Red no longer had the flawless body she possessed when we first got together, but she was still thick and her pussy was just as good as it had always been.

I pulled her on top of me and positioned her on my dick, then slowly guided her down.

"Yes, baby, this is what I need," she moaned.

As she began to ride me, our worries became secondary. Red moved up and down my pole with familiarity. I grabbed a hold of her bodacious ass and slammed upwards, meeting her desire with equal intensity.

As the fever in our bodies rose, we started fucking violently. We both peaked at the same time, and as we nutted together, Rocket and all the other shit that was going on seemed to be the furthest thought from either of our minds.

***

Everything would've been good if we could've fucked twenty-four hours a day and I never had to leave the room. But I did.

Two nights in a row, I chanced returning to Brooklyn to collect money niggas owed me. On the third night, I had this eerie feeling in the pit of my stomach that I should just count my blessings and not show my mug in the BK again until I had contacted the Narc and Rocket was locked up.

But greed was a demanding bitch. A nigga still owed me fifteen bands, and I wanted that. I hit him up and he told me to come by his girl's house in Crown Heights, and she would have my dough.

I tried to get him to meet me somewhere else because Crown Heights was Rocket's stomping grounds, but he said, "I can't do that. I'm on my way to Connecticut. I left your loot with Shawna. All you gotta do is swing by there and grab it."

I didn't hear any larceny in his voice, and as far as I knew, he didn't have a clue what was brewing between me and my brother, so I decided to roll with it.

"A'ight, let her know I'ma fall through," I agreed.

I was greedy but I wasn't a fool. Because I was out on bond I couldn't afford to catch another charge, so I wasn't strapped. Therefore, I took other precautions to protect myself. Before pulling up to Shawna's crib I circled the block several times to make sure everything was on the level.

Satisfied with what I had seen, I parked and went to her apartment. She invited me inside but I chose to wait outside the door while she went to get the money. With every passing second, my heart drummed in my chest. I was expecting Rocket or Trap to pop out of the shadows and start busting at me. But my worries were for naught. Shawna returned and handed me a Foot Locker bag.

"Thanks." I was out before she could respond.

As I left Crown Heights, a car began following me. I told myself I was being paranoid, but after a couple of impromptu turns the vehicle was still behind me.

It's Rocket! I could feel it in my gut.

I pushed the pedal to the metal, but no matter how fast and reckless I drove, I couldn't shake that muthafucka. I knew my gas tank was close to empty. All day, I had been meaning to stop and get some gas. *Now your procrastination is going to get you killed!* I scolded myself.

I wanted to blow my own brains out for not carrying a banger. With the shit I was involved in, it would've been better to get caught with it than without it. Shit! I couldn't outrun Rocket, so I decided to lead his ass to the police station. Right now, it was the safest place for me to go.

I stayed low as I steered my car around other vehicles. If my crazy ass brother started popping at me, I didn't want to catch a bullet in the back of my head.

As the thought passed through my mind, the car pulled even with me. "Die, bitch muthafucka!" Rocket leaned halfway out of the passenger door and started dumping at me.

Boc! Boc! Boc! Boc! Boc!

His tool coughed angrily. I couldn't see who was driving but I guessed it was either Trap or that crazy ass Jamaican bitch Jae. Not that it mattered, my problem was Rocket.

I swerved left to right, trying to duck the gunfire that pelted the side of my ride.

Boc! Boc!

My back window exploded. Air gushed inside, making it feel like I was trapped in a whirlwind.

Boc! Boc! Boc!

His gun continued to spit lead at me. I wished like fuck I had my hammer. I would've been busting back at their asses. Fuck going out without a fight.

God had to be with me, though, because I knew that by now my car was running on fumes. As I zoomed down Empire Boulevard, the car began slowing down on its own, putt-putting and all that shit.

Please, just let me make it another half mile, I prayed. The 71st Precinct was just up the street.

My blessings ran out right in front of the police precinct. "Shit!" I pounded my hands on the steering wheel. I wanted to bail out of the car and run for the door, but Rocket skidded up beside me.

I caught a quick glimpse of his face before I sunk lower in my seat. Facing him without a gun was the last thing I wanted to do. I knew first-hand how beastly he was. And when he was mad, he took being savage to a whole other level.

I had clapped a few niggas myself, but every killer ain't equal. Some niggas committed murder and then there were those, like my brother, who were pure murderers.

As I remained slumped down behind the wheel of my car, I told myself even Rocket wasn't fearless enough to murk me right in front of the police station. But I had underestimated his level of crazy.

Boc!

The gunshot rang my ears and the side window of my Lexus shattered.

"Fuck!" I sunk to the floor and scrambled over to the passenger side.

The next boom I heard was his deep voice. "Loyalty over blood!" He belted, standing right outside my car.

Suddenly the driver's door was snatched open and Rocket leaned inside.

"Don't kill me, man!" I pleaded.

His response came in another burst of gunshots.

Boc! Boc! Boc!

I felt a ball of fire rip through my side. The second and third bullets caught me in the shoulder and the face. Blood filled my mouth and my lungs, and tears filled my eyes as I felt myself drifting to the eternal other side.

My eyes blinked open and shut. And then a bright light shined in the car. I thought I had died until I heard the unmistakable sound of cops' voices. That's when I realized the bright light wasn't God, it was the beam of flashlights.

"Sir, don't try to move. We'll get you to a hospital soon."

Mere seconds later, I was being lifted out of my car and placed in the back of an ambulance.

"If I die, my brother, Rocket, shot me. His real name is Draymond Wallace," I managed to get out just before I lost consciousness.

Chapter 6
ROCKET

It was early Saturday morning and my cell phone was going berserk with calls. Finally, Jae couldn't take hearing it vibrate anymore. "A wi de bloodclath!" She rolled over and snatched it off of the table by the bed. "Hello?" She turned on the bedside lamp.

Even before she rolled her eyes and held the phone out to me, I knew it was my mother on the other end. Her voice boomed out of the phone and every other word was a cuss word.

"Give Rocket's black ass this goddam phone, right now!" I heard her hollering.

I put the phone on speaker. There were no secrets between me and my woman. "Yea, Ma, what's up? It's five o'clock in the morning."

"I don't give a fuck if it's five o'clock in Hell! Have you lost your fuckin' mind, Negro?"

"Ma, what are you talking about?" I played dumb.

"Muthafucka, you know what I'm talking about! You tried to kill Ricardo!"

"Oh, that pussy ass nigga didn't die?" I spoke boldly.

"You heartless bastard!" she hissed.

"Thank you." My sarcasm was thick.

"Rocket, that's your brother." She broke down crying but her tears had no effect on me. If she was waiting for me to apologize, she would grow old and gray wherever she was calling from.

"That nigga ain't my brother. I disown him, and he knows why."

"What? Did you say you disown him?" Her voice was so loud I had to move the phone away from my ear.

"Yea, Ma, that's what I said. I could never share the same blood with a stinking rat," I said with distaste.

Ro had come out of a different nigga's nut sacks than me. My pop was as official as could be. His daddy had to be cruddy because that bitch shit that ran through Ro's veins didn't run through mine.

Mom Duke was going off. I was only half listening because unless she was about to tell me Ro had just died, I didn't care to hear nothin' else that came out of her mouth.

"I hate you!" she screamed. "I should've killed your lowdown ass when you was a baby."

"Whateva yo." I had heard it all before. I already knew she despised me. There was no love lost between me and that woman.

"If Ricardo is dead to you, then you're dead to me! And if he don't pull through, you better watch your back. Because I'll spend every dime I have to pay a muthafucka to kill your ass!"

"Ma, you should know I don't take kindly to threats."

"Fuck you!" She hung up the phone.

Me and Jae looked at each other. Sadness shone in her eyes. She hated the way my relationship was with my mother, but I was very used to it.

"Don't let that shit bother you, baby girl. I peeped game at an early age," I told Jae. "Let me tell you how that bitch used to do it." I laid back with my hands folded behind my head and recounted one of many incidents from my childhood.

She had told both of us not to leave the house that day, but we snuck out anyway. When we returned, she was standing in the doorway with a belt in her hand.

"We're about to get our asses tore up," I said as we stopped ten feet from the door, shivering with fear.

"Bring y'all hardheaded asses in this house!" Mama yelled. "If you're brave enough to leave out when I tell you not to, be brave enough to wear this belt!" She flicked her wrist and made the leather belt crack like a whip.

"You go first." Ro nudged me forward.

Although I was only 9 years old, the hood had already taught me to man up and deal with whatever came my way. I stiffened my back and headed toward Mama. She stepped aside for me to pass by, and then she whirled around and lashed me across the back with fury.

Whack!

I felt a welt instantly rise up on my skin.

Whack! Whack!

My back was on fire but I didn't run or holler. I stood there, gritting my teeth and enduring the hot, sizzling pain while she commenced to beat me like a slave.

I forced tears out of my eyes or else she would've beaten me to death. Seeing me cry seemed to calm her rage. She let the hand that gripped the belt fall to her side. With her other hand, she slapped me across the face.

Whap!

"Now, go to your room and don't come out!" she ordered.

Inside my bedroom, I sat on the floor with my arms wrapped around my knees. Now, I let the tears flow freely. They ran down my face, into my mouth, as I listened for a sound that never came—Ro's cries.

"That bitch didn't even whoop him! Didn't yell at him or nothing?" I should've known way back then that she favored him over me.

"Yuh nuh badda worri bout dem, dem a gud get fi dem. Know dat!" She wanted me not to worry about what they had done to me, 'cause they would get that back in return.

"Facts," I said as I sat up and kissed away tears that spilled from her eyes.

The tenderness I showed my girl was in stark contrast to what I had planned for that bitch who gave birth to me and her snitching ass son if he survived.

Chapter 7
ROCKET

I knew for certain Ro's weak ass had told the po's who shot him, because the last thing he would wanna do if he lived was face my gun again. So, me and Jae hurriedly grabbed some of our things and bounced to this little hideaway apartment I had copped for occasions like this.

No one knew about the spot so we could chill there without having to worry about the door being kicked in by detectives. If they somehow tracked us down, me and my baby was strapped with enough artillery to make them regret coming for me.

We had a choppa, an AR-15 with an extended clip, mad semi-automatic handguns and a couple of bullet proof vests. Of course, none of this would've been necessary had I handled my business properly.

I should've popped that bitch in the melon! I chastised myself for not shooting him in the head.

"Fuck was I thinking, yo!" I sighed.

"What's wrong, babi?" Jae looked up from the blunt she was rolling.

"I was supposed to make sure that rat muthafucka was dead. I should've put my tool up against his cranium and knocked the sauce out of that bitch, yo." I shook my head at my own carelessness.

"I can sneak up in the hospital and finish that nigga off. A dead man can't testify." Ma's tone was dead ass serious.

I knew she would run up in that piece and do exactly what she had suggested, but I wasn't going to risk that shit. If something went wrong and Jae got knocked, I would die inside.

"Nah, ma, fuck that. It is what it is, nah mean? If I gotta do a bid behind this shit, I'm going to do it like the real nigga that I am. As long as you promise to hold me down, I'm good."

"Rocket, don't play with me!" Jae frowned as she put some fire to the end of the blunt. "You know damn well I'll hold you down. I'll go on the run with you and bust shots at the cops when they finally catch up with us if you want to do that. It's whateva as long as I'm by your side." She puffed-puffed and passed me the sticky.

I smiled at her loyalty because that shit was sexy as fuck. "My muthafuckin rider, yo!" I put the stick of gas to my mouth and pulled hard, allowing the strong smoke to enter my lungs.

As we passed the blunt back and forth, I thought over my options. A prison bid was most def' in my near future, but those muhfuckas would have to catch me first. I wasn't going to turn myself in or no dumb shit like that. And if they ran up on me at the wrong time, when my mind was on some savage shit, I was gonna paint the sidewalks with their blood.

Sensing that the situation was heavy on my mind, Jae tried to ease my worries. She put her head in my lap and unzipped me. Before long, I was rocked up with a whole lot of her spit on my dick.

Once she came up for air, I laid her face down and beat the pussy like there was no tomorrow. "Daddy, you're going to fracture a bitch's spine," she cried as I hit it hard and deep.

"Don't front, you love this shit!" I pulled my dick out to the tip, and then I plunged in with force.

"I do!" Baby girl threw that ass back at me vigorously.

Our bodies slapped together until we exploded at the same time.

"Your pussy is the bomb, yo." I kissed the back of her neck.

"And that dick is the bloodclath truth, rude boy," she said, panting.

I rolled off of her and we dozed off in each other's arms.

***

I was too amped to sleep long. I kept waking up, hopping out of bed and going to the window to see if the rollers were outside. Around noon, I totally abandoned all plans to sleep. I got up, jumped in the shower and let the hot water caress my taut muscles, while I gathered my thoughts.

Moments later, Jae joined me in the shower. We washed each other up, and then we rinsed off and stepped out. Jae fixed me with a questioning stare as she handed me a fresh towel. My quietness must've worried her.

"You okay, babi?" She kept her eyes on me while grabbing herself a towel and drying off.

"Yea, I'm good." I tossed the towel in the dirty clothes hamper and walked into the bedroom.

Ma was on my heels, drying herself as she followed me.

"I wanna spend some time with my daughters before those people come for me," I said, stepping into some fresh gear.

"Okay, babi. And their mothers better not protest or I'm going to do to them what I've wanted to do for the longest." Jae dropped her towel on the floor and went to the closet to grab something to put on.

I carefully watched her select a pair of ripped jeans, a Yankee's t-shirt and a pair of lady Air Max. The look on her face matched her outfit. She was dressing for a rumble and already talking mad noise.

When it came to my baby mamas, Ashanti and La'Quinita, Jae had run out of patience for the foolery those two hoes constantly tried to put me through. I was fed up with their bullshit myself.

Ashanti should've been thanking her lucky stars that I even let her breath after the foul shit she did before we broke up. I had caught that trifling bitch creeping with another nigga while seven months pregnant with my daughter.

It took every ounce of strength in me not to put hands on her punk ass that day. Just the thought of her letting the next nigga run up in her box while my bun was still in her funky ass oven was enough to almost make me pull out and leave her slumped. But that wouldn't have been playa at all, so I just kicked her trifling ass you the curb and moved on to someone better.

Two months later, a paternity test confirmed that I was indeed MiMi's father. From Day One I've been there for my princess, but Ashanti couldn't get over the fact that I didn't fuck with her bum ass anymore.

As for my other baby mother, I just lost interest in her because she didn't want shit out of life but some dick and a bag of weed. Both her and Ashanti constantly put bullshit in the mix and Jae was fed up.

I chuckled as I watched her strap up. "You just want a reason to wild out on 'em, yo."

"You're damn right. Especially that bitch Ashanti," she admitted.

"Calm down, killa," I teased. "I'ma try to do this without any drama."

"Good luck with that." Her sarcasm was mad thick.

She was probably right though. It didn't matter, I was ready for whatever, and my patience wasn't much longer than hers. Today would be the wrong day for them to fuck with me.

I grabbed my cell phone off of the table by the bed and dialed Ashanti's number. As I waited for her to pick up, I thought back to a time when things were peaceful with us. The good times hadn't lasted long because shorty was always on some extra shit— lying and stressing a nigga over dumb shit.

I was reminiscing about the day she gave birth to my daughter. I had wanted us to always be a family, but it hadn't worked out.

Ashanti's voice ended my walk down memory lane. "Hello."

"Ayo, I'm 'bout to swing through and pick MiMi up."

"Nigga, you all over the news and you talking 'bout picking my daughter up."

"Yo, I ain't call to argue with you over our child, or talk about that bullshit that you see on the news. All I want to do is spend some time with MiMi before shit turns ugly." I kept my voice calm because I really wanted to see my baby girl.

"Rocket, you on the run and my child is not going anywhere with you!" Ashanti blasted.

I took a deep breath and slowly ran my hand down my face. *Don't let her blow you*, I cautioned myself. But she kept on popping her muthafuckin' lips like I was one of those corny ass niggas she fucked with.

Fuck if I was going for that!

"Yo, who the fuck you screaming at?" I spat.

Before she could respond, Jae who was standing nearby, walked up and snatched the phone from my hand.

"Bitch, listen and listen gud." Jae cleared her throat. "Yuh 'eard."

Her Patwha was out. She was mad.

"I know you 'eard what deh bloodclath he said, all he wanna do is see MiMi!"

"No! Anyway, who the fuck is you to say anything to me?" Ashanti's voice boomed through the phone.

Jae looked at me with her brows creased. To my baby mama, she said, "Listen, Ashanti, I'm not trying to hear that shit. Just get MiMi dressed and ready. We on the way to get her!" She tossed my phone on the bed and sat down to lace her sneakers up. "That bitch gon' learn today!" Steam was coming out of her nose.

I picked the phone up to let Ashanti know that this shit wasn't a game, but she had already disconnected.

You better have your mind right by the time we pull up on you, yo. I didn't want my pit bull in a skirt to have to put hands on her, but I was not gonna stop it if Ashanti just wanted to test that shit.

Sighing heavily, I hit La'Quanita's line, hoping she wouldn't spazz out like Ashanti. Shit wasn't all lovely with us, but she wasn't too hard to deal with.

My first call went straight to voicemail. *Answer your phone, yo.* I redialed her number. This time she answered and I could hear my lil' angel MooMoo's voice in the background.

"Yo, Nita," I called my baby mother by her nickname, "what's good, yo?"

"Rocket, do you know you were just on the news?" Alarm resonated from her voice.

I quickly tried to quiet it. "I know, but that's nothing. I'm 'bout to come get MooMoo, a'ight?"

"Rocket, nigga, you're hot! I don't want—"

"Yo, don't do that shit to me, yo!"

Out of the corner of my eye I saw Jae pulling her hair back into a ponytail and tying her head up with a scarf.

Rude gal ready to go to war with her hands.

"No, Rocket, I'm sorry. I don't want my baby in the car with your crazy ass when the police pull you over," Nita was saying, but I wasn't tryna hear that.

"Fuck what you're talking about. I'm on my way!"

I hung up on her ass, grabbed my tool off of the table and tucked it in my waistband. I wasn't about to keep arguing with those bitches over the phone about my kids.

"You ready to roll out, rude gal?" I asked the only one who tried to bring peace to a nigga's life.

"Yea, babi, let's rock and roll." She headed for the door, ahead of me, stepping lively.

***

A half hour later, we pulled up at Ashanti's mom's crib. Jae was out the car a split second after she parked and cut the engine off.

I hopped out of the passenger side and caught up with her in three or four long strides. She was already seething and ready to get things popping.

"I be letting her smart ass slide sometimes, but not today. If she don't let you get MiMi, I'ma tag that ass and take your daughter," she said as her short, thick legs moved with purpose.

We had just reached Ashanti's front door when it swung open. "Why are you here?" She blocked the doorway.

"Weh deh babi, deh?" Jae asked with her hands on her hips.

Ashanti looked at me 'cause she didn't understand what Jae said.

"Where is MiMi?" I interpreted.

Striking a resistant pose with her arms folded over her chest, and her head cocked to the side, Ashanti replied, "Rocket, I already told you you're not taking my baby anywhere with you."

"Bitch, and I told you we weren't coming here to play games with your ass, didn't I?" Jae drew her fist back and clocked Ashanti dead in the mouth, busting her lip wide the fuck open.

"Awww!" Ashanti howled.

"Don't scream, bitch. Fight!" Jae swung at her again, connecting with her forehead.

Ashanti staggered back, allowing me a chance to step in between them and pull Jae off of that ass.

"Let me go, Rocket! I told that bitch not to fuckin' test me today!" Rude gal tried to break free of my hold but I held her tightly around the waist.

"Bitch, I'ma kill you!" Ashanti cried. Blood ran down her chin and dripped onto her shirt.

"What the fuck is going on?" Her mom, Pam, appeared at the door with MiMi on her hip.

"Dada!" My two-year old yelled when she saw me.

Pam was looking from Ashanti to me and Jae, trying to piece together what had happened, while my daughter was squirming out of her arms.

Meanwhile, Ashanti was talking mad shit. "Let that bitch go! I want some of that ass. Let her the fuck go!"

I heard her spitting that rah-rah shit, but she didn't really wanna tangle with Jae. Shorty would've tore off in her ass.

"Yo, shut the fuck up!" I screamed at Ashanti. It was hard enough for me to hold Jae back without her inciting her even more than she had already.

"Rocket, let me go, and I'm not muthafuckin' playing." Jae snatched away from me for just a second.

She took a fierce step toward Ashanti but I grabbed her again and pulled her back. "Calm down!"

"What the hell is wrong with y'all!" Pam's cry caused my little angel to start wailing.

Quickly, I whispered in Jae's ear. "Baby, this ain't the time or place for that, nah mean? Not in front of MiMi." If anything could make her chill the fuck out it would be that. Shorty had mad love and respect for my babies.

"Okay, I'm gonna stay calm." Her voice mellowed but her chest was heaving, and she was staring death threats at my baby's mama.

"Bitch, this shit ain't over!" spat Ashanti.

"Chill yo!" I continued trying to diffuse the situation.

"Nigga, fuck you!"

Ashanti must've wanted me to treat her like I treated niggas. I wasn't quick to put my hands on a female, which is why I had let Jae handle the bitch for me, but if she pushed me hard enough she could get her head split.

Nah, I'm not letting this bum bitch make me smack her in front of my seed.

I threw my hands up in the air, gesturing peace. "It's all good, baby girl. I just came to pick up my daughter. Let me do that and I'm out."

"I told your black ass you're not taking her no fuckin' where!"

"You buggin', yo." I turned from her and spoke to her mother, hoping she would intervene on my behalf. Things were good with us. She had mad respect for me because I took care of my seed. "Miss Pam," I spoke politely, "will you please talk to your daughter?"

"I told that damn girl not to hold this baby from you." She handed me MiMi without saying shit to Ashanti.

"Daddy's baby." I kissed my daughter's fat cheeks.

The heat on my back coming from Ashanti felt like an incinerator.

"Take her to the car, I'll bring her bag out," suggested Pam.

"Copy that."

I carried MiMi to the car and Jae followed me, mumbling venom underneath her breath. Shorty wanted to kick off in Ashanti's ass so bad her whole forehead was creased with anger.

"Baby, she's not even worth breaking your nail. You already showed her how you get down; she don't want none. She was just bumping her gums. Strap MiMi in her car seat, I'll be right back."

I passed my baby to her, and then walked back up on Ashanti's porch. A minute or two later, she came back out, holding a rag over her bloody mouth with one hand and a bag in the other.

She looked at me with eyes like hot coals. "You let that bitch put her hands on me?"

"Naw, you did that yaself. Ya' mouth got you fucked up!" I grabbed the bag from her hand. "I'll call you when I'm 'bout to drop her off!"

“I fucking hate you!” She screamed at my back as I turned and headed back to the car.

Jae rolled the window down and spat poison at Ashanti. “Good, ‘cause I’d hate to kill you if you loved ‘im!”

I chuckled at her feisty ass as I got inside and closed the car door. “Ma, you too turnt up. One day the two of us together is gonna cause this whole city to bow down,” I predicted.

And I was dead ass serious.

***

La’Quinita had MooMoo ready and waiting when I pulled up in front of the apartment building.

“I heard about that shit with Ro,” said Quinita as soon as I was within ear shot.

“I ain’t heard shit.” I creased my eyebrows and bent down to pick MooMoo up.

“How long you keeping her for?”

This bitch can’t wait for me to pull off so she can run the streets and chase after some dick.

“Just answer ya’ phone.”

“You can’t give me a better answer than that?” Quinita sucked her teeth.

“Nah!” I turned, and me and the little one walked off.

I didn’t want to chance getting snatched up by the po’s, so we drove straight to the hideaway and found something to do indoors with my baby girls.

For three days straight, I just spent time with them, trying to enjoy every moment I had left before a nigga got put in cuffs and taken away. A part of me didn’t wanna go out without making that thang clap, but shit really wasn’t that catastrophic.

Every time I looked at my two beautiful princesses, and my sexy ass girl, I realized that leaving them temporarily would hurt them, but if I ended up in a coffin, that shit would fuck them up bad.

“Bae, what’s on your mind?” Jae’s voice brought me out of my deep thoughts.

I looked up from the sofa, where I was combing MooMoo's hair, and flashed my shorty a confident smile, letting her know I was good. "I'm just thinking, ma. That's all."

Shorty wasn't fooled. The look in her eyes told me that she knew her and the girls were heavy on my mind. She walked around the sofa and wrapped her arms around my neck, from the back. Without saying a word, she communicated her love and devotion.

I tilted my head back and puckered my lips. "Let a nigga get some of that sweetness."

"Of course, babi." Jae pressed her soft lips against mine, and parted them to invite my tongue.

We shared a quick, wet kiss.

When our lips unlocked, MooMoo was feeling jealous. "Daddy, I want a kiss too," she sang.

"Come and get one, Daddy's girl." I lifted her into my arms and got a whole lot of that sugah.

Now, it was MiMi's turn to act jealous. "I want a kissy kiss, too, Daddy," she whined, making a gangsta's heart beat with pride.

Nothing felt better than being loved by my babies and my girl. I sat MooMoo down and gave her sister a big hug and a kiss, and then I finished putting MooMoo's hair in plats; something I had learned to do quite well.

Once I was done, my heart ached knowing that I couldn't keep them any longer 'cause I had to get back to the streets and make money. I conjured up a smile and announced, "Well, baby girls, it's time for Daddy to take y'all home."

"No, Daddy!" They wined.

"Don't worry, I'll come pick y'all up again in a couple of days," I promised.

It took a few kisses to quiet their little protest. After gathering up their things, we were out of the door and on our way back to their mothers' cribs. I just hoped I could keep my promise and see them again in a few days. But I had a strong premonition that things might not work out like that.

***

When I dropped MiMi off, I had a serious talk with Ashanti, ending it with a sincere request. "I know we've being through a whole lot of BS," I said. "But it's all good. Whatever happens, just don't take my seed out of my life."

The bitch just stood there and looked me up and down, not saying a word.

"I guess you can't even promise me that, huh?" I tried to murder her with my tone, but Ashanti was unfazed.

"Tell your bitch to give you a baby. Me and mine are good!"

I closed the little space between us in the living room and grabbed her by the face. "You keep itching for that ass whooping I owe your nothin' ass. If I was a different type of nigga I would snap your neck!"

"Get the fuck off of me!" She tried to pull away but I had a firm grip on her face.

MiMi was on the couch; she had fallen asleep while I was talking to Ashanti. The commotion caused her to stir. I didn't want my baby tc see me handling her mother like that, and then grow up thinking it was cool for a nigga to put his hands on a woman, so I let Ashanti go.

"One day you're gonna say the wrong thing to me, at the wrong time, and I'm gonna kick off on your ass for old and new," I warned.

Whatever slick response she uttered bounced off of my back. I leaned down and placed a kiss on MiMi's cheek. "Daddy loves you, baby girl. Always and forever."

"No, you don't! You love that bitch!" Ashanti spat.

I rose up and pushed past her with my mouth tight and my fists clenched. I had to get the fuck up out of there before I bodied her stupid ass.

***

MooMoo gave me hell when it was time to drop her off. Baby girl screamed, kicked, yelled and hollered, not wanting me to leave her.

"I love you." I kept saying it over and over again, but MooMoo didn't want to hear that shit. She wanted to stay with me. She grabbed a hold of my leg and wouldn't let go.

"I tried to tell you not to spoil her. Now look at what you have to go through," said Nita, shaking her head as we stood on her porch.

"You can't tell me not to spoil mine. That's what real fathers do."

Nita frowned, but her eyes betrayed her. She acted like my spoiling MooMoo raked her nerves, but deep down she was proud to have a baby daddy who loved his child, because a lot of niggas didn't.

Eventually, I was able to coax away MooMoo's tears. I kissed her goodbye, and then I leaned in and whispered to Nita, "Yo, whatever the fuck happens, hold my seed down with ya' life."

She nodded but I knew better. That shit went through one ear and out the other. With her, dick, bubblegum and bullshit would always be her main priorities. That's why I was so bothered about going to do a bid and leaving my children— their mothers could not be trusted to look after them like I would.

That shit had wrinkles in my forehead as I walked down the steps with my hands shoved down in my pockets and my shoulders sagging.

Jae held my hand when I got back in the car. "You okay, babi?"

"Not really, but it is what it is."

I glanced up on the porch and saw my little girl waving goodbye. I waved back and swallowed the lump in my throat, and then I told Jae what my concerns where.

"If dem sketals don't do as yuh sey, I'ma beat 'em pan everi set!" She made it clear that if them hoes didn't do as I say, she would beat them every time she saw them.

Her love and devotion squeezed a tear out of a gangsta's eyes. Knowing rude gal would keep an eye on those situations while I was a way gave a nigga the same feeling of protection as a bulletproof vest.

My mind was at peace now, but I was still hoping to get at that pussy, Ro, and serve him a fatal dose of my Nine before he could ever make it to court and take the witness stand against me.

Chapter 8
TRAP

When Rocket hit me up with the news that he had blazed Ro for talking about snitching, I knew shit was definitely real. But I expected nothing less from fam because we lived by the code: *Loyalty over everything*. Not even blood relatives could make a real street nigga compromise that.

Rocket's only regret was that Ro wasn't dead. "B, I should've clapped that pussy in the dome, son," he said. "That nigga still breathing, bruh."

"He must've had an angel on his muthafuckin' shoulder. But him *and* the angel can get it." We didn't have to be blood to be related. Our loyalty to each other was enough, and I was ready to ride on that. "Say the word, my nigga, and you know I'm in the next thing moving to finish that bitch ass nigga off." I was lacing my Timbs up, ready to go dispose of the rat for good.

Thinking back, I had never liked Ro, and I had peeped disloyalty in him from the moment we first met.

"Where you from, B?" Rocket asked me as I tossed the ball to my twin, Tray, on the basketball court.

"Crown Heights, son," I boasted as I studied the nigga standing behind him. Dude's eyes were all over the park.

"Word?"

"Word!" Tray was at my side with the ball under his foot. "You wanna shoot some hoops?" I asked.

"Hell yea." Rocket was anxious to show his skills, but the little nigga behind him intervened.

"You know momma gonna be mad if we stay out late."

"You always bitchin' and whinin' 'bout the wrong things, Ro," Rocket quickly checked him. He picked the ball from under Tray's foot and turned back to his brother. "You gonna play, bitch, or go home?"

I looked at Ro, waiting for his response as Rocket bounced the ball back and forth between his legs, ready to hoop.

"It's not like you gonna get ya' ass whooped anyway." Rocket continued, brewing with anger.

"I'ma go home." Ro walked off.

"Bitch ass nigga!" Rocket spat, dribbling the ball to the basket and laying it in.

I recalled thinking at the time, Rocket seemed solid, but his brother was soft. Because even way back then, my brother and I would never leave each other. We rocked with each other, good or bad, and if an ass whooping was the consequences, we would've taken one together.

"I knew that nigga was a sucka, and suckas, I don't fuck with!" I said now.

"Bruh, it's all good." Rocket sighed heavily. "But I never would've expected my own blood would turn out to be a rat nigga."

I heard the hurt in his voice, and his pain became my own. I had to let him know that all he had to do was say the word and I would be up in that bitch, finishing up what he had started. "Son, let me do what I do."

"Nah, blood. I can't risk you like that. I fucked up by not hitting him in the head. I respect your loyalty though."

I glanced over at the redbone sleeping peacefully. I had picked her up from a strip club last night and gutted her out. The dick had her hanging off the side of the bed with her mouth wide open, knocked the fuck out. Still, I got up, grabbed my strap off of the table by the bed, and went into the bathroom to assure myself she wasn't listening.

I closed the door and leaned against the sink before continuing the conversation. "It's never too late, Rocket. Never!" I tucked my tool in my waistband. "Just say the word."

"It's too hot right now."

"When the fuck did we start caring about the temperature?" I was ready to end his brother's life.

"The temperature is with the NYPD, not the streets, 'cause you already know how I get down, Trap."

Hell yea, I knew bruh was a beast. That's why I didn't understand why he was putting the clamps on me.

"Real shit, my nigga, we got stupid guns. Fuck NYPD! Let's take them to war, too!" I argued.

"Nah, family. Just trust me on this one," he said calmly.

"A'ight. At the end of the day, I respect your wisdom," I conceded.

"I'ma hit you up in a few, bruh."

"Smooth. But if you change your mind, hit my line."

"Copy."

"One."

I ended the call and walked back into the bedroom. Pound Cake's was still asleep. I reached in my pocket, pulled a few hundreds off of my grip and tossed them on top of her.

"That pussy was A-1, ma."

I headed for the front door and let myself out of her apartment.

***

The summer heat was scorching, and it caused my T-shirt to stick to my body almost as soon as I stepped outside. The block was quiet but I knew it wouldn't last long.

Our team had Crown Heights on lock with the werk, pills and green. Rocket had linked up with a plug a few years ago and the type of weight he was getting helped us gain control of major areas in the city since our product was superior. Our gunplay and our reputations usually kept mofo's in line, but occasionally we had to clap a fool just to remind the streets that we played no games.

My thoughts were heavy on our buildings and the dough, but heaviest on my mind was Rocket and the situation he was in, because a bitch nigga didn't want to keep it one hundred.

Ro has to die for that.

I hopped in my truck and hit up my twin, Tray, as I drove off.

"What's good?" he answered, sounding half asleep.

Knowing him as well as I did, I figured he was probably laid up with two big booty bitches. One was never good enough for him.

"Where you at?" I asked anyway.

"At the hotel with these two freaks, doing what I do. What's good though?"

"Bro, we have a problem."

"Speak on it." I could hear rustling on his end. I assumed he was getting out of bed and walking off to have some privacy. After a moment or two, he said, "Talk to me. Are we going to have to bring the hammers out?"

Like myself, Tray was sick with that gunplay. "Yea, it's that time again. But this time it's one of our own." I repeated everything Rocket had told me.

I didn't have to ask Tray to ride. Rocket was like a brother to us. From the time he was ten years old, he had lived with us because he had serious beef with his step-pop. Mom Duke welcomed him into our crib, and she grew to love him like he had come out of her womb. She had instilled in us the moral that if one of you fight, all three of you better fight. We lived by it, even as men.

"The nigga still living?" asked Tray, referring to Ro.

"Yea, he got wet up, but the pussy survived. Now, Rocket is all over the news, bruh."

"Say no more. Meet me at ma's crib."

"One."

I hung up the phone and patted the gun on my waist. It was cool to the touch, but I planned to make it hot real soon.

***

Tray

Niggas quick to scream how real and loyal they are, but as soon as they get caught up in some shit with time hanging over their heads, they switch up like a bleeding bitch, and that's when the cramping starts, and pussy niggas start snitching.

If Ro thought he was going to get away with that pussy ass shit, he couldn't have known how deep my love for Rocket ran.

I hit Rocket's line. As soon as he answered, I reiterated my loyalty. "Fam, I just got the news. That's some real hoe type shit!"

"True that, but I'm standing tall. Whatever happens I'm, gonna stay true to the code," he said.

"No doubt, son. That's how you're built. But Ro has to pay for that."

"Indeed. Snitch niggas can't ever be given a reprieve from the streets. Shit like that already has the game fucked up. You feel me?"

"That's one hundred. You already know me and Trap will handle that."

"Say no more. Right now, though, the team still has to eat. With so much heat on me, I can't move how I wanna move. So, you and Trap gotta hold the spots down, and I'll just collect the bread and make sure the shipments continue to flow."

"Copy. I'm on that right now."

"Cool. Hit me back after you handle that."

"A'ight." I ended the call, snatched my car keys up and headed for the door.

When I reached Ma Duke's house, Trap was already there. He was sitting on the porch, smoking a blunt. I walked up and took a seat beside him on the steps.

"Shit is crazy, right?" He passed me the blunt.

"Yea, but you and I always felt Ro wasn't official. I guess Rocket couldn't see that because that's his blood."

"True. And it's always a nigga close to you who will sell you out. But I'll die a fiery death before I would ever rat on anybody. That's a bitch move!" Trap said with distaste.

"Done by a bitch nigga to a real one."

As the weed smoke reached my lungs, I thought back to the first sign that Ro would cross his own brother.

Rocket told me he had a move to make with a nigga named Knight. The plan was to sell three bricks to some cats from Newark who Knight knew, but I just didn't trust him.

"B, let me come with you," I begged Rocket. "I know you can hold your own but I been hearing some cruddy shit about Knight."

"Blood, you worry too much. Fuck around and have a stroke," he laughed me off. "Anyway, as long as I got this four-pound on my waist," he patted his toolie, "a fool better not try me."

"But you know niggas will," I reminded him.

"If they do, you'll read about it. I'm good. Just hold the spot down."

"Mane, I don't trust that clown ass nigga," I repeated in a stronger tone this time.

I had spotted Knight chopping it up with Ro one late night behind the Jamaican Bashment place on Flatbush Avenue. Then, all of a sudden, Knight contacted Rocket talking about he had a sale for him with the Newark niggas. I felt shit was suspect, but Rocket wouldn't listen.

Trap begged Rocket to let him ride with him, but to no avail.

"If anything looks out of place, best believe I'ma bless those who aimin' for my downfall." He touched fists with us, and then went on the move alone.

Every minute my nigga was away, we kept looking at the screens of our phones, waiting for that text letting us know he was good. As the hours crept by at a snail's pace, we became more and more worried.

Finally, Rocket returned to the spot. He walked into the house and tossed the werk on the table. "Them niggas ain't show up."

I was relieved to see him but I could tell something was wrong.

"What the hell took you so long then, my nigga?" Trap asked as he wrapped rubber bands around the stacks of moola we had for the plug.

"Nigga had me driving around the city with the birds, talkin' 'bout the niggas ain't answering their phones and shit."

"What?" I jumped up, ready to go find that clown.

"That ain't the half, Tray." Rocket took a seat by the door.

"Run it down then, B." I urged.

"Nigga wanted me to drive to Newark, but I let him know straight up that, that wasn't happening."

"And?"

"Mufucka had the nerve to say how he was gonna look bad 'cause he told them he knew where to get the straight drop from. But the more I thought about that shit, the more I realized that the nigga had me on some fuck boy shit mission."

"Mane, I told you from the jump about that fool, yo."

"Yea, dawg, Knight be on that shit," Trap intoned.

"It's all good, 'cause he won't get to try the next nigga." Rocket chuckled. "I got his ass in the trunk!"

"You for real yo?" I asked.

Rocket nodded, and then he tossed me the keys.

Trap was on my heels as I walked outside to Rocket's whip. As soon as I popped the trunk, I saw Knight's bloodied body twisted up in there. When I touched him, he was as stiff as a board.

"That nigga, Rocket, don't play no games." I laughed.

"None at all!" Trap smiled.

Later that night, we tossed Knight's body in the Hudson River. Back at the house, I said, "On everything I love, son, I swear Ro had something to do with that move that Knight was trying to orchestrate."

Rocket stared me down hard as if he was considering the possibility, before responding, "If it ever comes out that he did, only God can save him."

Rocket never got proof that Ro had put Knight on him. He continued to fuck with his brother because Rocket was the type who wanted everyone to eat. Now, his mistake on judging Ro had come back to bite him.

"Bruh, we gotta fix this shit. Fuck what Rocket talking about this time." I passed the blunt back to Trap.

"I was thinking the same thing," he said. "We going up in Kings County hospital blazing!"

"Say no more. I'm ready!"

I didn't give a fuck what the outcome would be. I would lay my life on the line for those I loved.

Chapter 9
JAE

Whatever Rocket decided to do, I was strapped up and ready to ride for my boo. So, fuck that shit he was spitting about getting me caught up. A bitch been caught up since the day he made me his girl. I just had to convince him that I could pull off the murder without getting bagged.

"Please, just let me run up in that bloodclath place and give deh rat some cheese," I pleaded as I drove with one destination in mind.

I could tell Rocket was deep in thought 'cause he had yet to say a word since he got off of the phone with Tray.

"I'm telling you, by the time they find that nigga, we'll be long gone." I hit the exit to Kings County hospital.

"And then what?" Rocket looked over at me like I was out of my goddam mind.

"The muthafuckin' *informa* won't be able to tell or testify." I kept my eyes on the road.

"Babe, he already told. Now, what's gonna be is gonna be."

"You mean, you going to jail?" I asked bitterly.

"Yea."

"Bitch ass nigga!" Hot tears ran down my face. "How the fuck he gonna fold on you?" I screamed as I pressed the gas pedal down to the floor.

"Jae!" I heard Rocket's voice but my mind was made the fuck up. "Slow down before you get us pulled the fuck over, shorty."

I eased my foot up off of the gas and slowed down. "Why, babi, why? I don't want you to have to go away." Hot, angry tears scorched my cheeks. But Rocket remained calm.

"Sometimes it's just how it is. Muthafuckas not loyal."

Tears continued to jet down my face. Despite the pain in my heart, my level of respect for my man increased. No matter how many people turned their backs on him or tried to bring him down, he still stayed G'd the fuck up from the floor up.

"But fuck that, I'm not going out without a fight," he added.

"And you know I'm going to be right there beside you, fighting, too."

"Ma, I keep telling you to fall the fuck back, yo." He rubbed my leg gently to soften the sting of his demand.

No matter how loud, clear and direct he was about me staying out of this, the rider in me just wouldn't allow me to sit back and watch my man get fucked over by his snitching ass brother.

Hell naw!

"Fuck that, I'ma ride for you!"

I was only a block away from the hospital. The blood rushed through my veins like an electric current as I formulated a plan to put a quick end to Rocket's problem.

As soon as I reached the hospital, I slammed on the brakes and threw the car in park. Rocket's body launched forward but he recovered quickly.

"Baby, why you park?" He looked around, just for a second or two, and then recognition flashed across his face and his brows furrowed.

Before he could object, I was out of the car, moving purposefully. I was about to cross the street when I heard Rocket bark out my name.

"Jae! Girl, bring your hot-headed ass back here!" He ran up to me and held me back, pinning my arms to my side. "Fuck is you doing, yo?"

"Let me go, Rocket!"

"You can't just run up in that bitch," he whispered as I struggled to free myself from his stifling bear hug.

"Why?" Tears trickled down my face.

"Because you can't!" He bit down on his bottom lip in frustration at my defiance, but a bitch didn't give a fuck. I was acting on pure emotion.

I tasted my salty tears as I spoke from my heart. "Deh muthafucka tink seh it's cool to tell on you so it's gotta be cool for me to smoke that ass!"

"No, what he did, ain't cool, but you can't run up in that bitch." He turned his head around and glanced at the tall building. "Security is too, tight."

"Fuck security, they can get it, too!"

"Humph!" Rocket laughed, but I didn't see a damn thing funny.

I looked up at him through eyes like slits. "Man, let me go!"

"Shh!" He kissed me softly on the forehead. "It's a time for everything, baby, and right now is not the time. That coward is gonna get his."

"Fuck all that shit you saying right now, Rocket. Tomorrow ain't promise! Let go of me, so I can go pop that nigga."

He let my hands go and stepped out of the way. I was thinking I know my nigga ain't trying to test my bloodclath character. I'll never fall for what I stand for! If he thought for one second I was bluffing, he was about to find out that his bitch was true to the muthafuckin' game.

I re-tucked the jammy on my waist, ducked my head low, and headed across the street.

"Jae! Yo, shorty, bring your crazy ass back here!" I heard the patter of Rocket's feet behind me, but I kept on pushing.

As I reached the side of the street where the hospital sat, he finally caught up to me. I felt him wrap his arms around my shoulders, restraining me.

"No, man, let me go handle this!" Tears strained my voice.

"Ma, it's all good," he whispered in my ear as an older couple walked pass us.

"If it's all good, then let me go!" I struggled against him. "What, you thought I was going to bitch up? You testing my thoroughness, nigga?"

"Baby, it ain't that."

"So, if it ain't that shit, then stay here and I'll be back after I finish that snitching ass nigga."

"I can't let you do this shit right now, Jae. No, baby girl, I'm not letting you risk your freedom for me."

"I'm not just doing it for you, I'm doing it for us."

"Not! Now let's go back to the car!" Rocket tightened his grip on my little ass body and practically dragged me backwards. "Now is not the time. Goddamn! I see ya' loyalty and ya' gangsta, but I can't let you go out like that!"

People were walking by, looking at us with suspicion.

"Yo, you got a problem with your eyes?" Rocket challenged a middle-aged man.

The man looked from Rocket to me, as if he thought I was being kidnapped and needed his assistance. Luckily, he decided to mind his business because Rocket was already seething, and he was looking for a reason to clap at somebody.

"Yea, pussy, you better step the fuck on!" he spat as the guy walked off. Then, he placed his mouth an inch from my ear. "You out here acting up and you know I'm hot as fuck!"

"Fuck that shit you saying, Rocket!" I yelled as he dragged me back to the car and opened the passenger door, forcing me inside.

"Stay the fuck seated!" He slammed the door and dashed around to the driver's side.

I folded my arms across my chest and breathed hard. When Rocket was behind the wheel, he looked over at me reproachfully and shook his head.

"Why you so damn hardheaded?" He let out a heavy sigh of exasperation.

"If that nigga as much as breathe ya' name to dem boys, I swear on my life, I'ma end everything that he loves. Straight the fuck up!" I pulled my Glock from my waist and slammed a bullet in the chamber. "Pussyhole informa fi dead!" I reached for the door handle.

Rocket must've known that once out of the car, this time I would not let him stop me. So, he quickly drove off before I could hop out.

Several blocks away from the hospital, he placed a comforting hand on my thigh. "Don't be mad, rude gal. That nigga can't hide forever, yo."

I slapped his hand off my leg, turned my head and stared out of the side window. "Miss me with that shit!"

"A'ight, ma, you got that. But on some real shit, I need to hit up the plug and let him know how Ro rocking."

"You think?" I replied sarcastically. Until he let me end his brother's life I was going to be a real difficult bitch to deal with.

I could feel the heat of his gaze on the side of my face, but it was nothing in comparison to the fire crackling inside of me.

"Boss man, what's up?" I heard Rocket say into his cell phone. I knew he was talking to his plug, Cuba.

I blocked out their conversation as I tried to think of ways to get away from Rocket and creep back to the hospital. Ro had to die, point blank, period. And I was going to be his executioner.

A moment later, my anger turned to alarm when I saw a NYPD cruiser behind us. Nothing good ever happened when those bitches came around.

"Rocket, the jakes are behind us," I whispered out the side of my mouth.

"Say what?"

"The pigs, bae. They're behind us."

"For real?"

"Yes, babi."

"Boss man, I gotta hit you back," he said to Cuba. He ended the call and dropped his phone between the seats. His eyes found the rearview mirror.

"What you wanna do? If they hit those lights, I can clap at 'em and that should give you enough time to get us far away," I spoke calmly.

"Let's wait and see first," he replied.

I snorted because that wasn't the response I expected. "Fuck a hater, a snitch and a cop!"

"Pump your brakes, baby girl. I'm not trying to get you caught up."

"And I'm not trying to see you hauled off to jail."

"I know, but let's hope for the best."

"Fuck the best, give me the word I want to hear." Traffic halted and my leg was shaking, badly. Anxiously, I awaited on my nigga's word. "We can bounce to Jamaica, Rocket."

"This is it, baby girl."

"What?" I snapped my head around. Red and blue lights flashed.

"Tuck that shit, ma."

"Rocket," my voice cracked, "you gonna pullover?" I turned back around.

It was do or die time, as far as I was concerned. Fuck everything else. I was ready to go on the run with my nigga as fugitives from justice, or die by his side.

My hand gripped my steel as my heart raced with adrenaline.

Clap, clap, muthafuckaz. I'm about to show y'all crackers that you've never met a bitch like me.

***

Rocket

I saw in baby girl's eyes she was ready to make that toolie cough, but I wasn't about to let shorty go there.

"Jae! Stand down!" I said forcefully.

"Why? Rocket, we can take these muthafuckaz."

"No, ma. Just do what I say. Tuck that shit!"

"I can't believe this shit! What the fuck happened with us going on the run together?" She sighed heavily as she followed my orders.

I let out a long sigh of relief and steered over to the curb. I wasn't pulling over because I wanted to. I was doing it for her. I would never forgive myself if she had to do some time because of me.

With a scowl etched on my face, I watched as the officers exited the squad car with their hands on their weapons. They split up when they reached the bumper of the car. One moved to Jae's side and the other my way.

"Don't let them take you away from me, babi." She made one last plea.

The beast in me wanted to give in to Jae's pleas, but I knew it would've been straight reckless of me to murk a cop to avoid the shit hanging over my head from Ro. Even if I had to go do a bid for that, I would be in and out in a few years. *Why throw me and Jae's lives away over that?* I asked myself.

When the cracker knocked on the driver's window I looked over at Jae and saw that she had tucked the gun away. *Good, she listened.*

I hit the switch to let the window down with my left hand as my right hand stayed visible on the wheel. "How may I help you?" I asked, watching him stare inside the vehicle.

"License and registration, sir?"

I pulled my license from my pocket, wishing I had left Jae at the spot. If shorty hadn't been with me, nine times out of ten, I wouldn't have complied to the cop's demand. Instinct, along with the Jake's flat, officious tone, made me doubtful I would avoid arrest.

"Officer, can I ask you why you pulled me over," I asked.

"Registration please."

Yea, this shit is about to go north, I all but concluded.

Sighing, I lifted the hand console up and got the registration paper for him.

Po po studied it for a few seconds and then he read my name aloud. "Draymond Wallace, Jr.?" he asked.

"Yea."

"I'll be right back."

His partner from the other side walked off and they met up at the back of our car. I watched them say a few words before the other one returned to his position at Jae's window.

"Please just pull off." Her voice was low but I heard her.

We both knew what was next. I didn't look forward to leaving my daughters and Jae, but it was what it was.

"Nah. This ain't nothing but some small shit. You're a tiger, shorty. You'll be a'ight if I gotta do a bid."

I watched tears run down her face. Her leg started shaking and her fingers twined together like a braided rope.

"They can't hold me forever," I said softly, hoping to quell her worry.

Hurriedly, I instructed her to get in touch with Cuba, and I told her precisely what to tell my plug. When I saw the officer getting out of the car, I finished up with, “I love you.”

She faced me. “I love you to the stars and back to my heart, Rocket.”

“Yea, I know you do, love.”

Our sweet goodbye was interrupted by the officer’s stern voice. “Mr. Wallace, could you please step out of the car?”

“For what?” I asked, although I knew the answer.

“Step out of the car.” He had his gun aimed at me.

His partner had moved to the front of the car, where he was braced in a shooting position. “Slowly, with your hands above your head,” he barked.

Slowly, I did as I was told with a smile on my face. I would never give a muthafuckin’ pig the time of day to see me sweat. As I was coming out of the car, I realized that they had called for backup. I was a dangerous, wanted nigga, and under different circumstances I would’ve resisted arrest by clapping bullets at them. But nah, not this time. I wanted to live to extract revenge on Ro.

Chapter 10
RO

"Loyalty over blood!" Rocket's words attacked me like the bullets that he had showered me with.

"Baby, please don't die on me."

"Red, he's going to make it. They got him here just in time."

The way I was feeling, I prayed things were looking better for me.

"If he doesn't make it…" My mom took a minute before she carried on. Her words sounded like they had gotten trapped in her throat. "I swear to the man above that Rocket will be doing time just like his father."

I knew my mom had my back, but never like this. Rocket is older than me by almost three years. His father, OX, was locked up by the time he was one, so when my father came into the picture, our mother, Rachel, dropped him where he was. In prison. OX received a sentence of a 175 years for murdering his best friend, who was a confidential informant and also my father's brother.

Two years later, according to my pops, my mom got pregnant by him, and nine months later I was born. I'm my father's only child and the apple of his eye. I could do no wrong.

As far as I can remember and the older I got, I started to realize just how bad my father hated Rocket.

"Rachel, I'm not taking that little ugly muthafucka with me and my boy," my dad would tell my mom. Dad never took Rocket anywhere with us. Nowhere. When our mother would show Rocket any kind of attention in front of my father, he would go the fuck off and beat their asses.

I recalled one night my mom was bandaging up a cut that Rocket had gotten from playing basketball down the street.

"Ma, it hurts," Rocket whined as my mom poured rubbing alcohol over the wound so she could clean it.

"Baby, just don't look," she coached him. It hurt her to see Rocket in pain. I saw it in her face. "Turn your head towards the

door." But Rocket didn't turn his head. He bit his bottom lip and balled his fist up.

None of us heard my father when he entered the house until he knocked the bottle of rubbing alcohol clear across the room.

"What are you doing?" My mom asked, standing up to get the bottle.

"Bitch, sit the fuck down!"

"Ricardo, I'm cleaning his cut and I need the alcohol." Her head was down, facing the floor. My mom started to move around my father to get the bottle but he snatched her back by her hair. "You are hurting me," she cried, but that didn't stop my father. It made him madder.

"You sitting up in here catering to this ugly little muthafucka!"

Rocket stood to his feet and my father let my mom's hair go.

"Ricardo, please, don't," She begged from the floor, pulling on my father's leg.

"You think you grown, huh?" My father walked up on Rocket like he was his size.

Rocket didn't back down or look away. His chest puffed out and both of his fists were clenched together.

"Don't touch my baby," Rachel screamed, causing my father to turn his attention back on her.

"Your baby, huh, bitch?" He reached down and smacked spit from my mom's mouth.

Rocket attacked my father from behind with his little arms, but my dad didn't stop raining blows on my mom until she curled up in a fetal position. When he turned around, he punched Rocket so hard in his chest that he literally flew across the room like a balloon losing air.

"Damn, Ricardo!" My mom jumped up, hearing Rocket's body hit the back of the chair, but a punched knocked her back down and out.

Rocket moved his legs, but the hit had knocked the air from him, so nothing else moved. His eyes spoke volumes, and if looks could kill, my dad would've been dead.

"Dad, please don't hurt him." I stood in my his path so he wouldn't do anything else to Rocket.

"You lucky, your brother saved you!"

My father and I left the house that night and didn't return until the next day. Everything was in place like nothing had happened the night before, so to keep my mom ass-whooping-free, Rocket stayed in his room or down the street with the twins.

When it came to Rocket, everything that concerned him provoked my father. Rocket's father would send him letters all the time from prison, but when my father found them, he would rip them up and throw them in Rocket's face. My brother showed no emotions, but I knew he hated my father.

"That nigga ain't here to protect you, bitch!" My father would say to Rocket. "If you want to communicate with him, you get the fuck from under my roof."

My mom would put her words in. "He's just a child."

My daddy would spazz out and beat our mother, thinking she was still writing OX. Rocket got tired of living with us and stayed at his friends' house I would see him and his friends at the park, but my father made sure I never said a word to him.

Our mother didn't care that Rocket wasn't there because she didn't have to endure any pain from my father's hands, so I ended up getting all their attention. But in all reality, I missed Rocket. He would play with me, teach me card games, and shower me with his love like a big brother would.

Later in life, Rocket would come around with his friends to see me, but he never stayed around, or entered the house. It was like he was showing my parents that he was a survivor. My father stayed out of his way but I could tell that Rocket was just waiting for the perfect day to go the fuck off.

My brother would give me the shirt off of his back if I needed it. He made sure I had money in my pocket all the time, and when he got in the game, he put me on. No matter how bad my mom neglected Rocket or how my father treated him, he never took his hurt or anger out on me. I was his blood and he loved me.

“He better make it.” My father was present. “Muthafucka hit my son up like a practice target. But if he don’t make it, be prepared to bury them, both!”

And I knew he was talking to my mother.

Chapter 11
TRAP

"They got Rocket, Trap!" Jae screamed out in pain. She sounded like my baby mama did when she was in labor with Trap, Jr.

"What?" I jumped up, flicking the blunt in the ashtray on the table, almost knocking my mom's flower pot over. "Who got bruh, Jae?"

Tray was already heading for the front door, toting his hammer in his hand.

"Bloodclath pigs, Trap!"

"Where you at?" Tray was already in his car with the motor running, waiting on me to enter.

"No!" she hollered.

Shorty was Rocket's world on the low beside his kids and the ones he called family— us. He loved her more than he actually loved either one of his baby mothers, but he didn't want to get hurt like he did with them bitches, so he kept his feelings under lock and key.

"Jae, where you at?" Tray was looking at me like I had ten heads, so I hit the speaker button so I wouldn't have to repeat shit.

"Linden and Nostrand."

I knew what she was saying but I needed her to be more specific. "Where at? Top or bottom, Jae?"

"Over by Kings County Hospital."

Tray looked over at me and he knew what I was thinking.

"That nigga went to finish what he started," he said, reading my mind.

We were not identical but you had to know us to figure out who was who. We both rocked a low haircut full of waves, the same height of 6'1", and the color of 4 spoons of creamer in a cup of coffee. Tray had a piece of his left ear missing at the bottom 'cause we were so close together that we were connected by the ear inside the womb. When one of us got sick, the other would be sick that same hour.

Tray stayed fresh to death. Nigga matched from his draws to his socks. He was a pretty boy on the low. With me, I didn't give a fuck, as long as I didn't stink and my pockets were laced with big faces.

"Fuck that, they might as well take me too, yo!" Jae said, ending the call.

Lil' mama was a true rider. I wasn't surprised that she was about to act a fool. The bitch was plum crazy about Rocket.

Tray got us to the scene in less than five minutes without getting pulled over. The street was blocked off with police cars and some nosy mafuckin' people. We left the weapons in the car and ran to see what was cracking with our peoples.

They had Rocket in the back of a squad car with three officers around the car. A few fucking pigs were tearing Jae's car the fuck apart with a K-9's help. It was already hot as fuck outside, but being around all those pigs had my body overheated.

"I don't give a fuck!" I heard Jae's voice, but I couldn't spot her short ass until Tray pointed her out. She was surrounded by six police officers. "Yuh tink I give a fuck about disorderly conduct or jail?"

My eyes locked with Rocket's and he mouthed, "Calm her down."

I nodded and did as my bruh had requested. "Jae," I yelled and the law turned to face me.

"Step back, sir," one of them said.

"Let me just talk to her." He glared at his partners but I kept talking. "I can calm her down." It was like heaven to their ears when I said that.

They opened the circle and Jae made her way to me with tears running down her face.

"Bruh, said calm down." I whispered in her ear when she was in my arms.

"Ma called the lawyers and they said that they'll be down there before bruh get's there, yo," said Tray, joining us.

"A bloodclath snitch get more love than a real nigga, y'all," Jae cried pulling her face up off of my shirt, looking at Rocket as they drove him past us. She blew him a kiss and I watched her heart leave her chest.

"We gonna make sure that shit never happen, sis." Tray added.

"Never," I assured her, fist bumping my chest to my nigga.

***

Jae

My heart left my chest as I watched them bloodcloth pigs carry my man away. Seeing Rocket's face fade away, the only thing I could do was think about having revenge on the nigga and bitch who had crossed him. With all the attention that the cops were giving Rocket when they realized who he was, I'd managed to go unnoticed as I stashed my gun and his cell phone behind a fucking big ass rock. I wasn't in the fucking mood to go through all the bullshit about my gun and having the cops confiscate it, thinking it was the weapon that Rocket had used on his brother. I had to stay strapped. Legit.

Tray was on the phone with Ms. Judith as Trap hawked the cops down as they scattered from my car with nothing in their hands. They would never catch me riding dirty.

"Shotta, you straight?" Trap asked me as I tightened my ponytail back up.

"I'ma warp that nigga's coffin with a bow, bruh." I had it embedded in my mind to drive back to Kings County hospital and rock Ro's bitch ass to sleep. Fuck this setback.

"Shotta." I looked at Trap. "Be easy, sis." I dried my tears up as I waited patiently for the rastclath police to get fucking lost. "It would kill my brother to know that you're locked up, too."

"I might as well be, Trap." I felt my eyes watering again. "That nigga is my heart."

"Sis," Tray stepped in, "Ma wanna holla at you," he said handing me the phone.

I listened to Ms. Judith as she tried her hardest to calm me down but she could never understand that Rocket was the peephole to my soul.

"Thanks, and let me know what the lawyer saying as soon as they get in touch with you." I ended the conversation with her, handing the phone back to Tray.

One by one the officers pulled off, leaving us standing there. I needed a blunt to clear my mind and I needed one fast. Once the coast was clear from all the haters, I moved towards the rock and grabbed my belongings.

"What is the plan?" The twins asked me at the same time.

"I'm not sure." I eased my hammer under my shirt, inside my jeans. "Continue to chase that paper. Rocket wouldn't want it no other way."

Just saying his name without seeing his face had me fucked up.

"Let Ro breathe for right now until Rocket say otherwise," I added.

The twins stared at me like I was fucking crazy. I knew they wanted the nigga dead just like I did but we had to wait on my man's word.

"Slide through the spots and collect what is owed." I said, moving towards my car with tears streaming down my face.

I powered on mine and Rocket's phones just in time to see Cuba's call coming through.

"Hello." I answered as I started the car, but Cuba had yet to say a word. "Something came up but I'll be there to address the situation."

"Last table in the back on the left," he finally said.

"Say no more."

He disconnected the call.

***

I walked two blocks over and checked my gun to make sure it wouldn't fail me if I had to use it. Juniors was packed from the door.

"Excuse me," I said as I tried to get inside. A few people stepped to the side to let me through but a waiter grabbed my arm. "Bitch, why you touching me?" I snapped, reaching for my toolie.

"Do you have seat?" She let my arm go.

"Yes." I eased my hand up off of my baby and made my way to the back. I noticed Cuba's goons before my eyes landed on him at the last table on the left.

He had a table full of food in front of him as he leaned back in the seat. "Take a seat," he gestured with his hand.

I sat down even though I didn't want to. Plus, I only took orders from one man, and that was Rocket. "Rocket just got locked up."

"I ordered you something to eat," he said, ignoring my statement.

"No thanks." I replied, having taken the seat across from him. "I'm pretty sure you seen the news." I jumped straight to the point. The fried chicken looked good but my appetite wasn't present. He took a bite of the roll and gaped at me. "I'm taking that as a yes." But he didn't utter a word. "Well, Rocket tried to erase his brother for mentioning your name to him."

"Why would he do that?" He questioned me with a mouth full.

I sat straight up so I had enough room to pull my gat from my waist if I had to, plus I didn't want any unwanted ears in our conversation. "Ro and his bitch got jammed up. Rocket bailed them out but his brother had his mind made up not to do a day, so he told Rocket that he would sing on you." I kept it *one thousand*, studying his face, but he didn't stop chewing or even blink. "Loyalty is a must with Rocket, and death before dishonor is his lifestyle."

He took a sip of water, wiped his mouth and leaned back, still looking at me. "So where does that leave me?"

He had a good question. One I couldn't answer 'cause I didn't know what Ro was going to say. I pushed the plate forward. "I'm not sure what Ro will say, but I know Rocket will stop anything breathing that tries to dishonor him, and that includes dishonoring you, too."

He smiled, and all I gazed at were his golds. "How will I get my pay?"

"Whenever I get that time with Rocket in private, I'll find out what's owed and make sure you get yours. Anything else?" I needed to smoke.

"When will you find something out?"

"Whenever I get that time with him, one on one, in person." *I know this muthafucka heard me the first time.*

"And?"

I pushed my chair back, standing up. "I'll be in touch."

I left the table, and headed for the door. Muthafucka had yet to offer any help towards Rocket. Not that it mattered, it was just the principle of it.

***

Ms. Judith informed me that Rocket was denied a bond, and he had to wait to see the judge on Monday.

"What the lawyers saying?"

She took a deep breath and I felt the bad news before she said it. "It doesn't look good because Ro is alive and he's already told the police who shot him."

I took a puff of the Haze. It was my seventh blunt for the day. "Okay." Smoke danced from my mouth.

"Jae?"

"Yea."

"He's gonna be fine."

"That I know, Ms. Judith."

Hours later and three more blunts, my phone rang. "You have a collect call from…" the operator said before I heard my man's name. I smiled at it. "Press five to accept." I pressed five, not wanting to hear shit else the bitch had to say.

"Babi, I love you."

"I already know. How are you?"

"Truth or lie?" Hearing his voice had me fucked up all over again. I needed him home with me.

"Truth."

"I'm G'd the fuck up." I lied. I was distraught. He was going through enough and I didn't want him to be stressed over me.

"Good. Have you talked to the twins?"

"You already know I did, babi, and the meeting was crazy, but we'll talk soon." I wiped the tears that were running down my face.

"I just wanted to touch bases with you." I heard his voice crack. "Know that I love you."

"Rocket," I paused, "I love you more than you'll ever know."

"Now is that time to show me."

"You ain't said shit."

He laughed 'cause I used his own lingo on him. We chopped it up for a few minutes before he got off the phone, leaving me more fucked up than before. The phone call left me with a heavy heart, but nothing would ever make me waver on him.

***

Rocket

I'm cool on those that I'm related to by blood. Niggas broke the camel's back with the shit they pulled. There's no forgiveness when loyalty is tested and failed.

As I dialed Trap's number on the payphone inside the holding cell, all I could think about were my girls. The shit had just gotten better for Ashanti and La'Quinita with holding my seeds from me, but Jae promised otherwise.

When Trap didn't answer, I hung up and hit Tray's line.

"Bruh, how you holding up?" he asked, the second the call was connected.

"You already know, everything is real and nothing is cozy."

"Mane, hold ya' head. We riding with you," Tray assured me.

"I tried to holla at bruh," I was referring to Trap, "but he ain't answer."

"He making a few moves with Shotta."

"Y'all watch over her, yo."

"Bruh, Jae walks like a shotta, she talks and acts just like a shotta. No disrespect bruh, but she's a bitch that play by no rules when it comes to you and the ones that you love, so know that she'll be straight."

I couldn't help but crack a smile. They were going to have their hands full with her. They loved Jae like a sister, and she loved them because of their loyalty to me. "Collect and breathe easy, bruh."

"Already my nigga."

"Death before dishonor."

"Death before dishonor."

Mufuckin' magistrate denied me a bond, professing that I'm a danger to society, but it's all good. They couldn't hold me forever. It didn't matter where I was, I would always be the realest nigga ever.

During the twenty minutes I had with my lawyer, he let me know I was going to do some time. Nothing major 'cause the DEA had owed him a huge favor from way back, and it was time to return the debt if my cash was right.

"Like how much time?" I questioned him.

"Probably three years, no more than eight," Borowitz responded. None of the numbers that he mentioned was shit. I would rather do that shit than fold. "You did a lot of damage to your brother in front of the station, Wallace."

"Fuck that nigga. I should have toe-tagged his ass." The more I thought about it, the more I got heated that the nigga wasn't dead. "The bread gonna be what you want. That shit will be straight!"

He smiled. "Bond hearing is Monday. I'll let your family know that you are okay."

"Bet."

The next morning, I was changed out and shipped to Rikers Island with a van full of niggas. I couldn't wait for this shit to be over with, even though I knew the shit was just getting started. *Damn!*

Chapter 12
JAE

Tray was at Ms. Judith's crib counting up the dough we had gathered up from a few of the spots, while me and Trap continued to collect, when I recognized Red leaving her sister's house on Nostrand Avenue, by herself.

I parked the car directly in front of a fire hydrant and popped the truck when I saw her.

"Nobody is off limits. Not even this bitch!" I seethed at the sight of her.

"I'ma murk that fat bitch, sis," growled Trap.

There were a few people posted in front of the apartment building and I couldn't afford my man's bruh to get caught up with a body.

"Not right now, bruh. Let me introduce her to these hands." I hopped out the car and grabbed my cricket bat from the trunk and ran across the street.

The small crowd of people were looking at me like I was crazy, but I didn't give a fuck. This bitch was about to feel my bloodclath pain. I hadn't been able to function without Rocket, so for that, the bitch was about to pay.

"Bitch!" I called out behind Red, and when the thot turned around, I swung the bat with all my strength. It caught her on her upper shoulder.

"Arrgghh!" She hollered in pain. I swung on that bitch again but she ducked and dropped her purse. I was trying to take her head off.

"What the fuck?" Someone yelled.

I released the bat from my hand and squared up on the hoe.

"Bitch, you crazy!" She screamed, holding her shoulder.

"Yuh nuh seh nuttin' yet!" That bitch hadn't seen shit yet.

I moved my arms back and forth like a boxer. My blows were stiff, slow and firm. She blocked one of my left hooks with her right forearm, but my right jab caught her dead in the eye. She staggered back, and my left fist caught the other eye.

"Bitch, yuh and yuh man a informa!" A fist connected with her mouth. The bitch was big and I used that to my advantage. She tried her hardest to hit me but my movements were too fast. I was the baddest and I wanted this bitch to know. I kicked her left knee in, and down she went.

"Dayumn!" A voice sounded off. I was about to give these people a show of their lives. A free one.

"Send that bitch to lay beside that nigga, sis." The excitement I heard in Tap's voice amped me up.

I caught her with an uppercut under her chin when her fat ass was descending. I swear I saw a tooth fly out of her busted ass mouth. When she hit the concrete, the bitch rolled over on her stomach and curled up in a ball. *Pussy ass hoe.*

I stomped her hands as they covered her head. "Yuh bloodclath bitch!" The more I thought about Rocket behind bars because of Ro, the harder I trampled the bitch. "Yuh…" I kicked her head like a soccer ball. I watched it bounce up and down before I moved my foot again, landing another kick. "Fi dead!"

"That's enough, lil' mama," cautioned an unfamiliar voice.

"Nigga who the fuck is you?" Trap said coming up to us.

I turned around to see him ready to send a nigga on his way to the other side.

"Easy, yo." Dude's hands were raised above his head. "All I'm sayin' is that she won." He licked his lips backing away from Trap's gun.

I picked my bat up and clocked Red one more time in the head before I spat on her. "Bloodclath informa fi dead! Snitch ass bitch!" Blood leaked from her head.

"Mind ya' muthafuckin' business, B, before you get fucked over what don't concern you!" Trap told the nigga.

"Bruh, let's go! Too many eyes." I schooled him, but he didn't move until I pulled his hand down. Today was this nigga's lucky day, for sure. "Bruh!" I called out. The crowd had gotten bigger but they stood afar, watching the show. "Come on, yo."

Trap backed up, with the pistol still aimed at the nigga's head. We crossed the street and got inside the car.

I tossed the bat in the backseat and checked my face out. I was still flawless. "Let's go before I change my mind and body that bitch and the Superman wannabe!" I re-pinned my hair up and pulled off to collect the rest of Rocket's bread, sparking up a fresh blunt.

Chapter 13
TRAY

"You ain't gonna believe this shit, yo," said Trap the instant he saw my face. I had just secured two hundred and fifty thousand in cash.

"Believe what, bruh?" Jae dropped a black book bag at my feet and walked off to take a seat. Trap's face let me know that something wasn't right. "Nigga, what's good?" I stood to my feet, ready to take on whatever he had to say.

"Yellow Man hit two of the spots, bruh."

"What the fuck you mean?" I wasn't comprehending shit my twin was spitting.

"Deh disloyal mufucka showed up at two of the projects and claimed that Rocket sent him, so the workers gave the bread up, not thinking anything about the request," Jae explained.

I glanced at Trap, waiting for him to tell me it was a joke, but his facial expressions stayed the same. Which meant it was murder time.

"I've been calling and texting that nigga and he has yet to hit me back!" Jae snapped.

"What the fuck?" I reached for my phone in my pocket to call the nigga myself.

"He ain't gonna answer, bruh," my twin said, taking a seat beside Jae.

Shotta was always rolling a blunt up when she had shit on her mind. I hit Yellow Man's line but the nigga sent me straight to voicemail.

"I know we ain't gonna let that shit slide." I hit send, hoping the nigga would just answer, but when I got the same result, I knew shit was fucking real.

"Imagine that shit, Tray," Jae spoke, licking the blunt paper. "Imagine that," she laughed. "Niggas crossing over like it's a game and Rocket ain't judged yet!"

"How much he bagged?"

"About five hundred thousand," Trap answered me.

"What?"

"Boy, why you up in here screaming?" My ma walked in on us in the basement.

"Mufucka just robbed us!" I clapped back.

"What?" She smiled at Jae. "For how much?" She didn't like what we did for a living, but she still had our backs. I was too heated to speak, so Trap told her what had taken place. "Damn," she expressed before she continued. "That's what the lawyer asking for to represent Rocket."

"It's all good," Jae said in a calm tone, puffing on the blunt. "All I'm worried about is paying Cuba off." Smoke circles escaped from her mouth.

"Fuck that nigga!"

"I agree, but it's Rocket's character on the line." She passed the blunt to Trap. "I won't allow no nigga to go around throwing salt on his name over some green backs."

I saluted Jae. She was about loyalty and principles.

"How much is that?" I asked, pointing to the bag that she had dropped at my feet.

"A quarter million!"

"How much y'all owe Cuba?" My mom questioned, fanning the weed smoke from her nose.

We all looked at Jae. "Rocket didn't say and when I talked to Cuba, he didn't give me a number."

I hit Yellow Man's line again, but all I got was voicemail. "We gotta pay that nigga a visit, yo!"

"I'm ready. What we waiting on?" Jae snapped. A true shotta for real. She was down to ride at any time and cost.

"Ma, count and stash the bread up. We'll be back!"

My nostrils flared as I headed for the door. Ro had to pay for that bitch shit he did.

***

RO

I was awake but still medicated when I overheard the doctor updating my mother on my condition. I had lost a number of teeth thanks to the bullet that lodged in my face from Rocket's burner. The left side of my jaw was wired, so they had to feed me everything liquid. A colostomy bag was now my new intestine. My shoulder was straight; the bullet entered and exited without any major problems.

"When will he be released?" My pops inquired.

"In a couple of days. High dose medication will be prescribed for the pain," the doctor explained to my parents.

"Thank you." My mother expressed her gratitude.

I had got the message from Rocket but I wasn't going to take heed and do any time. Fuck him and his plug. I was going to snitch his plug out for me and my woman's freedom.

"They got Rocket, son. The police called me a few days ago and delivered the news. He was denied bond," my mom spoke. "But..." She took a breather. "But Red got caught by Jae."

I flicked my eyes open as I felt a throbbing pain travel through my upper body. My heart. "Whaa?" I pushed through the pain, trying to find out what had transpired with my lady.

"Shhh." My mom placed her finger to my lips. "She's down the hall and she's okay," she said, leaving the room.

My pop's leaned over my bed; his face was hard. "When the time comes for you to point that nigga out, don't hesitate. Show that mufucka no mercy!"

"I'm not," I muttered, squeezing my eyes shut as the image of Rocket squeezing that trigger replayed in my mind.

***

When my mom wheeled Red into my room in a wheelchair and I saw her, it crushed me. Red explained to me that Jae had caught her leaving her sister's house and beat her with a bat. Literally. Jae used Red's size to her advantage and trashed my lady. Red had a broken arm, two black eyes, a sprained ankle, a gash in her head that required twenty stitches, and bruises allover her body. She looked like a dump trunk had hit her. That crazy Jamaican bitch fucked my woman up.

"I can't inform on them, Ro." Tears ran down her face. "I have kids that I need to protect out here."

My father walked out the room. The ass whooping scared Red not to tell, but not me. Our freedom was on the line, so fuck Rocket, his empire and his plug. I was 'bout to sing the national anthem, a cappella.

***

TRAP

When a real nigga shows love to the streets, mufuckas always show their true hands. Rocket didn't have to show love, but the real nigga in him did. Every person around him ate, hands down. That's why my hammer was loaded and ready as I pulled a mask over my face.

Jae didn't want to wear one but she did rock a hoodie. "I'ma kill the nigga for disrespecting my nigga, so fuck wearing one! I want this nigga to remember my face."

I shook my head. There was nothing that I could say to change her mind, so I kept silent.

"Leave the keys in the ignition." I opened the back door.

"This ain't my first trip, bruh. I already know," she snarled, opening up the driver's door. "I'm true to this!"

The house was in the middle of the block with a front porch light on. Me, Tray and Rocket had been there about twenty times to either drop off or pick up, and the layout hadn't changed. I hoped tonight it'd be the same way.

Yellow Man made his bitch leave the backdoor unlocked, so if he was in any trouble it wouldn't take him long to enter the house and run for cover.

I was leading the pack with Jae behind me, and Tray followed as we moved alongside the building. There was no movement or light coming from inside as we traveled around back.

I stopped dead in my tracks when the sensor light for the neighbor's house came on.

"Damn, take my back off," Jae whispered loudly for Tray to hear her.

A chuckle slipped from my mouth. I hoped she popped that hammer the way she popped her gums.

"Stay right here." I looked back at Jae and Tray. "I'ma see if the joint is unlocked." Before Jae could say a word, I was off.

Luckily, we found the backdoor unlocked. I shook my head at Yellow Man's stupidity, which allowed us easy entrance into his spot. Once we were inside, it took less than a minute to grab his woman and introduce a nightmare into her life.

***

"But I have a child," she begged, looking at me. "I'll make sure he pays you!"

"You got ya' silencer?" Jae questioned Tray with her eyes and voice.

"Yup." He handed it over to her.

"Please, I'm begging you, don't kill me."

Shorty was wasting her breath. The Jae I knew was letting that shit fall on deaf ears.

"Please," she screamed, and before she could utter another sound or word, Tray's toy spat venom from Jae's hand.

Tu! Tu! Tu!

"A loyal nigga protects his family with honesty!" She spoke to the dead corpse before letting two more rounds off into shorty's lifeless body.

Jae was a savage; I had never met a bitch whose gangsta was on her level. Rocket had done well by choosing her.

Chapter 14
ROCKET

The muthafuckin' judge declined my bond without my physical appearance in court. I had a feeling that I wasn't going to get one, but to reject me without me being there in the flesh was some other shit.

"Mr. Wallace." My lawyer sat behind the glass, giving me the news. "Look at it this way: at least if you have to serve some time, the time you're spending in here will count."

"I hear you, but damn!" I had mad things that I needed to do.

He shuffled through a stack of papers before he stopped. He read over the sheet before he slid it through the slot to me. "Ricardo Johnson identified Draymond Wallace as the shooter."

"It's all good," I said as I stood, pushing the papers back to him. "I'm ready for whatever."

"I'll do my best representing you." He pulled at his beard. "I'll make sure your sentence isn't that long." He winked at me.

"You better, with all that bread you asking for." I stood up and walked out the door so the officer could escort me back to the block.

I couldn't sleep the night before visitation day for shit. I paced the 9 by 5 the whole night. My bunkie was an old head who had been down for two years. He was knocked out as I walked from the door to the wall, wishing morning would appear.

I was too amped the fuck up to see Jae. Somehow, she figured out how to put money in my account, so I was extra straight. When they got me, I had a band in my pocket, so they posted it on my books. I used that to get what I needed.

Morning finally came and they unlocked the doors. I was the first one in the shower. An hour later my name was called for visitation.

As I stared at my bitch walking across the room to me, all I could do was give her the utmost respect. Without the money and power, my woman was still standing beside me, holding me down.

It's mad crazy how a bitch I met through a traffic stop had my mafuckin' back more than those who shared the same blood as me.

"Babi!" she jumped in my arms. "I love you." She tilted her head up and our lips danced together in perfect harmony.

As I gazed into her eyes, I could see and feel her undying love and loyalty for me. "How you holding up, baby?" I asked when we pulled away.

"I'm a hitta and a trapaholic. G'd up from the floor up for my man!"

"Is that right?"

"Rocket," she stepped closer, "I'ma stay devoted and ride this wave with you." Her lips touched my mouth again and my hands cuffed her ass like we were in our bedroom. "I'm all about showing, building and winning," she pulled away to say. "Know that you'll always be the realest in the streets, whether you present or not." Her lips were back on mine.

I welcomed her tongue. *Damn, I can't wait to make love to her again.*

My eyes scanned the busy visitation room quickly, looking for the two female officers. They both were posted up at the door, seemingly deep in a conversation. My dick jumped. I had to pull away before we fucked around and got the visit terminated.

"I can't wait," she licked her super moist lips, "for you to come home."

"Word?" I walked around the table to take a seat.

"Yuh already know, babi."

Her outfit was simple but gotdamn, it was shouting to the heavens to be saved. *Free Rocket* was inked on her white plain shirt across the chest. The fitted, tight jeans showed every curve that there was to see. And even though I loved her in heels, I liked the sexy way she rocked the all-white Air Force 1's she had on. She twirled around, giving me a full view before she took her seat. I couldn't wait to tear that pussy the fuck up.

"What's the word on the streets?" I slouched down in the chair, stretching my legs out so they could touch hers.

She leaned over the table between us and whispered, "Yellow Man tested ya' gangsta." She licked her lips. "He got two of the spots and got ghost."

"What? I've shown that nigga love from day one and this is how he repays me?" My mouth curled with anger.

Jae leaned closer do that her words wouldn't carry beyond our table. "Yea, he violated, but his bitch paid with her life."

"Say what?" I lifted an eyebrow.

"It's never just you, or me, it's always us!"

"Say no more." I understood exactly what she was saying.

With pride, I looked at her and nodded my head in appreciation of her thoroughness. She sat back in the chair. Rude gal wasn't but so tall, but she had the heart of a giant.

I erased the small hint of a smile off of my face and looked her in the eyes. "Island gurl, you've gotta stay out the way."

"And let niggas disrespect you? Fuck outta here. Not on my watch, babi," she vowed.

"Jae, listen to me."

She looked away, causing me to kick the fuck out of the table. The niggas on the side of me and their visitors jumped. Her eyes came back to me.

"Let that shit go till I touch! Do you hear me?" I snarled.

"Yes." That's what her mouth said, but I knew better. She was fucking hard headed.

I gave her a few seconds to let my words sink in before I carried on. "What the plug had to say?"

Her eyes closed. "All he's worried about…" Her eyes popped open. "…Is his bread."

"Word?" I wasn't surprised that he wasn't worried about me. *Mufucka, count me out, 'cause my back is against the wall.*

"Yup. Mufucka didn't ask if you needed any help or nothin'."

"It's all good. Make sure he get his paper." *Nigga won't be getting another dollar from my hands.*

"How much?"

"A mil' and a half."

"Say no more."

"If it's not all there, let 'em know I'll be home to get him the rest."

Jae gave me a look like I was crazy. Her brows arched instantly. She tapped her chest. "I'ma make sure he gets all his, even if I have to shed some blood."

"You don't fuckin' lis—"

"I won't give no nigga the time to talk or disrespect you," she cut me off. "He gonna get all his. Trust me, Rocket!"

"Let that shit go!"

"Rocket—"

I needed her to know what I said still flies. I sat straight up, rubbing my hands together. "Jae," I spoke through gritted teeth, "let that shit go, til I land! That's not a request, ma, it's an order."

She nodded her understanding. I just hoped she would obey me on this. For a few minutes, neither one of us said a word. I eyeballed her as she checked her surroundings.

"That bitch Red wasn't so lucky, though," she declared with a smile plastered on her face. "Caught that bitch leaving her sister's house on Nostrand, and trashed that ass proper."

Jae's hands were that nice. I didn't second guess for a second that she whooped Red's ass. I was glad that's all she did and nothing more.

"Sent that bitch to the hospital with her snitching ass nigga," she disclosed.

"You've got to start thinking for the both of us now, yo. I need you out there to hold a nigga down," I lightly reprimanded her.

"What you saying ain't nothing I don't know, Rocket."

"A'ight. Get on point and stay on point. I'm the gorilla; let me get out and do what a gorilla do. You just play the background before you end up doing life in the pen."

"Okay, damn!" She folded her arms across her chest.

I couldn't help but chuckle. "Cute ass mufucka." I leaned over and kissed away some of that stubbornness.

After that, we vibed for the rest of the visit, and she promised me that she would be back to see me next week, and stay clear out of harm's way.

"Five minutes!" The officer by the door announced.

"Damn, time moves too fuckin' fast." Her face dropped.

"It's all good. Come give ya' nigga some sugah."

She bounced up and into my arms. I hated that she was leaving but I was glad that she was in my life with me on this trip. But I wondered if she would ride the wave all the way. Only time would tell.

Our lips parted and I swore that shit hurt me more than I expected.

"Tell the twins to be here next week," I said when she removed her lips from mine.

"I got you!"

"Visitation is over!" the fucking haters screamed.

"I love you." She kissed me one last time.

"I love you, too, Jae."

When she walked off, she gave me a show with her ass better than a stripper on a pole. Lil' mama was bad as fuck and she was mine. That alone made my heart shine as I made my way to get searched so I could return to the cellblock.

Trust is earned, love is shown, and loyalty is proven. Jae— my bitch, my rider— gave me all that and more.

Chapter 15
JAE

St. Elizabeth, Jamaica, West Indies, 25 years ago, I was saying my times table in a closet, out loud with the lights off and that shit didn't scare me.

My grandparents would say, "If yuh nuh seh nuttin', yuh a guh stay pan track." Meaning, if I didn't have any distractions around me, I could stay focused and concentrate on the task at hand.

People would think that it was cruel how I learned my times table, but my grandparents called it structure. My father's parents raised me from birth 'cause my parents were too busy doing them.

At age 5, I was in primary school and it was my job to learn and pay attention because education is the key to success. We lived on a farm, so my other job was to help take care of the animals and crops.

"As a family, Jae, we are one." My grandma taught me. We live together, we eat together, we die together.

Getting up on Saturday mornings to witness one of my favorite animals prepared by my grandfather's hand under a tree, because he was the butcher and our provider, didn't move me in tears 'cause everything living must die one day. My papa would say that.

My grandparents took their vows seriously at ages 16 and 17. Now they were 97 and 98 and still together, happily married. Their words of honor expressed love and loyalty until their last breath.

That's how it was where I was born. A Jamaican at heart but an American by paper. To this day, I still lived by my grandparents' words of knowledge. "Loyalty over everything, even love."

I had a man who I was truly devoted to. He's all I wanted, and anyone who crossed him was going to get a reaction from me. I always told people: *Please understand this because I won't repeat myself. He's precious to me, and what we've built is sacred.* I valued loyalty and love, and not even death could change how I felt. Fuck the walls that he was behind.

***

"Ms. Judith," I greeted her at the door, "glad you could come over." I shut the door behind her. "How are you doing?" I asked, walking past her.

"I'm good, can't complain," she responded, taking a seat on my sofa.

"And if you could, would you?"

Water formed in her eyes. "How could a mother disown something that was created inside of her?"

I knew she was talking about Rocket 'cause I've never discussed my life with her. Only Rocket.

Her question caught me way off guard, but I understood the love that she had for her boys and Rocket. Her eyes poured water when studying A picture of me and Rocket in Times Square.

"It doesn't matter what happened back then, Ms. Judith. I'm just glad that you were there to show him love." I walked off to get the money for the lawyer 'cause I had to meet up with Trap and Tray in an hour to give Cuba what was owed to him. "It's all there." I handed her the Johnson Sport book bag.

"Thank you, Jae," she whispered as tears continued to race down her face.

"No need to thank me, it's my job, but thank you." I reached down and hugged her, showing my appreciation.

***

"All the bread there?" I grilled the twins the moment they got in my ear.

"Yea!" They answered together.

Minus the money that Yellow Man had taken from the spots, we were still sitting pretty while he was feeling the death of his child's mother, according to the twins. Listening to Rocket's words repeatedly in my head, I was going to let the nigga live, but he had better stay out of my way and out of sight. If he came around my way, I was going to touch that ass, on my life.

"You strapped?" asked Tray.

Daydreaming, I pulled Rocket's phone from between my legs, wishing it was his dick.

"Jae?"

"What?" I took my eyes off of the road to see what Tray needed.

"I asked was you strapped?"

"When do you know me *not* to have my shit on me?" I rolled my eyes at his ass. My shit was legit, so there was no need to be without it.

"You always poppin' shit," Trap said from the backseat laughing.

"My youth, whateva!" I laughed back.

"*My youth, whateva*!" They mocked me in unison, and we all cracked up at their fake ass accent.

Cuba wanted the meeting to go down in Prospect Park.

"I'm 'bout to pull in," I said when he answered my call.

"I'm in the far back by the gate, Black Denali."

"Bet." It was my time to end the call.

My lip gloss popped, but my pistol would pop better if shit didn't go down right with this muthafucka. I pulled into the parking lot. I heard Trap cocking his hammer. Tray double-checked his as I looked around for Cuba's ride.

"Let's get this shit over with," I said when I spotted Cuba's the truck.

I knew his goons were around. Even though I didn't see them, I felt eyes on us.

I left the car running as we opened our doors. The back door of the Denali opened and out came the Cuban. The book bag was strapped on my back as my Glock kept the crease in my jeans straight. I walked ahead of the twins.

"How are you doing?" asked Cuba.

"Good and you?"

"Great. Twins." He acknowledged them, and they just nodded.

I slipped the book bag off and handed it to him. "A mil' and a half." I handed the book bag to him.

He raised his right hand and the passenger door of the Denali swung wide open. A thick, tall, black haired Spanish woman sashayed out the truck to get the bag from my hand, and disappeared back inside the truck.

"Is it all there?" he asked, staring me down.

"Was Rocket ever short?" *Who the fuck does this nigga think he is to question my man's loyalty over some money that he risked his freedom for?*

"I take that as a yes," he spat when I didn't answer.

I counted to 10 in my mind to see if he would say something about still doing business, but when he didn't, I turned and walked off. Business was done. *He ain't the only bloodclath plug in the world.*

***

Hours after the meeting with Cuba, I was on the phone with Rocket's slime-ass baby mother.

"Ashanti?" I got her number from Rocket's phone. "How are you doing?"

"Who the fuck is this?" The bitch was so ratchet, but for Rocket to see his little one, I would do whatever to make sure it was done.

"Jae."

"Bitch, I know you ain't calling my muthafuckin' phone?"

"Look," I cracked my knuckles, "I know what occurred the other day could've been prevented," I lied. I always wanted to show that bitch my hands pop just like my gums. "I want to get MiMi on Saturday so I can take her to see her dad, or you can make thc trip ya' self."

"Bitch, what role you playing?" she yelled. I had to bite my lip just so I didn't go the fuck off.

"Yo, real talk, I don't appreciate that bitch shit, and it ain't about me—"

"My child ain't going nowhere with you!"

"Listen to me." I rubbed my hands together as my left leg shook. I was mad. "I'll be there at seven thirty to pick MiMi up on Saturday morning."

"Bitch, fuck you!" She hung up on me.

My first thought was: *Now, when I beat her muthafuckin' ass, I better not hear Rocket's mouth. If she knows what I knows, she better have MiMi dressed and ready on Saturday.*

Next, I hit La'Quinita up. Unlike Ashanti, she agreed to let me take Rocket's seed to visit him next time.

"Thank you, yo," I said, relieved

"No problem, Jae."

With that out of the way I was finally able to call it a night. As I closed my eyes, I wondered what the twins were doing to keep things good on their end.

Chapter 16
TRAY

With all the bullshit that was going on with Rocket, his plug didn't mention shit about doing business with us, which was cool, but at the same time, a fucking headache. We needed a connect and we needed one fast to continue holding the spots down.

I had run into this nigga Wayne through his sister Tasha. I used to fuck with shorty but she wasn't ready for a relationship, so we ended what we had but still remained really good friends. "What's up stranger?" I rang her end.

"Tray," she sang, "how're you doing?" I could hear her smiling through the phone.

"Shit, just chilling."

"What did I do to deserve this call?" She flirted. Even though she refused to be in a relationship with me, she couldn't turn down my dick.

"Tryin' to see if you can link me up with ya' peoples?" We had talked about me making moves with her brother's operation before, but since I was down with Rocket, nothing ever came of it.

"I've gotta hit him up and see, so let me hit you back."

"Bet."

I hoped the nigga would fuck with me, 'cause if he did then me and Trap could still run Crown Heights until something else came up. Twenty minutes later, my phone rang and it was Wayne. "What's gud, son?" The nigga must've remembered me. "My sister said you tryna holla at me on some business shit?"

"Hell yea."

"Aite, say no more. Meet me at Coney Island park."

"An hour." I checked my watch.

"Yea. That's good."

"One."

Trap was at Ma's, spending some time with Trap Jr., so I wouldn't call and interrupt him with his seed until shit was official with this move. Then, I would let my brother know I had found a new plug.

***

I was twenty minutes early, waiting on this nigga to show up so we could discuss business. As I waited, I texted Tasha, asking her if she wanted to link up tonight. I missed the pussy.

Her: *Just say U miss me.*

Me: *Naw, I want U 2 tell me dat when I'm N dat thing.*

Her: *:)*

Me: *U ain't sayn' nuttin'!*

Her: *I'ma call U when I get off 2night.*

Me: *Aite.*

The hour came and that nigga Wayne had yet to show up, but since I wanted what he had, I sat tight. I had a gut feeling that I should leave, but the thought of getting more money kept me seated.

Jae's number popped across my screen just when I was about to hit Wayne up to see what was good.

"Yo, I'ma beat that bitch Ashanti."

"Calm down, sis." I knew Ashanti didn't want no problems with Jae. Ashanti spoke that rah-rah shit, but Jae *lived* it "What happened?"

"Deh bitch a chat 'bout—"

Her Patwha was out. She was mad. "Sis, I can't understand you," I stopped her.

"She talkin' 'bout how I can't get MiMi. Bruh, I'm telling you, you better call and talk some sense into that bitch, for real."

I spotted a black on black BMW, pulling in the park, then my phone beeped. It was the nigga. Bout time. "Jae, let me hit you back, sis."

"Whateva!" She coughed and I knew she was probably blazing. I shook my head as I clicked over. "Yo."

"I'm here, my nigga," said Wayne.

"Me too. Is that you in the BMW?"

"Yea, where you at?"

"Come on down. I'm about to step out." I dropped the call and climbed out of my money green Lexus truck.

Another white BMW followed deep for a regular meeting. This nigga is riding, I thought.

Wayne removed himself from the BMW, and so had two other niggas who were clearly strapped the fuck up. I could see the hammer prints through their shirts.

"Long time since I saw you." He dapped me up as I checked his goons out.

"I know, ya' sister dropped me." I released his hands. "She ain't ready for a real nigga."

"I can't comment." We shared a laugh. The nigga was blinged the fuck out and fresher than a dead muthafucka on their going away day. "So what's good?" He continued, scanning the parking lot.

"I'm in need of a plug, yo." I told the truth.

"On what?"

"The Girl for right now." I wasn't gonna jump in and say all that the team needed. I would flip the cocaine a few times before I added the rest to the list.

"Let's take a stroll," he suggested.

As we walked at a snail's, Wayne said that his product was the truth. "Everything that I supply is the truth, son. Believe that!" He boasted.

He wanted 18 stacks for a bird. And if the cocaine was that, then I could step on it and sling it through the projects for 21 stacks, making a few dollars, and out of town niggas had to pay $27,000. But I needed a constant flow.

"How many you want?" he asked.

His goons were posted up at the vehicles talking. We were on our way back to the rides.

"About twenty-one," I said, and he stopped walking.

"Word?" The look on his face let me know that he was surprised.

"Yea. And I need that joint like today."

"Aite, let me make a few calls and I'ma hit you up in a few days."

"Cool."

When the nigga dapped me up, I felt a vibe, a bad one, but I brushed that shit off and blamed it on paranoia, and the fact that sudden change always made a nigga uncomfortably.

"Fuck with me, son," I said, right before bouncing.

Chapter 17
RO

Me and Red were released on the same day. My parents were there to pick us up and take us to their house. Even though Rocket hated our mother, I knew he would never put her life in jeopardy, so it was safer there than anywhere else.

"So, what now?" Red asked when we were alone in the back room.

"I don't know," I lied. Rocket wasn't going to just let this shit slide, but I didn't want her to start flipping out.

"I'm scared, Ro. I'm so scared," she whined.

I was fucking tired of hearing about her being scared. I kept telling her that I was doing this for us.

"Ain't shit else gonna happen to you," I snapped. "Just shut the fuck up so I can think and gather my fuckin' thoughts!"

Red started crying harder, but I damn sure didn't give a fuck. I didn't reach out and try to comfort her. I knew what I had to do to seal Rocket's fate, but I had to come up with a plan for us to stay free. A real fucking good one.

"You promised me that nothing would happen to me, didn't you?" Red got up off the bed and walked in front of the TV to block my view. "What about my fuckin' kids, Ricardo? Have you thought about them?" she screamed, holding her head. This bitch was more worried about her kids than my muthafuckin' freedom.

"I told you from day one that I was doing this shit for us!"

She paced in front of me before she wigged the fuck out. "You got me in this shit and you better get me the fuck out." She faced me.

"Or else what, Red?" *How fucking dare this bitch*, I thought. She wasn't saying shit when I was giving her money for her kids and her family. "Or else what, bitch?" I was fed the fuck up with her no-good ass.

"You know what, Ro?" Her tears returned. "Fuck you!" she said, and then she stormed out of the bedroom, she slamming the bedroom door behind her.

Needless to say, shit was real tense.

***

Three days later, the Narcs came knocking. Thank goodness Red wasn't around. She had called to let me know that she was at her mother's house with her children.

"Mr. Johnson, how are you doing?" One of the Narcs asked as we stood in the center of the living room with my mom and pops nearby.

"Good to be alive." They smiled but I was dead ass serious.

"We are glad that you are alive, because we really need your help." The other detective chirped in.

"How can he do that?" My father jumped in the conversation.

"We need to know who the connect is, sir."

"Can't he just handle one thing at a time?" my mom asked, holding my hand.

The Narcs glanced at each other, and at that moment I was glad that my mother was there, giving and showing support.

"After the case with your brother is settled, Mr. Johnson, we'll be back," replied the gentleman closest to me.

"Thanks," I said with relief.

My father escorted them out as I dropped my head in shame, knowing I'd rather tell on the next man than do a fucking day behind the gates of hell.

I just hoped Rocket couldn't reach out from jail and have me touched.

Chapter 18
TRAP

I was on the hunt for that shady ass nigga Yellow Man, but the he was nowhere to be found. I showed up at his baby's mama's funeral and the pussy ass nigga wasn't even in attendance. *Straight bitch!* I avoide scoffed silently. *Nigga bit the hand that was feeding him, now he better run for his fucking life.*

Sitting around the house a few days later, I still had the thirst for blood in my mouth. Niggas just couldn't keep it solid.

"Daddy, can I go over to your friend's house this weekend?" Trap Jr. asked, standing in front of me as I counted up the bread that Tray said he needed for a move that he wanted to make.

"I've gotta find out if Pound Cake has any plans." I moved my eyes off the dough to check my little nigga out. Trap Jr. reminded me so much of his mom, Tara. Shorty was my world and more before she died on the delivery table, giving birth to our son six years ago.

"When is that going to be?" He had Tara's attitude. Always wanted an answer right away. He loved staying at Pound Cake's house 'cause she had a little nigga the same age as my son.

"Some time later." I rubbed the top of his head affectionately.

"Find out for me, 'cause I ain't trying to be stuck over here with grandma all weekend."

"What?" I chuckled.

He had a huge mug on his face. "Dad."

I leaned my head to the side to get a better view of my kid.

"Don't get me wrong, I love grandma, but I be bored over here, yo." He took a seat beside me.

I wanted to laugh but I held it back. "Aite, I got you." I used my left hand to mush his head in a playful manner. "Now take ya' ass back upstairs so I can handle business."

His little eyes roamed over the bag of money before he stood to his feet.

"Let me get a face to put in my pocket." He fondled his pockets.

I pulled a $20 bill from the pile and gave it to him, kicking him out the basement.

"Twenty these days can't get you nothing!" he yelled, going up the stairs.

I didn't comment 'cause my little man couldn't help it. He had that shit in his blood, thanks to his mom.

I took a nostalgic trip down memory lane.

"You giving me just a stack, Trap?"

"Come on now, Tara. I gave you twenty-five hundred two days ago, ma."

"So what?" She rolled on top of me.

"That shit ain't growing on trees, boo."

She grinded her pussy on me, biting down on her bottom lip. She was nine months pregnant with little man. "Well, I'm 'bout to work for it." She removed her from her panties and fucked us back to sleep. When I woke up, I gave her five stacks.

A few tears dropped from my eyes as I reminisced about my baby. She was a down ass bitch for me and I missed her. My thoughts were cut off by my cell phone.

I cleared my throat, wiping the mist from my eyes. "Yo."

"Trap, I just saw that nigga Yellow Man, yo!" said Swave. I had let a few niggas know that I was hunting for the him.

"Where at?" I stuffed the money in the duffle bag, shoving my feet in my Timbs at the same damn time.

"The nigga just left the trap, talking 'bout how he checking for you."

I wondered why the fuck this nigga didn't text me when Yellow Man was right there. I didn't say shit about it, though.

"Checking for me?" I pushed the bag full of loot under the table, grabbing my hammer.

"Yea, bruh."

"Where you at?"

"Over on Empire."

"Bet." I dropped the call, running up the steps. "Ma," I hollered.

"Yes!" She screamed back.

"Put that bag up for me!"

I was out the door before she responded, but I knew she had it covered.

***

I was on Empire within minutes. I circled the block as I dialed Swave's number back. "What the nigga pushin'?"

"A white Crown Vick."

"Bet."

"And he had two niggas with him, too."

"Aite."

I didn't give a fuck if Yellow Man had an army with him. I wanted that sucka dead for fucking with my family, especially with all that Rocket had done for his ungrateful ass.

I slammed a bullet in the chamber and smashed the gas pedal down, looking everywhere for the Crown Vick with three pussies.

"Fuck!" I punched the pedal.

I circled the block over from Empire with my machine in my grip when I noticed a white Crown Vick coming up the street towards me. I let my window down and floored the gas pedal towards the car.

Boc! Boc! Boc! Boc! Boc!

My hammer was clapping thunder and lightning from about ten feet. The Crown Vick swerved, and the driver ducked, but the passenger in the front seat was leaning out the window, clapping back at me, and it was none other than Yellow Man.

I hit the brakes and watched the Vic' crash into a parked car. The driver didn't come back up, but Yellow Man kept sending lead my way. I knew my Mac 11 wouldn't fail me, it was my bible; the truth. The banana clip held 100 bullets and I was going to rain every single one on him.

Yellow Man and another nigga jumped out of the parked car, limping. I put the car in park and jumped in the backseat, only to exit through the back door, still busting fire at them niggas.

Sirens filled the air as I hunched down behind my car. I stopped fucking the trigger for a moment to see if they were still firing.

When I didn't hear anything, I eased my head out slowly. I saw Yellow Man and one of the niggas running down the block.

The sirens were getting closer and closer, so I dashed back in my car and reversed down the block, pulling my phone out of my pocket.

"Jae!"

"Yo," she barked loudly.

"Come get me! I'm 'bout to be at Pound Cake's crib."

"Say no more." I knew she heard the urgency in my voice.

Chapter 19
JAE

If I called a muthafucka my friend or my family, I meant just that. I'd ride and die for mine, so when I got that call from Trap, I knew shit had gone down or was about to go down, and I was ready to ride.

Since Rocket got locked up, shit had gone stupid crazy. Muthafuckas that he thought wouldn't try him had shown him different, but it was all good. They couldn't hold him forever. Especially a real nigga.

As I turned on the block that Pound Cake lived on, I spotted Trap behind me in his car with a cracked windshield. I found an empty parking spot and parked, waiting on him to do the same. I pulled my Glock from under my leg and rested it on top, just in case I had to let a few bullets go.

"Sis, let's go." He jumped in my car, out of breath and I pulled back out on the road.

"What the fuck, nigga?"

He slipped the Mac 11 from under his shirt and sat it at his feet, leaning the seat all the way back.

"Nigga, what the fuck is up?" I hated being in the dark or the last to know something.

"Got a call that Yellow Man was looking for me, so I showed up and got the party started."

"Without me?"

He palmed his whole face. "Anyway, I didn't get that clown but I got one of his boys, though."

"That's good, but you did this shit without me, Trap."

"I ain't have no time to think, sis, real talk, so don't take that shit personal."

I drove to the spot, not saying a word. I knew Rocket didn't want me in no shit, but damn, I couldn't let his brothers fight the war by themselves.

"I'ma get that nigga before it's over with, I swear." Trap professed once we were in the house.

"I think Rocket want us all to stay low until he touch," I said, sparking up my half a blunt.

"When is the visit, again?"

"Saturday."

***

Saturday morning, the twins were at my house, waiting on me to get dress so I could go get the girls. La'Quinita answered my call and said that MooMoo was dressed and waiting.

The dumb bitch Ashanti, on the other hand, had her fucking phone turned the fuck off. Every time I called and got the same thing, the more I got mad.

"I swear to God, I'ma smoke this bitch!" Tray was driving as I sat in the back. "I told this bitch since last week that I was coming to get MiMi, yo."

We were almost at her house, 'cause I called Ms. Pam's phone and she said that she wasn't there with her.

"Let me ring the bell first, Jae," Trap had the nerve to say. Rocket couldn't tame me when it came to trashing his baby's mama's ass, so Trap had no chance.

"Naw, bruh, I'ma ring the bell!" *I'm 'bout to show this bitch, again.*

If MiMi wasn't ready, I was going to show her mama that my words were just like my hands. I rang the bell and tapped my right foot.

This bitch right here is out of fucking control when it comes to MiMi for real. I banged on the door the second time and still nothing happened.

Breathe, Jae. Breathe. I coached myself. I needed two boxes of Dutch Masters just to tolerate this bitch on a good day. I hated that it came down to this for this bitch. I placed my hand on my hip as I looked around, making sure there wasn't anyone outside that was going to point me out.

The door snatched wide open right before I pulled my toolie from my waist.

"Damn, Jae," Ashanti said, wearing a pair of boxers and a white oversized t-shirt.

The bitch was lucky I didn't spray her door down with bullets before I knocked. "MiMi ready?" My foot was still tapping.

"Yea, let me get her." She rolled her eyes.

I can bet a million dollars that the bitch heard me knock the first bloodclath time. I walked back to the car to wait. Trap and Tray were talking about a move that would continue to bring in some funds.

"Bruh, just be careful fuckin' with that nigga," said Trap.

"You know I am."

"As long as you good, then shit will be straight."

"We gonna run the move down to Rocket, too."

I smiled, 'cause no matter where my man was, they still made sure he was connected in the growth of their empire.

Minutes later, Ashanti brought MiMi out to the car to me.

"Hey, pretty girl." I crouched down and hugged her.

"Hey, Jae," she said in her baby voice.

"Ready to see Daddy?"

"Yes." She smiled. These girls were Rocket's heartbeats.

I stood up, still holding onto MiMi's hand. "I'll 'call you when we're on the way back." I stared Ashanti the fuck down, waiting on her to talk some shit.

All she came back with was, "Okay."

MooMoo was outside when we got to her house. I didn't have to climb out the car to get her. She walked to us. Having the girls together made me feel extra good. I couldn't wait to see Rocket's face when we walked through.

***

ROCKET

My niggas took a seat as I watched Jae and my seeds from afar. I loved how she catered to them like they were hers.

"Yo, Shotta is a muthafuckin' handful, B." Tray followed my eyes.

"Y'all gotta keep her out of the way, yo."

"My nigga, that's like talking to a dead muthafucka." Trap paused. "Ashanti almost got her neck knocked off earlier."

That bitch wasn't going to learn until it was too late. Jae wasn't the one to be fucked with.

I rose up out of my chair when I saw my three ladies walking towards the table.

"Daddy!" MooMoo and MiMi screamed, running to me at full speed.

Jae had a huge smile on her face. I swooped the both of them up in my arms as I placed kisses all over their faces. Jae sat the snacks and drinks on the table as she took a seat between the twins, smiling.

"Y'all better not tell him shit, either," I heard her mumble underneath her breath to the twins.

I sat down and held both girls. One was on one leg and the other on the other as we vibed as a family.

Tray told me he had a nigga that was going to supply them until they could figure everything out.

"Just be careful, B," I cautioned him

"You already know, we have each other backs covered," Jae added.

"I already told you to stay clear." I knew she wanted to say something, but she would never challenge me in front of my boys, so she licked her lips. "I mean it, Jae."

MiMi and MooMoo snacked away while we talked about everything that was going on in the streets.

"If that nigga Ro cross all the way over to the left, let him be 'til I touch," I told my niggas. "I wanna handle that shit myself."

"Yellow Man?" Jae questioned.

"Let him stand, too."

"Already," Trap agreed.

Everything else was a go if they were in the way.

Visitation ended so fast that I didn't want them to bounce. I showered my little ones with a lot of love before I handed them over to the twins with some hood love. I had to taste Jae's lips. I didn't sample them when she arrived and I'd be damn if I didn't before she left me.

"Stay clear and out the way, yo." I kissed her lips, gazing into her eyes. "And thank you."

She closed her eyes and welcomed my tongue without a response. *Damn.*

"I love y'all." I called out behind my family as they walked away. MooMoo and MiMi were crying when they realized that they had to leave. That shit fucked me up bad. My fucking blood had caused my seeds to cry, and for that the muthafucka had to pay with his life.

Chapter 20
RO
6 months later…

As I walked into the courtroom with Red at my side and my parents behind me, I held my head down. The room was packed from top to bottom with nothing but street niggas. Red squeezed my hand and I squeezed hers back. The twins, Jae, and the hood niggas were on the left side of the courtroom behind Rocket's attorney. The DA and my lawyer were on the right side and that's where I took my seat. I got a deadly look from Jae, but I smiled that shit off, showing my new grill.

"You sure about this?" Red questioned me, looking over at Jae and the twins.

"You damn right," I whispered in her ear before I took my seat with the DA and my lawyer leaving her to sit with my parents.

"Please stand," a bailiff announced, "for your honorable Judge Pryer."

The white judge entered the courtroom through a side door and took his seat on the throne before the rest of the room took their seats.

Less than a minute later, Rocket was escorted into the courtroom by two guards. That nigga had swelled the fuck up with muscle. *Damn*. His face seemed relaxed but I could tell that he was still dangerous.

Jae wiped tears from her eyes as she blew a kiss at him. The twins pounded their chests and saluted that nigga.

"You ready?" My lawyer asked.

I couldn't even answer. I just nodded with a blind stare. *Fuck! Am I really about to rat on my own brother?*

***

ROCKET

I took my seat beside my lawyer and smiled.

"Mr. Johnson," the judge announced, and Ro and his lawyer stood up. "Raise your hand if you swear to tell the truth and nothing but the God's honest truth."

Ro raised his right hand and repeated to tell the truth and nothing but the whole truth.

Niggas swear all the time under oath and still lie. I just had to wait to see the outcome.

"Please take a seat on the witness stand." The bailiff told Ro.

"Bloodclath informa," Jae murmured. My bitch didn't give a fuck.

The DA asked Ro his name and he told the courtroom his government.

"What is your relation to Mr. Wallace?"

"He is my brother," Ro respond to the DA without looking at me.

As the district attorney replayed the event that night with me and Ro, my head thumped. I was fucking mad that it came down to this and not that nigga's death.

"Mr. Johnson, do you see the person who shot you?" The DA asked my brother as he paced in front of the courtroom.

The courtroom was silent as we all waited to hear his response. I looked up on the witness stand and pierced his eyes with a hard stare. *Snitches get stitches*, I wanted him to know.

The hood was there in abundance. I let my eyes travel around the cold courtroom, taking in all of their faces. I hoped Ro would do the same. Maybe the presence of niggas he respected and feared would dictate the answer he provided.

As my eyes circled the room, they fell on our mother. The bitch was seated in the front row smiling at Ro encouragingly. My blood boiled from just looking at that hoe. The hatred I had for her was immeasurable. Ever since we were kids she had taken Ro's side in every dispute we had.

"You ain't shit," I mouthed as I stared at the side of her face. I tore my eyes off of her and looked back at the nigga who was pushed from the same pussy as me. He hadn't ever been a stand-up dude, but I held on to a small amount of hope that he would live by the code of family over everything. But that hope was quickly dashed out.

Ro turned in his seat and our eyes locked again. He popped the collar of his dress shirt and smirked at me. *Fuck you, nigga*, his look read. I knew it was a wrap even before the DA repeated his question. Ro stood up and pointed a snitching finger directly at me.

"Yea, I see the person who shot me. He's sitting right there. My brother, Draymond."

Jae let out a loud scream from behind me. She knew Ro's identification of me had sealed my fate. My baby's pained cry seared my soul and I couldn't contain my anger a moment longer. I shot up out of my seat at the defense table and tried to rush up to the witness stand, but a large bailiff grabbed me and held me back.

"You snitch bitch!" I growled.

Ro smiled triumphantly. "Fuck you! I got you back, nigga!" he mouthed.

"Order! Order! Order!" The judge hit his gavel.

"Let me the fuck go, Trap!" Jae kicked and screamed, trying to get to Ro, too.

"Order!" The judge was standing up.

"Get her out, my nigga," I shouted to Trap. Shorty was mad and there was nothing I could do to calm her down.

Red was shaking. My mom and her disloyal ass husband was in shock.

"You've got to relax, Mr. Wallace," my lawyer was standing up in my space. "Just remember what I said."

I shook my head. From signing the paper to pointing me out in court had done it for Ro. He was a dead man breathing.

Ultimately, I was sentenced to three years, with five years on probation. But in my heart, Ro had sentenced himself to death.

Chapter 21
RO
A week later...

They never found the gun, there was no witness, just my words against his, so hell yea, I took the stand and pointed that nigga out as the shooter. *Fuck Rocket!*

Red and I were present in court for the drug charges.

"Relax, babe. I got us." It was my time to reassure her that things were going to be great.

"One-year probation." The judge handed down to us, thanks to all of the information that I had given the DEA about Rocket's plug, Cuba. The icing on the cake was me describing Cuba to a sketch artist. I had seen the nigga four times while I was with Rocket.

"Thank you," Red told me as we left the courtroom.

"I've told you from Day One that I had ya' back covered, didn't I?"

"Yes." She rewarded me with a kiss.

"How about we celebrate?" I suggested. We were free to walk and go as we pleased.

"Hell yea." Her whole disposition had changed back to the Red that I knew and fell in love with before all this bullshit.

***

After two straight days of love making, Red decided to go grocery shopping, so we could move back in our own spot.

"You want me to come with you?" I watched her getting dressed. She had lost about twenty pounds from stressing and looked great without the extra weight.

"Babe, I'm good. How about you meet me at the house?"

We had been shacked up at my parents' house, just in case the twins and Jae wanted to retaliate.

"Okay. I love you."

"I love you, too." She blessed me with another kiss before she left the house.

I rolled back over in bed and shut my eyes, drifting off to a sleep. But there was a knot in my stomach, like a feeling of disaster.

***

TRAY

The move with Wayne was a good move. The product, was that ill, so I didn't complain. We were still running Crown Heights just a man short, but Jae made up for that shit, easily. Whenever we wanted to make a run and couldn't do it, she made sure she was there, putting in some hella work. Rocket had a true soldier on his side for sure.

"Bruh, you good?" Me and Trap was out collecting from the spots.

"I'm straight, B."

But I knew my twin better. Something was on his mind, heavy. "Nigga, cut the bullshit and spill the beans. What's good?" His silence worried me. Whatever he was facing, I wanted him to know that I would be there with him facing that joint, too.

"I still can't believe that nigga took the stand and pointed our bruh out, yo." Trap finally said.

What Ro did had affected us all, but Rocket had said that he wanted to handle that nigga himself, so we had no choice but to let him live.

"Three years, my nigga," Trap expressed.

"Thank God it ain't more."

"I know, right. But damn!"

We were waiting on the nigga Swave to pull up in the grocery store's parking lot when I spotted the fat bitch Red without Ro.

"Say it ain't so." I pointed the hoe out to my twin.

"You ain't gotta say it. That's that bitch!" His toolie was in his hand.

The parking lot was crowded with people. We watched her enter the store without seeing us.

"Yo, B. Where you at, son?" I hit Swave up.

"'Bout to pull in, fam." And he did.

"On the left by the dumpster, son." I directed him.

"Bet."

The little nigga was a true hustler. He ran through two birds in less than two days. I smiled as he slid into the back seat and passed us a bag of money up front.

"What's this?" Trap asked, meaning how much.

"That's for the two that y'all fronted me and the money for my two."

"Aite, I'm holla at you in a few, son."

Little nigga had been grinding.

I hit Jae's line up as he bounced up out the car. "Sis, what's good?"

"Just got off the phone with Rocket." I could tell that she was crying. Her voice was shaky.

"How's bruh?"

"He straight."

"Good." But I knew if he wasn't he wouldn't tell her or us. "I need you to go to the spot and get two fried chicken breasts for me." She knew I meant two birds, rocked up.

"Okay."

"Then call me."

"Anything else?"

"Naw," I laughed at her smartass remark. We were a team, and a team that grinds together, shines beautifully together.

"Aite." She disconnected the call.

"There go that bitch."

Red had just exited the store with a shopping cart full of groceries. We watched her from the back as she loaded the car up without a care in the world while my brother was sitting behind a gate, thanks to her nigga.

***

"Pull up beside that hoe, Tray."

We had been trailing the bitch for about five minutes. She had just pulled onto her street, which was Bedford Avenue.

Bee! Bee! Bee! Bee!

My brother was hanging out the fucking window, blazing.

Bee! Bee! Bee! Bee!

Trap turned her car into Swizz Cheese with lead. The bitch didn't even see death coming. "Testify that, bitch!" Trap declared as I pulled off.

***

RO

"Ricardo, wake up!" My mom was shaking me from my sleep, screaming like a mad woman.

"What?" I snatched the covers up off of me.

"Red!" Tears were gushing down her face.

My father stood in the doorway with a pitiful look on his face.

"Red, what, ma?" I was sitting up in the bed, holding onto my mom's arms, trying to calm her down so she could explain to me what the hell was going on. "Dad," I looked past my mom for answers from my father, but his face held that same hopeless look. "Somebody tell me what the fuck is going on!" I snapped.

My mom threw her body in my arms and cried. Right then, I knew something bad had happened, but I didn't know what.

"Red is dead, Ro. She is dead!" My mom's words were so low but they were so damn loud.

I tried standing up but my knees buckled under me and I collapsed on the bed with tears streaming down my face. "How?" I screamed. "How?"

My father's head dropped and he walked out the room.

"How, Ma? How?" I pulled my mom's head up as I stared into her eyes.

"A drive-by, Ro. A drive-by," she repeated.

I let her go from my grip and reached for my phone off of the nightstand. I had over fifty missed phone calls, all from Red's mom and sister. Not even two hours had passed and my woman was dead. I knew Rocket's people had something to do with her death. I felt it. Red wasn't built for the streets. Why had I dragged her into that life?

***

For days, I stayed cooped up in the room without nothing to eat or drink. I ignored every phone call that came through to my phone.

"Ricardo, you've got to talk to her family," my mom preached, but I ignored her words. Red was gone and I couldn't get her back.

Days later, not one person went forth with any information about her death, and to make shit worse, I didn't attend her funeral. I was scared that whoever did her in was waiting on me to show my face. I knew her family didn't like me 'cause I always had her doing something illegal, but I knew for a fact they hated me now.

Chapter 22
ROCKET

"It's the ones that are closer to you that does the most damage," Killa explained to me after I returned from court. Over the time of us living together, I told Killa my story. "Blood is supposed to be thicker than water, but the green-eyed monster, envy, is a real muthafucka."

I shook my head in disbelief, thinking back to see if I had done anything fucked up to Ro, but nothing came to mind.

"Don't wreck ya' mind tryin' to figure out what you've done to receive this treatment from your own blood." I picked my head up, staring at the old man on his bed. "Mufuckas are born to hate, mufuckas are born fake; it's in their DNA. Just thank God that ya' pop's bloodline was stronger than that bitch that birthed you. Revenge is a real bitch, know that, and when you get that time to show your hand, show no fuckin' mercy!" He left the room to give me some space to clear my head.

Instead of sitting around, moping in the cell, I gathered my shit and headed to the shower with Jae on my mind. As the water cascaded over my body, my wood rocked up in my hand, thinking about my gangsta bitch's love and support. Within minutes, I was sending my seeds down the drain, along with what Ro had done, but that shit was far from over. I was going to make that nigga's family— 'cause they weren't mine— suffer the consequences of betraying me.

***

Later, I joined Killa at a table in the day room as he trashed another old head in chess. Seven tables were mounted down in the concrete with four metal seats on each one. Three televisions were hung from the ceiling around the pod. Niggas were either playing cards, shooting dice, watching sports or hugging the phone.

The officer's station was above us in a bubble. My eyes shot up only to find Officer Anderson smiling at me, dumb hard. Shorty was bad as fuck, I can't lie, but she didn't have shit on Jae, so I turned my head from the box to the table.

"Niggas wanna act like they 'bout that life, but they ain't! Me? I'm all the way 'bout that!" I was saying when I heard a commotion in front of me.

The crowd around the phones was getting bigger by the second. A few mufuckas disconnected their calls and stepped back from the problem.

"I'm not getting off this jack until I feel like it!" A little nigga banged the phone against the wall after he spoke, mean mugging six guys in front of him.

"Blood," he responded with the phone in his hand. He laughed out mad loud in their faces. "Ma, I'ma hit you back!" He hung the phone up.

The second the jack left his hand, he stuck the leader Pupu with a four piece so fast that it shocked everyone, even me.

"Oh shit!" Killa yelled.

I jumped to my feet to watch the show.

"Guards!" Someone yelled. I looked up to the bubble to see that Officer Anderson was gone. She was on her way to the pod. The announcement didn't stop the little nigga from throwing his elbows.

"Damn!" Killa's chess partner said with excitement over his face.

"Lockdown! Lockdown!" Control announced, but no one moved until the doors popped as guards rushed the day room, deep.

As the other officers ran towards the fight, Officer Anderson ran straight in my direction. "Lockdown, Mr. Wallace."

I looked around for Killa, but he was not in sight. I was never the type of nigga to take orders from a bitch, but with her, I had to. The bitch had a badge.

***

Trap, Jae, and Tray showed up the following week. Soon after we were seated, Jae stepped away to get me something to eat and drink.

"So, what's good, family?" I asked my mans.

"It's a dog-eat-dog world out that bitch right now, B," said Tray.

"Yellow Man thought he could come looking for me and I wouldn't show up." Trap spoke in a hushed tone. "I know what you said, but I can't just let that nigga rest easy, B."

I respected his gangsta and loyalty, but I wanted to handle that nigga myself. "What happened?" I asked as Jae returned with my food and beverage.

"Bruh left that nigga one man short," Tray informed me, "but that's not all either."

I watched Jae open up the hamburger bag and added Mayo and mustard to my sandwich.

"I sent that bitch Red to wherever she's supposed to be!" Trap let me know.

"Thanks, baby." I took the sandwich from Jae's hand. "Word?" I faced my niggas.

"Word!" He assured me with death in his eyes as he replayed the events to me.

"Why the fuck that bitch keep staring over here?" Jae asked.

I turned my head to see where she was looking at only to find Officer Anderson's eyes locked in on us.

Tray and Trap laughed and I made a mental note to let baby girl know that flirting with me was one thing, but to disrespect my bitch was something I didn't and wouldn't allow. I didn't give a fuck how much power she had with that badge, don't try me.

"She them people, Jae." I tried to downplay the problem by leaning over and sampling her lips, but I knew if it continued, Jae wouldn't be scared to address the issue.

Jae grilled shorty the remainder of the visit. Before we said our goodbyes, I assured her that I would check the bitch about disrespecting her by only sweating me.

"Handle that, babi. Or next visit I'm going to handle it," she huffed.

"I got you, ma." I kissed her goodbye.

***

CO Anderson made it her business to escort me back to the pod, making sure I was the last nigga to be dropped off. More was the opportune time to set things straight.

"That flirting shit that you be pulling in here, I let that shit slide, but when I'm out there with mine, don't cross that line."

"Draymond—"

"'Cause lil' mama," I referred to Jae, "is all the way 'bout that life, and not even ya' badge could save you if it comes to fuckin' with me."

"It's not—"

Control popped the door to my pod and I walked off on that bitch.

Back in my cell, I laid across the bunk and thought of Jae, the streets, and all that I was missing out on. I couldn't wait to return and mesh out proper punishment to those who had it coming to them. In the meantime, I wanted to strengthen my mental. That way, when I touched down, my wisdom would match my gangsta.

So, as the time passed, I began to pay attention to and calculate everything, even the smallest shit.

Chapter 23
TRAY

It'd been a year and the business was booming with Wayne. Jae was standing firm when holding Rocket and his seeds the fuck down. Trap was chopping down the projects with me with the work as the money piled back up.

"I'm 'bout to double up, bruh." I said to Trap.

"Aite. Hit me when you done!"

I was supposed to meet Wayne, but at the very last minute, he advised me that he had to handle some other shit, so one of his right-hand men would be linking up with me.

I'd never dealt with no one but Wayne. I wanted to let the nigga know that I could wait, but the way the hoods were blowing up my phone, I canceled the thought of waiting.

"My nigga, Spazz, gonna let you know where to meet him." Wayne informed me. "Just answer ya' joint. I gave my nigga ya number." He disclosed.

"Bet."

Minutes later, Spazz rang my line and gave me the location on where we should link up. Coney Island. The only time I went to the island was the first time discussing business with Wayne. Other than that, the nigga always brought that shit to one of the spots on my side.

Instead of picking up the bread from my mom's spot, I decided to check shit out first, just to be on the safe side.

***

I showed up at the barbershop and waited for him to show up, but instead, a thick ass bitch greeted me in the parking lot.

"Spazz said to follow me."

Hearing the nigga's name, I relaxed and followed the bitch through a side door. My gut told me to turn around, but the greedy bitch money flashed across my eyelids and I continued to follow her.

"Where that nigga at?" I asked as I entered the dark room behind her.

"He'll be here in a minute." She flicked on a light switch and everything seemed to move in slow motion in front of my eyes.

I reached for my hammer, but my reaction was too slow.

Whack!

Something connected across my temple, sending me flying down to the floor.

Whack!

And I blacked the fuck out.

Chapter 24
JAE

"Yo, I haven't heard from Tray since earlier, Jae." Trap woke me up, banging on my front door with his pistol in his hand.

"What?" I stepped out of the way so he could come in. "What you mean?" I rubbed sleep from my eyes as I closed the door.

"Bruh said he was linking up with the plug 'bout the work six hours ago."

I sat down and opened the drawer so I could roll a blunt.

"That shit ain't never took that long, sis!" He paced the room with the hammer at his side, shaking his head. "Something is off beat, yo. I can feel it." His voice cracked with emotion.

"You called his phone?" I broke the Dutch down so I could get my mind right with this Orange Haze.

"Been callin' his phone, but that shit is off, yo. I'm tellin' you, something is wrong." He took a seat across from me.

Six hours and that nigga didn't vibe with us. Yea, something was fucking wrong. I kept my thoughts inside as I said a prayer to watch over my brother by loyalty.

"Nigga didn't even collect the bread from Ma's crib."

I sparked the blunt and puffed real hard.

"What the fuck, yo?" I leaned my head back on the sofa with my eyes closed as the herb hit my lungs. I took another puff and jumped up on my feet, handing the blunt to Trap. "Let me get straight so we can burn these streets down." Smoke clouds flew from my mouth as I spoke.

In less than five minutes, I was dressed and ready with my 9-millimeter tucked in my jeans. "You ready, bruh?"

Trap had smoked the whole damn blunt. He had his phone glued to his ear. "Ma, I still ain't heard from him." Tears ran down his face. "I'm not tryin' to think fucked up, but I'm tellin' you, yo. If anything has happened to him, it's about to be blood stains everywhere!"

"Let's hope for deh best, and if not, I'ma ride with you on every set!"

He nodded and led the way out the door.

***

For three days straight, we barely slept. We burned the streets down nonstop. No one had seen or heard nothing from Tray. It's like the nigga had just disappeared. His car was nowhere to be found.

Ms. Judith called and filed a missing person's report, but still, nothing happened.

Trap was in the same clothes, he hadn't ate, shat or took a shower. He was literally sick, constantly throwing up all the water that he was drinking. "Sis, I can't handle losing my twin, yo." He hugged the toilet, letting the water flow from his mouth.

Tears dropped down my face, thinking about Tray somewhere laid the fuck up or dead.

"Fuck!" He let his head hit the seat as I wrapped my arms around his upper body on the floor.

***

TRAY

I don't know how many days had passed but I was still breathing by the grace of God.

"Where the money at nigga?"

They had beaten me so bad that I could barely see. My hands were tied behind my back while I sat in a chair. Every time I dozed off through the pain, someone woke me up with a hit to my body. Blood filled my mouth, and my head felt like someone had taken a baseball bat to it for days.

"Spazz, that nigga ain't givin' shit up!" A voice said. I couldn't see a face.

"Boss man said that this shit was going to be easy, bruh," spoke Spazz. I recognized his voice. "But this nigga ain't crackin' yo."

This was a set up. Fucking Wayne had put his niggas on to do this shit. But why? Business was great between us. I thought.

Whack!

A pistol cracked against my head.

"Where the money at?"

I'll never give my people up. *Never!* "Fuck you!" I spat blood everywhere. "Fuck you!"

Whack! Whack!

"It's been three days, Wayne, and this nigga ain't said shit, son."

I've been missing for three fucking days, so I know my twin been going ham with Jae at his side trying to find me.

The nigga Spazz tossed his phone to a nigga and pulled his hammer from his side as he walked towards me.

I'm a G. Been one from the egg and I'll die a G. "I'll never crack under pressure." I coughed as he got closer to me. "My blood gonna make sure all y'all get yours!"

"Word?" He jammed a bullet in the chamber, staring down on me.

"Yea, bitch, word!" I smiled, looking up at these haters. "Bitch ass niggas!"

Boc!

Chapter 25
TRAP

Jae passed me the phone to talk to Rocket, but I couldn't walk, much less talk so I handed that shit back to her. There was nothing that Rocket could say to me to uplift my spirit right now. I didn't mean no harm. I just wanted my twin back at my side.

"Babi," Jae said as she walked away. "He don't wanna talk right now," she whispered.

Tomorrow would be day number six, and there still wasn't a word about Tray.

"Aite, I love you, too." I heard her tell Rocket.

My mom's name and number flashed across the screen of my phone and I held the last breath in my body as I answered her call. "Hello."

"The police just called me," she informed me, and I knew the news before she said another word, thanks to the cry that she sounded off in my ear.

I dropped the phone and clutched my chest. My brother was gone and so was I. I know Tray would never put anyone's life in danger, so my nigga took the easy way out. Death. Death before dishonor was a code that he took pride in. The wail of anguish that I heard from my mother will always be with me.

I remember seeing Jae picking the phone up off of the floor as she fell to her knees at my side. "I'm so sorry," she said as her arms comforted me.

***

My mom and I took the trip to go identify Tray. I'd shed all the tears that I had to shed. Now it was time to shed some real blood behind mine. I griped my mom's body as the examiner pulled the sheet over Tray's body. My nigga was fucked all the way up and I could tell that he had endured a horrible death.

My mom's body rocked from side to side in my arms as she stared down at her seed. "Why?" She asked, but I knew God wasn't going to answer right away, but I was. “Why?” She let all her weight go as I held her up.

According to Tray’s autopsy, he was beaten and starved for days before his enemies finally shot him in the head at point-blank range. A smile was covering my twin’s face. He took death like a real G.

“I’ma get ‘em all, yo!” I dapped my twin up as I carried our mom out the room.

***

I sent my brother away in a real hood style, a week later with me, Jae, Ma, my son, and Pound Cake in attendance. I didn’t want the streets to see my twin the way I saw him last. He rocked a fresh white tee shirt with a black NY fitted hat, True Religion’s and Jay’s on his feet. His favorite Uzi was lying beside him.

“I love you; know that! You already know the streets gonna bleed for this shit!” I closed his coffin as tears pour down my face. *Gotdamn!*

Once Tray was in the ground, I sat my mom down.

“When I get the word about who did this to Tray, know that I’m going to send everything that they love on the way over.”

My mom hadn’t slept in days. She looked like she had lost 50 pounds in the week.

“I’m giving you all my rights over for Trap Jr.”

Her swollen eyes dripped with tears, but she nodded. She was that down ass mother and I couldn’t thank God enough for her.

“Their family’s gonna mourn more than you.” I packed the duffle bag up with a few belongings of mine. “I love you.” I walked over to her and kissed her forehead. I knew I’ll never be able to comfort her or bring Tray back, but I’d be damn if I didn’t slaughter whoever and theirs that did this to mine.

Trap Jr. was fast asleep when I entered his room. Gazing around the room brought me back to when me and Tray had to paint the walls blue. I kissed my little nigga’s head. “I love you.” I didn’t know when I was going to see him again. The streets were about to be my home until everyone that was involved in my blood's death was dead.

I exited the room but I didn't close the door. I was taking a break from parenting to become a menace to society for mine. *Niggas bled Kool-Aid, I bled concrete when it came to my loved ones!*

Chapter 26
ROCKET

Since I've been down, I've seen my girls, thanks to Jae. As soon as I was free, I was going to get them, and if their mothers wanted to act stupid, I was going to fold their asses. I was tired of those bitches.

I talked to MooMoo all the time, but Ashanti stayed trying to handle a nigga on the phone when it came to MiMi.

"Hello," a nigga answered Ashanti's house phone, and accepted my call.

"Yo, where Ashanti at, B?"

"So, you callin' here, askin' 'bout my bitch!"

I pulled the phone from my ear to make sure I was hearing what I was hearing. I had that bitch first, but fuck that, I wanted to holla at my child, and in order to do that, I had to talk to the bitch.

"Who the fuck is this?" I saw red through the walls.

"Nigga, you called my spot. You tryin' to play daddy from behind the wall. Homie, you need to concentrate on doing time instead of being a prison father. I got this!" The clown ass nigga disconnected the call on without me talking to my seed.

That bitch Ashanti had it coming. I couldn't wait till the weekend to tell Jae to handle that hoe.

***

The look on Trap's and Jae's faces let me know that something wicked had happened. I looked around the room for Tray but I didn't spot him anywhere. Jae's eyes were bloodshot red, and dark lines rested under Trap's eyes.

"Tell me it ain't what I'm thinking." I was still standing up. My bitch or my nigga had yet to move. Jae's eyes watered up and I knew Tray was gone. I pulled my brother up and hugged him.

"Our brother is gone." He said in my ear.

My knees bent, but Trap held me up. We held each other up. I wanted to crawl under a rock and cry because I wasn't out there to help Trap— my nigga, my brother. I wasn't free to help comfort Ms. Judith.

"How?" I let Trap go as I wiped tears from my eyes.

Jae held her face with her hands. Thugs cry.

"Niggas beat and starved him for days before they shot him at close range."

"Say it ain't so, B." I slouched down in my chair. I felt my breakfast coming up in my throat. I closed my fist, tight.

Jae excused herself from the table to use the restroom.

"Gotdamn, son!"

"It's gonna be alright." Trap pledged. "Niggas gonna wish they didn't pull that shit, son."

"What's the plan?" I felt useless. It wasn't shit I could do right then, but as soon as my feet touched, I was going to rain blood.

"I'm waitin' on the streets, B."

Family isn't always your blood relatives, but with me and Trap, we were family.

"I'm smokin' everything breathin' that had something to do with it, and those that didn't!"

"Save me some, my nigga!" Fuck probation, I had to put some work in for my brother with my brother.

"I can't promise you that anything will be left."

I understood. Jae joined us back at the table.

"How you holdin' up, baby?" I touched her leg. Tray was family to her, too.

"I'm good, but," she paused as the tears returned. "But I'm 'bout to put in work with Trap."

How the fuck could I tell her no? I smiled, 'cause no matter what, she had a nigga's back.

"I'm cool with that, and tap Ashanti's head for me while you at it."

"Pistol or hand?"

"Hand for right now."

"Say nuh more."

Chapter 27
TRAP

Word spread fast around Crown Heights about Tray's death 'cause he was a well-respected individual. Wayne was responsible for my blood's blood.

"You don't have to come, Shotta." I'd got word about where his baby's mama lived.

Jae was in black from head to toe. "Nigga, fuck what yuh spittin', B!"

Trap Jr. was staying with Pound Cake. My mom was having a real hard time dealing with Tray's death, still.

"I ain't tryin' to get you caught up in no shit." I tossed a shirt over the vest.

"What you preachin' ain't the gospel. So, is you ready?" She asked, pulling her ponytail to the back. Rocket was a lucky ass nigga to have Jae.

"You already know!" We bounced from her crib.

Niggas gossiped more than bitches, so it wasn't hard to get a location on one of Wayne's baby's mothers. Tameka was the first one that I had planned to visit. The nigga had her all the way in Queens, stashed away, but hell wasn't far away to travel if that's where he had her.

"I can't kill no babies, Trap," Jae announced as we got off the Belt Parkway.

"It's all good, I'll handle it all."

"My youth," her Patwha popped out, "yuh tink seh mi just come fi warm deh seat?"

"Naw, I know you ain't just going with me to warm the seat." I answered and repeated her question.

"Good. All I said was that I'm not touchin' no kids. Anything else will be touched, son."

The nigga had two kids by two different women. I pulled right in Tameka's driveway and parked. I cut the lights off before me and Jae exited the car. 918 Grove Street. I checked the information on my phone from Pound Cake to make sure I was in the right spot. We were. We traveled up the porch together.

"You gonna knock or you want me to?" Jae asked.

"You knock."

I looked around at the neighborhood. It was the suburbs. I heard Jae as she tapped the door lightly. The space between the houses were about 20 feet. Wayne had this bitch stashed away, but not well enough. I still found her.

"Ring the bell, fuck that!"

And Jae did just that. Seconds later, a light came on inside, then we heard the bolts turning. My hand was already on my strap. The bitch didn't ask who it was, she just opened the door and Jae's fist cracked that bitch with her knuckles, sending her flying backwards.

Whack! Whack!

Jae jaw-checked the bitch.

Tameka swung, but Jae ducked and caught the bitch under the chin with an uppercut, knocking her on her ass.

I pulled my silencer out and silenced that hoe right where she landed. Blood splashed all over Jae as she looked down on the bitch. She didn't have shit to do with what Wayne did, but she was his baby's mother, and she had to fucking pay for what he did to mine.

We searched the house and found a beautiful baby girl sleeping.

"Trap," Jae looked at me but I shut that shit that she was about to spit to me with two shots to the little girl's head.

She closed her eyes for a moment before she walked out the house with me behind her.

"Two down!" I entered the car, smiling up at the sky.

***

JAE

Night number two, Trap found the other baby's mother and kid, and left them stinking. Every time the nigga pulled the trigger, he smiled. "Mufucka gonna feel my pain," he professed.

"When am I going to put in some work?" I was jealous that he got to do everything.

"You can do the sister, tomorrow."

Rocket called me that morning, telling me about what he had seen on the news.

"That shit crazy," he said lowly over the phone, "but how are you doing, baby?"

"I'm good. Ready for you to come home."

"I'm ready, too."

I had to pay Ashanti a visit. Not that I forgot, but this shit with Tray was very important.

"How the fam?"

"Twin straight, ya' mom good. She's getting better." Seeing Wayne's family dropping picked her back up a little. An eye for an eye.

"I love you and be safe."

"Don't stress. I'm the female version of you, and I love you, too." That caused him to laugh before he got off of the phone.

I was ready before the sun set to get to Wayne's sis, Tasha. We found out that the bitch worked late nights at a production warehouse downtown. I was parked beside the bitch's car with my seat all the way back as Trap blazed some Kush on the passenger's side with the window cracked.

"What time this bitch supposed to clock out?"

He passed me the pack before he answered, "In less than two minutes."

I had to use the silencer because a police station was only two blocks away.

I puffed the ganja back to back as I stalked the front door for this Tasha bitch. I had got her picture off of her Facebook account, along with a picture of her car. Dumb bitch posted everything on social media.

Ten minutes passed before the bitch staggered out the building. Majority of the workers had left already.

"Finally!" I sat up and let my window down. The closer she got, the faster my finger fucked the trigger.

Tac! Tac! Tac! Tac! Tac!

Her body did the Harlem Shake, but I didn't stop until she hit the concrete. I glanced over at Trap as I pulled around her ride to dump two more shots in her head. A smile plastered his face as I fucked the trigger.

The next night, Trap did Wayne's parents real dirty. He killed them in their bed and put the house on fire, starting in the bedroom where he shot them. "Mufuckas gonna remember you, bruh." Trap looked up at the sky full of stars, talking to Tray as we pulled off from the house.

"Now we've got to find Wayne."

"Swave told me that he heard the nigga skipped town on a vacation."

"Oh yea?"

"Hell yea, sis."

"He comin' back tuh a nice parti, den."

***

As I was out putting some money on Killa's books for Rocket, I ran right into Ashanti's no-good ass.

"What's up, Jae?" She addressed me like we were good friends from high school.

My mouth didn't respond, but my fists did.

Bop! Bop! Bop!

I went straight for her mouth and eye.

"Ahh, you fuckin' bitch!" She screamed like a real bitch.

I didn't waste any breath talking back to the hoe. I needed all the energy that I could to beat that ass.

Yack!

I throat-chopped that hoe with the side of my hand. She held her neck instead of swinging back. Dumb bitch. And I tagged her ass one more time for calling me a bitch.

Bop!

She fell to the ground with my last punch. I got in my car and pulled off. My knuckles hurt as I gripped the steering wheel.

Chapter 28
TRAP

My blood broke bread with a nigga that was shady, and in the end, he lost his life. Pound Cake did some homework for me and got me an updated photo of the nigga Wayne so I could spot the nigga in pitch black dark, myself.

I searched hell and heaven for that bitch ass nigga, but he was nowhere to be found. I drove to the hood Coney Island with Jae at my side and still couldn't locate the nigga. Niggas claimed they hadn't seen or heard from the nigga, but I knew niggas and bitches lie, so I left a few of niggas leaking just to let him know that I was looking for him.

It's been a month since I laid Tray to rest, but my brother wouldn't rest in peace until that nigga was dead. I was laying on Jae's sofa when my phone rang.

"Terrell." My mom was the only person to call me by my government.

"Yes?" I sat up.

"NYPD came over here, looking for you."

"Huh?" I got up off of the sofa and peeked out the blinds. Nothing seemed strange, so I shut the thought down because no one knew about this spot but Jae and Rocket.

"What they want?"

"Talking 'bout they had to ask you a few questions."

"Fuck for?"

"About some shooting in Coney Island."

"They ain't talkin' 'bout nothin', Ma." I laid back down and picked up a rolled Spliff that Jae had twisted up. "How you holding up?" I changed the subject.

"Good. Taking it one day at a time." I heard the pain still echoing in her voice.

"How is Junior?" My son was back with her. He kept her up and alive, according to her.

"He's good. He's right here. You want to talk to him?"

"Yes, Ma."

"Dad, what's up with you?" My heart beat extra fast hearing his voice. I missed him.

"Nothin'. Makin' some moves."

"Word?"

"Yea, little nigga, word."

He laughed. He reminded me so much of Tara it wasn't funny.

"Aite, bet that."

"I love you."

"I love you, too, Dad."

Fuck the NYPD. Them pigs better bring enough bacon to get me.

"My youth, yuh up in here blazing without me?" Jae sat across from me in an over-size tee shirt and shorts.

"Shit, you smoke so damn much. I'm surprised ya' lungs haven't given up on you."

"Son, I was born and raised in Jamaica. Wi smoke ganja all day." She snatched the blunt out of the ash tray and added fire to the end.

"I'ma skip town for a minute, sis." Her face expressed sadness. "I want that nigga to resurface, plus Ma said the NYPD on my ass right now."

She took four puffs before she leaned over and passed me the blunt. "Make sense." Smoke escaped from her nose. She was a professional weed smoker. "Where you plan on going?"

"Pound Cake got a spot in the A."

"That's a good place to lay low."

I pulled on the blunt with my mouth as I listened to her.

"Split that bread up in three. I'ma use my part and hold Rocket and his seeds down. Give Ma hers and use yours to help you out in the A." This bitch was the truth, and I didn't think there was another like her, alive.

"I'ma go back to my old job at the insurance place and lay low till Rocket touch, but if I run into that nigga Wayne, I'ma send his head to you in a box."

I knew she meant it.

Chapter 29
ROCKET

"Mufuckas either gon' feel me or kill me. That's on everything I love, yo!" I vowed to my rider. She was seated across from me in visitation, slaying 'em as usual. Jae had on black Balmain cropped tuxedo pants that had her ass sitting up like two over-sized watermelons. The white button up V-neck shirt fit her perfectly to the T.

When it came to visitation day, my bitch made sure she went all the way out for me. She had on a pair of six-inch black, patent leather, pointed-toe Jimmy Choo shoes that allowed her to be my exact height. Her hair was pulled up in a slick ponytail, exposing the diamond studs and David Yurman's white gold necklace that I had bought her for our first-year anniversary. But her beauty hid the viciousness she was capable of dispensing to anyone who violated me.

My declaration put a smile on her face. She placed her hands in mine on top of the table and held my stare. "I wouldn't expect anything different from you, babi. But does the same apply to your family?"

"Family?" I spat. The word tasted like dog shit in my mouth. "I'm cool on all of them. There's no forgiveness. Not a gotdamn drop!"

"Say nuh more, babi. However you want to roll, I'm rocking with you. To the grave." The sincerity in her voice fueled my ambitions.

As I looked into the windows of her soul, my heart thumped with love. Even when sugar turned to shit, baby girl still stood by my side. Whatever I needed behind these walls, Jae provided.

"And I'll never forget that, ma," I uttered unconsciously.

"You won't forget what, babi?"

"The depth of your loyalty. I promise you I'll repay you with the same."

"I trust that yuh will." She squeezed my hands tightly, and I could feel the love she had for me surge through her fingers into mine.

"Come give your nigga some of that deliciousness." I whispered to Jae.

"Yuh ain't said shit!"

We leaned over the small table between us and our lips locked. Jae slid her tongue inside my mouth, 'causing my dick to jump. Her lips were soft and she smelled good as fuck. I wanted to strip her out of her clothes and ravish her right there. But I forced myself to pull away.

"Damn, Island Girl. I can't wait to get all up in that." I reached under the table and squeezed my bulging dick print as my eyes caressed her body.

"Only six more days, babi, and I can't wait either." She licked her glossed lips.

It was hard to believe that in less than a week I would be home, holding Jae in my arms. I had dreamed about my release day every day for the last past two and half years. Many of those dreams had been tinged with hot bitterness over the fuck shit that caused us to lose all of that time together.

"My own fucking blood."

"Yea, babi, that bloodclath gotta pay," said Jae.

I nodded in agreement, and then I added, "Not only him, though. This time, the whole borough is going to bow down to my gangsta."

Just six more days before I would bring pain to Brooklyn.

***

My baby mothers held my kids from me for the last six months, but I was cool with that. The ride was basically over, and I couldn't wait to see them bitches. With my absence, Jae did almost everything for Ms. Judith and Trap Jr. out of love for me, and that made me love her more. She said Trap stayed in touch with his mama and seed.

"He said he'll link up with you as soon as you touch, but until then, hold ya' head." Jae gave me his message.

The noise at the door brought me back to reality.

"Rocket?" I looked over at the cell door, seeing Ms. Anderson squatting at the trap door for the food. She was a bad ass female guard. If I didn't have Jae on my team, I would've given her the dick from the first day she tried to get it.

I acknowledge her with a nod 'cause I didn't want to wake Killa up.

"Your mail was in D unit," she said as she pulled the envelope from her back pocket.

I got up off of the bed and headed towards the door to get my shit.

She unlocked the trap door. "I wish you the best, and if you ever need me," she stopped and licked her lips. "My number is on the back. Call me."

I got my mail from her hands without a word and walked back to my bunk. She shut the flop and left. There was no return address on the envelope. I stood by the door as I opened the letter.

Rocket,

My main man, you at your last days. Congrats. Three years is a long time for your first time to be caged up, especially when your blood snitched. I salute you for standing with your toes flat. I've seen your family and that beautiful Island Girl of yours, but I haven't paid them a visit because I know you don't tolerate disloyalty. Solve the problem or the problem will cost you a lot. Sending love from my country, Cuba, to yours.

Ps. You have a rare diamond in that woman of yours. Three years and all she did was work and live around you. Cherish her.

I got the message. My brother had to go, but who the fuck Cuba thought he was sending threats at me. Plug or no plug, don't disrespect me or mine. I ripped the letter up and flushed the number along with it. Fuck that nigga!

Chapter 30
ROCKET

I had learned many painful lessons from the streets, but my family topped it all. My mother had me but the streets helped raised me into who I am today— a real nigga.

I loved New York. It meant a lot to me. It was my stomping ground. Especially Brooklyn. It was a tough place to live and survive, and with the help of Ms. Judith and her twin boys, I survived.

I had less than two days before I graced the streets to see my so-called family, my kids, my woman, and the family that helped to raise me.

"This is it, son." Killa dapped me up. Goon was a part of me now.

We clicked when he came out of the hole on the first day.

"This ain't it, pops." I was going to hold him and Goon all the way down.

"You know how many times I heard that, Rocket?"

"I'm leather. I can't be cut with a butter knife. My actions will show for itself." I had split everything I had in my possession between Goon and Killa.

"B, I see you home, son." Goon had less than six months left.

"Bet!" I walked through the door, leading me to freedom.

***

The sun was out, and so was I. No more chains. No more locked doors. Free at last.

Seeing Jae strutting in the parking lot with her hands on her hips had my big man hard as a brick. I can see the *LAST OF A DYING BREED* tattoo on her chest, and I'd have to agree; she was the last of a dying breed. When the judge gave me my time, I never thought in a billion years that she would have stayed around my entire bid. We were only together for a year, and then the fuckery happened.

She showed me that she was definitely one of a kind the very first visit after I was sentenced. "Look, I'm not going to sit here and expect for your life to stop." That's all it took for me to say before she went in on me.

"Whenever you come at me, come correct. I said I was with you no matter what! When shit was sweet, I was there! Now that it sinks, I'm still going to be here! You know what? I'm not going to explain shit else to you. My actions will speak for itself."

And her actions showed me.

A fitted white wife beater cuffed her 34D's perfectly. The skinny leg black jeans had her hips looking like the old Twin Towers— solid. On her feet were the latest J's, and just like that she was perfect for me.

Her honey golden complexion had her looking flawless. No makeup on, only lip gloss. The blonde high lights in the front of her shoulder length hair was the icing on the cake for me. *My bitch is bad!*

A smile spread on her face and I could that she was missing a tooth. Tears ran down her face. "'Bout time dem let yuh guh," she said as tears continue to run. "I was ready to run up in that bitch and go ham!" She was my down ass bitch.

I dropped my bag that had all my pictures of her and the kids inside as she leaped into my arms. Her legs were behind my back, locked together as her happy tears wet my neck. I pushed my face into her collarbone, taking in her scent. Strawberries; my favorite.

"You going to let me get some sugar or not?" I asked, knowing she didn't want to let me go, but 160 pounds wasn't light.

She lifted her face from my neck and pressed her lips against mine. I could taste her tears. She unwrapped her legs and slid down my body, but our lips never came apart. Her heels hugged my torso like her life depended on my body.

Damn I missed her! I had to push her off me just so we could get the fuck out the parking lot.

"Welcome home, babi," she told me as she walked in front of me. She was 5' 7 and thick as fuck. I had to admire her ass for a minute before I picked my bag up off of the ground. She knew how to walk and make her ass clap at the same damn time. I couldn't wait to slay that pussy.

Jae was riding clean as fuck in an all-white Audi on 4's. She turned and tossed me the key. I caught it in midair with my right hand. "You drive."

I walked around the hood, admiring the ride. When I left, we had a 2012 Impala. The inside was white with our names engraved in the headrests. I looked at her, wondering what she was doing that I didn't know.

"Get in and stop staring. I'll tell you in, in due time," she said, reading my mind.

I got in, got comfortable and pulled out the parking lot. Jeezy's *Pretty Diamonds* was playing.

"Make a left at the stop sign, then a right at the light," she said as she typed the address in the GPS.

After that she took her Jay's off, she dove head-first into my crotch. My dick was already semi-hard so it didn't take long for it to get hard. I eased up a little so she could slide my pants under my ass.

"Follow the GPS," was all she said before she went to work.

***

JAE

My favorite little sister claimed that I was crazy as fuck to just work and cater to Rocket while he did his time. "You put ya' sexual life on hold, all together?" she asked me.

"You damn right. Three years ain't shit. Plus, I have other shit on my mind besides some nigga's funky ass dick."

I needed to prepare for his arrival and it was my goal to see to it that everything was on point for his touchdown. It would be four years in February that we'd been together.

His family, fake ass friends and enemies thought I would have bailed out on him right after the judge banged the gavel. But all I did was show them differently. They didn't know that I was a rider. A real one. Time couldn't erase or divide the time that we shared. Nothing could.

On my knees, I leaned over into Rocket's lap with my head inside his boxers. I put a real deep arch in my back. I knew my ass was sitting up high so he could see it. The closer my lips got to the head, the more I realized how much I had miss sucking his dick.

"I missed you so damn much." I pronounce much so hard that spit flew from my mouth. I was close enough to where he could feel my lips moving as I spoke into the mic. The cool sensation from my breath caused it rise and become hard as a rock, just how I liked it.

I licked the head just to watch it rise again, then I followed it like a predator stalks its prey. I kissed it real slow before I spoke to it again. "Did you miss me, babi?"

He used his muscles and made his dick answer me by making it go up and down. I licked it from the head to the balls before I attacked it by putting all 9 and 1/2 inches in my mouth.

Chapter 31
ROCKET

I had to lean my seat back just a little, or I would have wrecked the fucking Audi with how she was sucking my dick. I had one hand on the steering wheel and the other on the back of her head. Her ass was up in the air as her face was knee-deep. I took my eyes off of the road and smacked her ass. Both ass cheeks jumped. *Damn!*

I turned my attention back on the road as my right hand roamed through her hair. When she started talking to my big man, my body turned the fuck up from the warm air from her mouth. When her lips locked around the head, I had to close one of my eyes.

Jae used her left hand to beat my dick as she sucked it, while her right hand rubbed my balls. She bounced her ass up and down as she pounded my dick with her mouth. I was feeling heat, then cold air as she moved her gums.

"Fuck!" I screamed like a bitch. Before I got locked up, she used to suck me for breakfast and dinner, fuck me every night except for when she was on her cycle, and when she was bleeding, her jaws was her pussy. I loved Sundays, because I was hitting that *pum pum* as she say, five times a day.

She knew she had me gone with her head game. Her shit was that damn good. I didn't know who taught her, but if I did, I would thank them my-damn-self.

"Turn left onto I-95 North." The GPS sounded off.

I could not turn left, so I kept straight. I was about to bust, and I refused to fuck it up over some turn.

"Rerouting." The GPS went off, again.

"Baby." I hit the gas pedal, switching lanes, trying my hardest to keep my eyes open and on the road. Her head was moving so fast that I had to pull the fuck over.

Horns were blaring, but fuck them. This nut was the best, and I'd be damned if I didn't enjoy it.

"Jae!" I yelled her name. "Fuck." My foot was still pressing the brake down to the floor. I felt my body shaking from my toes to my legs, straight to the head of my dick.

Not once did she come up for air. I came so damn good that I stuffed her head down further as I let my seeds flow. I closed both my eyes, tight. It wasn't until I heard her breathing heavy that I let her head go.

"Welcome yuh home with some good jaw, and you wanna stifle a bitch," she said as she licked the head of my dick, getting the little left overs that she didn't gulp down.

I couldn't reply.

"Can you just get us home safe, please?" She added with a laugh.

It took me a few minutes before I pulled back out into traffic. *Damn, I'm free!*

Chapter 32
RO

Fuck! For the last two and a half years, I hadn't been able to get a good night's sleep, 'cause I knew Rocket was coming for me. I looked at my phone. It was 3AM and I still couldn't sleep. *Fuck!* I tossed the phone beside me as I closed my eyes, trying my hardest to get some Z's.

I had just gotten off the phone with the prison that Rocket was confined in and was informed that he was released this morning at 8. I was sitting at the kitchen table, watching our mother prepare breakfast for us.

"Mom, he is out." I uttered, hoping she couldn't hear how scared I was.

"Who is out?" She stopped flipping the pancakes to face me. My look alone let her know who it was. "When?" I could see fear written all over her face.

"This morning at eight."

We both looked over at the clock on the wall above the microwave. It was 9:18. We hadn't talked about him since that day in the courtroom.

"Fuck!" I slammed my fist against the kitchen table, 'causing the dishes to bounce.

My mother jumped. The look I got from her let me know that she was tired of my shit. It was 3 years later, and I still hadn't gotten my life together.

Truth be told, I was afraid to show my face in the daytime to the world, so at night I ventured out to handle my business, but not for long. I got tired of looking over my shoulder.

"Ro, you have to get yourself together and face him. You can't keep living in fear. Three years and you haven't accomplished anything." She went back to flipping pancakes.

"How can I not live in fear? Look what they did to Red! I know they had something to do with her death!"

"Y'all knew the lifestyle before y'all joined it. You knew the consequences more than she did."

"Yea, we did! But it wasn't like I was telling on him. I was telling on his plug!" I watched as she shook her head before she turned around and locked her eyes on me.

"But you still ended up telling on your blood!"

"That nigga tried to kill me!" I was more scared when reliving that night.

I dropped my head with shame knowing that Rocket would never hurt me. He had the chance to when I first told him, but he let me walk out the door, breathing.

"If he wanted you dead, he would have killed you that night, Ricardo, but he didn't."

I couldn't pick my head up. Tears were dropping from my eyes like a water hose. Guilt had been eating away at my soul for years.

"But you took the stand and pointed him out. You snitched on him."

I was shocked as fuck. This was the first time she ever took Rocket's side. I lifted my head with tears streamed down my face, but fuck it.

"You told me to do what I thought was best for me, didn't you?" My voice was above the normal level.

Soon, my drunk ass father joined us. I could smell the liquor before I could see him.

"Didn't you?" I barked again. I'd never raised my voice at my mother until this moment.

I could see the hurt, the pain written all over her face. "Yes, I told you to do what you thought was best for you, but I would've never imagined that you would tell on your own blood."

I couldn't believe the shit that I was hearing.

"You the same person that was behind me that day in the courtroom, when I pointed him out. "Wasn't you?" My tears were gone. "Fucking answer me, ma!" I screamed at the top of my lungs.

My mom's eyes were full of tears, and at any time, they were sure to fall. "Yes," she answered, and as I expected, the tears were flowing. "I was there with you."

My father entered the kitchen just as I was leaving. *Fuck breakfast.*

"Son," I heard my father's voice as I passed him on my way to my room.

I didn't answer. I couldn't answer 'cause I couldn't think.

Chapter 33
ROCKET

I hit the turnpike, ecstatic to be free, and that nut I released couldn't have been any greater. I'd been waiting years for that day to arrive. Mufuckas counted me out like I had received a life sentence and not three years.

My brother had it coming, for sure. The nigga Wayne had to be found. He had to pay for killing Tray. There was no way in hell I was letting that shit go. *Fuck outta here!* Yellow Man, a nigga I showed love to in the streets, vanished with a few of the spots' money that I was supposed to pick up. By the time Trap and Jae got to the joints, it was too late. I damn sure wasn't charging that loss to the game. *Fuck no!* Niggas needed to know firsthand that loyalty was everything and respect was free, but disrespect would cost them their lives.

"I'm so glad you home; I can relax now," Jae said as I switched lanes, "but you know if you need me, I'm right here." She touched my side.

She'd had a lot on her plate, but through it all she held shit down, all the-fucking-way. She made sure my kids got birthday presents, Christmas gifts and school shopping money from me like I was free. She made sure the world was revolving around me; no lie.

Jae was the first woman to ever make me want to give up the bullshit and settle down and plant roots as a family. Truth be told, I never felt I was worth it since I never had shit to live for until Moo-Moo was born, then came MiMi. They were all I had before Jae entered my life. Now I was so gone off her. I was going to marry her and spend the rest of my life with a boss bitch and not some hoe that would do anything for a buck.

"Those that are here standing with you now, are the ones that you should be dedicated to," was one of Killa's jewels that he threw at me.

Jae definitely fit that description.

"I'm home now, so you can relax," I said, rubbing her leg. I could feel the heat coming from between her legs, so I let my hand travel to her oven.

"Sellin' dope out the pot, straight drop. It's all there."

"Oh shit," she said as she pushed my hand away leaning over into the back seat.

"Yea, I just ran through the bag, it's all there."

"Fuck!" She yelled over the ringtone. "Hello? Hello? Hold on!" she sang out as she sat back in the seat, handing me the device.

I looked at her as if to say, *"Who the fuck is that?"* All she did was smile, showing me her missing tooth. I took the latest iPhone from her as I returned my attention to the road. Traffic was moving slow.

"Yo."

"My nigga, welcome home, bruh!" The voice on the other end screamed with excitement.

"My brother, what it do, yo?" Hearing Trap's voice, I couldn't help but to smile inside. It had been a long time since we had vibed with each other.

We started chopping it up like I wasn't gone for years. I remembered back in the days when I didn't have shit to wear, him and Tray would share their clothes, even their draws with me. Anything one had, we all had it.

"I wish Tray was still alive," Trap said as I was about to pull up at the crib.

I could hear the sadness in his tone. When one twin got sick, the other was sick within the next hour. That's how close they were. "Nigga, you know he watchin' over us." A tear fell from my left eye.

Jae had fallen asleep since I got on the phone with Trap, so she didn't see me as I wiped it away. I missed that nigga Tray. Us three together were always trouble. The neighbors would call us the Triple Threat when we were growing up. You fight one of us, you had to fight all three of us.

"Bruh gonna rest in peace, soon," I said.

"Oh, I already know," Trap stated with confidence.

I was back, and the only way I wouldn't find Wayne would be if the man above called me home.

"I love you, my nigga; no homo! I know you have a lot of catching up to do with Shotta," said Trap.

I had to laugh 'cause that nigga knew me well. I parked the car and tapped Jae on her leg. She sat up, slowly rubbing her eyes.

"Oh, you already know." We both laughed before I continued. "I love you, bruh."

"Hit me up."

"One." I ended the call.

Jae was out the door. I unlocked the back door and grabbed my jail bag as I followed my woman into our house. I still couldn't believe that she hadn't moved. Crown Heights, Brooklyn was home for us. That was where we met each other, four years ago. Only thing different was that she was living in an apartment then and was going through a breakup.

I had just picked up twenty bands from Yellow Man and was on my way to drop it off at Ms. Judith's house. I was driving solo on Sterling Street in Ms. Judith's BMW when a NYPD cop car got behind me and hit the lights for no reason. The police fucked with Blacks, period. Rich, poor, young or old, all were getting harassed.

One thing about me, I always put my money in a Johnson Sport book bag, just in case I had to strap that bitch on my back and run. Today was just another day that my book bag came in handy.

I didn't pull over properly. I stopped the car suddenly in the middle of the street, bolted out, and hauled ass. I knew the apartment building at the end of the block by Kenny's Fried Chicken front door was always open. Mad little hood niggas were living there, 'cause I stayed dropping work off for them to sling around the hood.

Once I hit the steps to enter the building, I dashed up the stairs, taking two at a time. It was a six-floor building. I refused to just stop on the first floor, so I skipped all the way to the third floor. One of the young boys that I served lived on the fifth floor. *Just 2 more*, I kept repeating over and over in my head. I was running out of breath fast. I refused to just give up $20,000 like that, knowing that the officers weren't going to turn it in, but pocket it themselves.

I heard the police's radio going off. They were in the building, finally. Just as I was about to hit the steps to go up to the fourth floor, a door flew open by the steps.

Our eyes locked. "Can I," was all I said, and she moved her head up and down.

I walked inside and she locked the door.

"Who you running from?" she asked in the sexiest voice ever.

My breathing was heavy, my heart was pumping fast. "Police," I replied as I bent down, trying to catch my breath.

"Follow me." She moved around me and I couldn't help but to look up at her ass.

Damn, she thick.

She took me to the kitchen and told me to have a seat as she pulled a bottle out of her cabinet.

I dug my phone out of my pocket and called Trap. "Bruh, call Ma, and tell her to report the car stolen," I whispered.

"You good?" he asked with concern.

"Hell yea." I breathed heavily. "I'm over here on Sterling Street. I'ma hit you back in a few when the coast is clear. Aite?"

"Aite, B. I'ma hit Ma up now. One."

All I could smell was black pepper. I took the bag off my back, sat it in the chair and followed the smell. My guardian was shaking black pepper at the bottom off the front door. Niggas do that shit when the police dogs are out so they lose the scent of whatever they were looking for. I heard mad chaos in the hallway, so I stepped back into the kitchen, picking my bag up.

"Stay here," she said as she left me with the black pepper.

"Coast clear!" I heard a male yelling.

"We are going to knock on each door, starting at this one to see if anyone's seen or heard anything."

That's the police. I picked the bag up again as I stuck my head in her sink. I drank some cold water from the faucet.

Boom! Boom! Boom!

Fuck! I was sweating like a river. I saw the shadow of old girl's body when she went for the door. "What the fuck?" I mumbled to myself, standing back in the cut, in front of the refrigerator.

The locks on the door turned and I held my breath. "May I help you?"

"Ma'am, we are sorry," the officer said, stumbling over his words, "to disturb you, but did you see anyone unfamiliar running throughout the building?"

"What?" I heard attitude in her voice.

"Have you seen anyone?" The officer said again, not making any sense.

"Can't you tell I am just getting out the shower?" She paused for a second before she continued, "I'm getting dressed for work."

"Yes, have—"

She slammed the door in his face and locked it. When she entered the kitchen in her bra and underwear, I didn't know if I should have looked or not, but her *LAST OF A DYING BREED* tattoo had my attention. "Dem gone!" she said as she left me standing there, holding my bag of money and my extra leg. *Gotdamn!*

A few minutes later, she returned dressed. She told me to make myself comfortable and I did. She had just saved me. I watched as she poured me a glass of Coke while I dialed Trap's number back.

I ran the incident down to him and he told me to sit still, so I did. As darkness settled, old girl fixed me a healthy plate of ox tails with butter beans and white rice with gravy. Over the meal, she told me a little about herself. I told her my name, but that was just it. She escorted me to her living room as she cleaned the kitchen up. Pictures of her and a few females were posted up along with on older couple. There were pictures of her and some males, but they looked like they could be her brothers.

The spot was clean from the table to the floor. I sat down and turned her television on to Sports Center while I waited on the twins. I heard her on the phone, talking away in her language; Patwha.

"Yuh can luk pon it like dat." Her Jamaican accent had my dick hard all over again. I blocked her conversation out as I tuned into the basketball highlights.

Minutes later, she joined me. Tray hit me up and said that they were on their way to get me, so I gave him the apartment number. I wasn't ready to leave. I was actually enjoying her company, even though she was quiet. The food was good, and her personality was something I'd never encountered in a female. Most bitches ran their lips.

When Tray and Trap entered her apartment, they couldn't take their eyes off her. She was that beautiful, and still is. I tried to pay her, but she wouldn't take a dime from me. I thanked her a million times and all she said was, "No problem."

The next day I had red roses and a card delivered to her front door. Weeks went by and I couldn't get her out of my mind, so I paid her a visit, and from that day on we'd been together.

Jae had the crib looking and feeling vibrant. My favorite colors— blue and green— were the living room colors. The walls were blue, the furniture was all black and a pic of us was posted up on the wall within a green frame.

"Daddi finally home," she sang as she approached me with a black duffle bag in her hand. I closed the door as I let the bag fall from my hand. "Thirty bands— twenty from me and ten from Trap." She dropped the money bag at her feet.

Fuck the money, I need some pussy.

I respected the strength that she possessed in every aspect. God really broke the mold when he created her, because the qualities she manifested were those of which I both fell in love with and never encountered in all my years on earth.

"Take me to the bedroom," I told her.

I kicked my Jay's off as I pulled my True Religion shirt over my head. I unbuckled my jeans, pulling them and my boxers off at the same time. Fuck playing around. As Jae walked, she took her shirt and bra off. I didn't want to just fuck her, I wanted to make love to her mind, body and soul. She deserved that. As soon as the bedroom door opened, I attacked her from the back. I took her ponytail holder off so that her hair could hang. Then, I sucked on her ears and neck.

Loud moans escaped her mouth as she stripped out of her jeans. No panties on, like I told her. She turned around and backed onto the bed, rubbing her nipples. I laid on top of her as I tasted her lips, then showed her breast some love.

"Ohhhh," she cried out with pleasure. Her nipples rocked up like a brick. Her hands are holding my head.

I licked her from her breasts to her stomach, skipping her navel to get to the pot of gold. I flicked my tongue across her clit as I glanced up at her. Tears grace her angelic face. I flicked my tongue again to make her back rise. She was begging me to devour her fruit. I placed my hands under her ass, lifting her up in the air towards my face.

"Ahhh!" she screamed.

I licked her ass before I returned to the center of the pie. I pushed my face all the way in as her body tensed. I nibbled and blew, blew and nibble as I sucked and licked her, trying to take her breath away.

"Ugghh!" Her hands were locked onto my head, fucking up my waves. "Rocket!" She screamed as she tried to pull away, but she was no match for my strength.

"I miss you!" I repeated her words to her, but with the kitty in my mouth.

I placed her legs on my shoulders as my face worked hard for the gold medal. Her legs are locked. When she didn't make any noise, I knew she was near her nut, so I worked my mouth faster and steady. Her body had become stiff. I looked up at her with the clit slapping against my tongue. Her body rose and fell beautifully, I knew she was near the end. It wouldn't take me long to taste her waterfall

Shortly, she blessed me with the gold. I sucked every drop up that her body descended from the nut. *Damn, I haven't lost pleasing her*. I kissed the cat with love, nice and slow. Her legs were shaking uncontrollably. Having to beat my dick all those years, I had to visualize me punishing the pussy, stroking it with precision just to get a good night's sleep.

I removed my hands from her hips as I came up for air. Then, I climbed up, but stopped to slap my dick against her pussy to watch a smile appear on her face. She knew what time it was. Daddy's time.

Her legs were already spread. I grabbed my dick, guiding it to her entrance. I was trying to put the head in but it wouldn't go. I placed one of her legs between mine and the other was on the outer, so I could get more room. When I tried again, I could see the pain on her face. She hadn't been touched in a hot minute. My heart beat with pride.

"I haven't had anything in me; not even a tampon."

I can surely tell. I grabbed my dick to guide it in.

"Arrggghhh!"

"Push back, baby," I said as I sucked on her neck.

Finally, I got it in. She was throwing me the pussy in slow motion as her pum pum expanded to my size. She held me like a glove. *Damn*. The heat and wetness alone had me wanting to tap out. That's how good she was working her muscles.

I had to switch positions before I ended up being a 1 minute nigga. Rolling her over on her side, my dick stayed in place. Jae was always flexible. Her body ended up in a fetal position as I stroked her from the side. I grabbed a hand full of her hair as I stacked one finger inside her mouth.

"Fuck me!" She demanded, so I laid the pipe down like a plumber.

It was so soaking wet between her legs that it was talking to me. *"Ta, ta, ta."* The way she arched her back gave me enough room to smack her ass.

"Face down, ass up!" She yelled to me.

I slipped my dick from her and she got mad.

"Yuh know I could have turned around," she said, getting back into position. She hated me out of her. She held her ass cheeks so far apart that I thought she was going to rip them. I stuffed my face in before I put the pipe back in her. "Uggggg!" she whimpered.

The way her body was rocking had a nigga on cloud nine. Now I had to treat the pussy, the gangsta way. I kneeled on the bed to enter her from behind. Wet was an understatement to describe her. She bounced her ass backwards as I pounded forward. Sweat was running down my face as I watched her ass slap against my skin. I moved her hands and I spread her cheeks myself to I get real deep inside her.

"Babi," she yelled. Her body fell onto the bed. Her cheeks tighten as I drop with her.

My knuckles held me up as I sucked the back of her neck. She lifted her body up a little just to put her hand on her kitty so she could rub on her clit.

"Cum with me, baby," I whispered in her ear as I sucked on her earlobe. "Cum for daddy."

She shook her head. "I'm 'bout to bust!" Her pussy muscles locked and I couldn't hold on anymore.

"Arghhhhh!" I hollered like a mad man while I watched her body jerk away. "Fuck!" I collapse on top of her with a smile on my face. "I love you."

"I love you, too, Rocket."

I knew she meant it. It was us versus everybody.

Chapter 34
JAE

If it wasn't in connection with Rocket, I didn't give a fuck about another nigga. Since there's only one him, wasn't no man a factor. One key, one heart, and it was his.

The way he had just blown my back out had me in a daze. I couldn't even breathe much less stand. All I wanted to do was go to sleep with my thumb in my mouth but I knew there were a lot of things to get done today so I rolled over to face my man.

Just taking in his scent gave me goosebumps all over again. My body responded to him in a different way than it ever had with any other man. I'm glad that I waited all those years for him, although I didn't think it was possible. I believed God had that forever growing emotion, love, in His plans for me. I saw timing was everything with The Most High.

"When do you plan on paying your probation officer a visit?" I asked. Rocket kissed my forehead.

"As soon as I get this sex smell off of me," he replied, giving me a smug smile. I eased from under his arms so I could hit the shower. He let me go freely.

"Check that bread out." I stopped before I entered our bathroom. His eyes were open and looking up at the ceiling and I could tell that his mind was working overtime. "I stored Ms. Judith's and MooMoo's number in ya' phone. Trap stay switching up so no contact is set for him." Seconds passed before he responded.

"Bet." I heard him shout as I pulled the glass door open to enter the shower.

I replayed my baby sister's words in my head as the hot water hit my body.

"Three years, Jae, and you plan on waiting all that time. Isn't no love that strong these days!"

She wasn't raised by our grandparents so she didn't know any better.

Our father had eighteen kids by fourteen different women. Wherever he laid his head he called home. Three of us were raised by his parents— his first two boys and me.

I was number six on the kid list for him and Chessan was number seven. We were real close, even though we never lived in the same house.

My mom was very young when she had me so my grandparents opened up their home to her. Her parents kicked her out when she got pregnant with me. She accepted their offer, but she wanted to do what young people did which was live without a care. So, she left them to raise me. According to my oldest brother, TT, her life was ruined the day she found out she was having a baby.

My father lived blocks away from my grandparents by himself so I saw him on a regular basis, to and from school, but that was it. My grandparents did everything for me.

Any individual who needed the attention of more than one person is a person who lacks self-esteem, self-respect, confidence, loyalty and security. Real men and women who are not committed to someone are free to be sketals in Patwha, or thots in American. But I believed, when you gave a verbal contract titled commitment to someone, everything you did as a single person stopped. I groomed my favorite little sister, Chessan, the same way my grandmother groomed me.

I gave Rocket my word from Day 1 so I had to stand beside him. My word was all I had in this world.

***

ROCKET

I had so much addition and subtraction to do that I couldn't help but to get the fuck up. I was up and off the bed as soon as I heard the shower water running. In need of clothes, I unlocked the first door to the left of our bed. It was a walk-in closet. A motion sensor light came on immediately

My clothes, sneakers, Timbs and fitted hats were on the left and the other side was hers. All my belongings were updated, even my undergarments were name brand and hanging up. My bitch knew my style. The best way I could describe how Jae made me feel was like I could take on the world with a butter knife and win. I had never been with a woman who made me feel this way which lead me to truly believe she was the rib taken from me at birth.

Fuck washing her scent off of me, I was 'bout to rock that shit all day like the latest cologne. I got dressed in no time. I donned a fresh white T-shirt with a pair of True Religion jeans on my ass and Timbs on my feet. I looked myself over one last time before I exited the bedroom. Handsome and still wealthy.

Within minutes, I had been in every room of the house checking to see how she updated the crib. Shorty had skills, but I wondered how she funded all this shit by herself.

I found my pants at the front door with my phone plus the duffle bag of money. Thirty bands were nothing compared to what I had when I left, but from the lawyer fees, to doing this and that, it ran out. But Jae made sure I had something when I hit those gates. *Mane, I love that bitch.*

It took me a while before I got the contact icon to appear on my screen. I hit MooMoo's number as I counted out a few thousands.

"Hello?"

I dropped the money back in the bag, hearing my baby girl's voice. My kids were my heart and my weakness.

"Who is this?" She snapped sounding just like her mother.

"It's me, baby," I said, clearly, so she could pick up my voice.

"Daddy! Daddy, when you get out? Where are you now? Where is MiMi?" She slammed me with question after question. "Where is Jae?"

Hearing the excitement in her voice let me know that no matter how long I had been gone, I still held a special place in her heart.

"I just came home. I'm at my house with Jae and you know I'm coming to get you and we're going to get MiMi. Matter a fact, pack some clothes." I didn't give her time to respond. "Ya' mom still live in the same spot?"

"Yes, Daddy." She started yelling. "Mom, Daddy is home and he's coming to get me!" "Mom, you heard me?" I couldn't hear Nita but I wished I was a fly on the wall to see that hoe's face. *Yea, bitch, I'm home.*

"Okay. I will be there, love you."

"I love you, too."

I ended the call and dialed my other baby mama's number. I used to worship the ground that Ashanti walked on, but after she fucked three niggas while we were together, my love for the bitch went out the window. Now I had a hate for the punk ass bitch so deep it was indescribable. I used to respect her even though I moved on, but she knew what it did to me when La'Quinita went M.I.A. with MooMoo. So for her to repeat what was hurting me made me want the bitch's head on a platter.

"Hello," she answered in a raspy voice like I had awakened her.

"Ayo, where MiMi at?" I got straight to the point. I got silence in return. I moved the phone from my ear to check and make sure she didn't hang up on me.

Ayo!" I barked again.

"Who is this?"

I wanted to reach through the phone and grab the bitch by her neck and squeeze until she turned blue.

"What nigga you think calling for her?" *Dumb ass bitch.*

"Hold on," she whispered. I would bet that 30 bands that the hoe had a nigga beside her.

"Rocket?" She questioned in her normal voice. I heard a door close.

"Ashanti, where my baby at?"

Jae was now across the living room in the kitchen with one of my T-shirts on.

"We need to talk," said Ashanti

"The only thing we are going to be talking' 'bout is MiMi."

Jae stopped what she was doing and pinned her hair up on top of her head.

"Well if you don't want to talk, I guess—"

"You guess what!" I screamed. "I'm not going to see my daughter? Bitch, try me and I swear on my kids, your life and everything you love, you won't live to see the next day."

"Your threats don't scare me."

"Good, I don't want to scare you but that's a promise coming from every fiber of my body."

"All I want to do is talk."

"You want to talk? Talk!"

"In person."

I had to laugh cause this bitch was serious. I rubbed my temples and ended the call.

"She lives over there on Kingston Avenue right across from the old Wingate High school." My baby informed me.

Jae was always on point. I low key wanted to thank the nigga that she used to fuck with for dropping the ball so a real nigga could claim her.

"You taking me to see my P.O. and get the girls, so get dressed."

"You not hungry?"

"After we finish running around, you can cook."

I hit the number that Trap hit me from. The nigga answered on the first ring.

"Yo, thanks for the bread, my nigga."

"Son, that's what you hit me for?" he said, laughing his ass off.

The nigga hadn't changed in all those years. I didn't trust niggas and I would knock a bitch down as fast as any nigga but Trap was the only nigga I knew who would never rotate on me.

"Just want to let you know, I got you!"

"Nigga, I'm out!" He ended the call on me and it was my turn to laugh because there was still a few real niggas alive.

I dialed Ms. Judith's number as I waited on Jae to get dressed. The old lady's voicemail picked up and I left a message for her to hit me as soon as possible.

Twenty minutes later, Jae and I were on the way to see my P.O on Fulton Street, downtown Brooklyn. I was out the door within minutes of my arrival. I had to report every Monday at 8AM and I had to stay away, five hundred feet from Ro. I couldn't wait to see that nigga, son had it coming.

As we were driving to get MooMoo, Jae gave me the rundown about everything. She went back to work for the same health insurance company on Church Street. She had been there since I met her.

"Whenever I get a client that's spending a good amount of money on health or life insurance or both, I give them my worker's discount without them knowing. I pay half price, so I pocket the other half. I transfer it in an account that belongs to my little sister in the UK."

Jae and Chessan had a beautiful bond.

"Chessan collects the money and sends it Western Union back to me with a little deduction. Then I meet up with this other girl I met from New Orleans and give her an amount. Within days she hits me back with double. I pay her a stack for each transaction that she processes for me, no question asked."

"What?" I asked, dazed the fuck out with what she was telling me. "Money fraud?"

"Yea, easy money."

"You don't need to do that shit no more. That's too much of a paper trail."

"Okay."

She was so submissive and I loved how she didn't question my ruling. Daddy was home and a lot of shit was about to change.

***

MooMoo was outside waiting on me with her book bag on her back as her mom looked on from the porch. I didn't have to get a paternity test done with MooMoo, because Nita was a virgin, but with MiMi, I did because her mother had hoe tendencies.

I opened my door and my little one ran and jumped into my arms.

"Daddy!"

We hugged for a minute or more before I placed her back on her feet.

"You ready?"

She hopped in the car and closed the door without a reply. Her actions said enough. I could hear her and Jae chopping it up as I walked to the porch.

"I see jail time did you well," Nita sassed. I worked out every day except Sundays. I had to give my body a day to rest. I heard Nita's remark but I dusted that shit off my shoulder hoping she could smell Jae all over me.

"First, let me say thanks for holding my seed down." She started to talk but I put my hand up, stopping her. "I'm home now and I want to build a relationship with Moo. I'm asking that you don't get in the way of that again." Because truly not seeing my girls for six months had fucked me up. "That's all I want."

I headed back to the car so we could pick up the other princess. Jae and MooMoo were in full conversation and I admired their relationship.

"We going to get our nails done and do some shopping," Jae told MooMoo.

Chapter 35
JAE

As we approach Ashanti's spot I had this gut feeling that today wasn't going to be any different from our previous run-ins with each other.

Disrespecting Rocket's baby mamas was never in my plans, but over the years of him being away, their true colors had surfaced. I had to remind Ashanti, especially with my hands that Rocket was still the same nigga that he was before he got locked up. He was also a great father.

I watch Rocket out of my peripheral as he placed the phone to his ear. I pulled in front of the house on the curb while MooMoo was texting away on her phone.

"Yo, I'm outside ya crib, you can bring or send MiMi out."

I twisted my ponytail over, hoping this bitch would just comply to his request.

"Ayo, I'm calm so don't let the beast come out."

And I knew from his comment that the bitch was saying some fucked up shit. I was out the car before he could say another word. I was tired of this bitch holding MiMi as a pawn all the time.

"Jae!" Rocket bark from the window, but I was not stopping until I was at the front door.

Bam! Bam! Bam! I thumped the door with my fist. *This bitch better hurry up before I start kicking this blood clot door.*

Seconds passed, still nothing. Just as I was about to kick the door, it flew open. Not MiMi, or Ashanti, but a nigga. I heard the car door slam and I knew Rocket was on his way. I cracked my knuckles, one by one with my eyes on the stranger in front of me.

"Is Ashanti here?" I asked in a respectful manner. You give respect to get respect. My grandfather taught me that.

Rocket was standing beside me. I watched the nigga size my man up, but for real that nigga didn't want any problems. I didn't give a fuck if Rocket was trashing his ass, I was still going to jump in and get a few licks.

"Yea, hold on," he answered as he closed the door.

A minute later, Ashanti was at the door wearing two black eyes looking like a straight raccoon, with the same nigga behind her. *She better select her words correctly because one fly remark is going to have her leaking blood all over the place.*

La'Quinita didn't give me problems. Her and Ashanti had an okay relationship, so the girls knew each other.

"Is MiMi ready?" Rocket asked in a cool tone and I could tell from Ashanti's facial expression that she was wondering how we found her. Little did she know, I knew the day she moved here.

I was twisting my neck from side to side. I stared the bitch dead in her eyes waiting for her to say something stupid.

"Yes," her voice shook. "Hold on, let me get her ready for you, Rocket." The nigga stepped back.

"Aite, we'll be waiting right here." He pointed to where we were standing. Rocket's hand was on his hip. He found his surprise in the bottom of the bag full of money, a Glock .40.

***

ROCKET

I'd be damned if I allowed those corny ass bitches to play yo-yo games with me and my seeds! All I ever asked of them weak ass bitches were to never take my kids from me or allow anyone to put their hands on what's mine, that's it. But they couldn't even do that.

The bitch was wearing the black eyes good and I was wondering if this was the same nigga that tried to play me on the phone months ago when I called to talk to MiMi. I guess it was some ego shit, but I hadn't let it go.

"Homie, you need to concentrate on doing time instead of being a prison father, I got this!" the nigga boldly told me. Whoever the clown ass nigga was had it coming.

I was loyal and faithful to the bitch when we were together because it was my nature. So, when I fell, I expected her to keep my daughter in my life. What I didn't expect was for her to play the games she had been playing with MiMi. I was disappointed because we vowed to always have each other backs no matter what but I guess the saying was true: Out of sight, out of mind.

"We can't put expectations on people, now do you understand why I expected you to sprint on me?" I talked to Jae as I waited for my little one.

"I told you before but I see I have to tell you again." Her tone was low but yet comforting to my ears. "I'll never neglect nor betray you. I won't abandon you like everyone else did. I promise I'll always be that peace you need to get you through any storm."

Before I could reply to her comment, the door unlocked and there stood MiMi with her mother behind her.

"Daddy!" MiMi yelled. No matter how hard her mom tried to keep us apart, it would never happen.

"I missed you." I reached down and picked her up. "Ready to go with Daddy?" She nodded.

"MooMoo!" MiMi screamed into my ear. I turned around to find MooMoo standing outside the car with her little hands on her hips. Jae's head didn't move. She had my back covered when my head was turned.

I put MiMi down as Ashanti handed a bag to Jae and I was wondering if it was MiMi's clothes.

"Take her to the car," I told Jae and she did as she was told. Ashanti was still standing in the door and so was her nigga, now.

At the end of the day my kid lived there and I wasn't digging my baby mama rocking two black eyes even though the bitch had dogged me out. I had never put my hands on a female unless I was pushed to the edge. I remember watching my mother getting her ass beat by Ro's father and that shit fucked me up. I didn't want my daughters to grow up thinking that a man loves them because he beats them.

"I don't give a fuck what you have going on over here, but keep your hands off her!" I spat to the nigga. "You want to beat on a bitch, find a bitch ass nigga and square shit out." Our eyes locked. "Take this as a warning, if my daughter ever mentions anything to me about you putting your hands on her mom, you can go ahead and buy a casket-sharp outfit."

Ashanti knew I would address the issue. She knew what my mother went through and I told her, if I ever put my hands on you, leave me. Her smile said, “thank you,” but fuck her.

I waited for the nigga to respond, but nothing escaped from his lips, just like I thought. A bitch ass nigga was in my presence.

I moved to the ride with my hand on my strap. Nigga better had gotten a clear head shot if he had the heart, and if he did and missed they both would be laying there with no air traveling to their lungs.

***

The car was full of life. Jae and the girls were having a joyous time with their talk. MiMi was all the way under MooMoo’s arm. The ride to the crib was great. I had all my ladies in my life that I would die for, except one, Ms. Judith. It was almost midday when we arrived at the crib.

Jae was cooking up a storm in the kitchen as the girls were making themselves comfortable in their new home.

“Before I continue, I want to tell you I love you.” I watched as she continued to season the chicken breasts. “It’s you who makes me a great man. You are one of a kind. This journey we’ve been on has been not only beautiful, but a well learned experience. You motivate me to want to improve our relationship each day because as long as we are happy, nothing can stop us from reaching the pinnacle of life. The only thing that will get us there is time, patience, persistence, and daily application of undying love.”

She moved around the kitchen like a fish in water.

“No concrete, distance, nor the challenges of what we had to face or those to come will ever separate this union. I’ve been through hell and back since birth, so turmoil is a part of my life, but victory has been a faithful companion, along with you.”

She hadn’t said a word. “I hope you didn’t take it as a direct shot to you about what I said earlier.” I regretted saying to her that I expected her to sprint on me. I was human so I knew when I had fucked up, and I apologize with my head up and chest out. “I know you are good for me. You tell me when I’m wrong, but you still have my back. I know you’d sleep in the trenches with me and grind till we up, so don't judge me by what I said." She faced me with a grin from ear to ear, but I could still see the pain within her eyes.

"I will love you until my last breath, Rocket. Imperfect and all."

"I value that, Island gurl." I kissed her on the forehead.

Love was definitely all around me, and I was cherishing it. But not far from the joy in my heart was the heat in my soul. Red hot, sizzling heat for the nigga did had caused me to miss years of this joy.

Chapter 36
RO

I was in a dark tunnel with nowhere to run, no light switch to turn on so I could figure out what I was going to do. Nothing. I wished I had never told on Rocket, but I couldn't take my words back.

Here I was, drinking my father's dark liquor. Henny for breakfast with my .38 in my hand. Self-condemnation and regret had taken over my life, because the only person who truly loved me was betrayed by me.

Damn! Tears gushed from eyes.

Years ago, my parents wanted me to attend school, but I wanted to enjoy the rush from the streets that I witnessed Rocket having. I got tired of being a leech and a burden to him when my parents turned me down, when I asked for money, so I begged him to put me in the game, and he did.

Rocket would preach to me all the time, *"Loyalty makes a man."* Now I was wishing I never took him up on that offer years ago.

There was only one way to fix all of my misery, I thought. With sweaty palms, I spun the barrel around with my eyes closed, saying a prayer, hoping God would forgive me.

Red is dead! I don't have shit else, so what do I have to live for?

I thought my mother had my back, but all that was a show. My father was an alcoholic. Dishonor was killing him slowly, too, so all he did was drink. He forced his own brother to tell on his best friend, and because of that, he lost his blood by death and Rocket's father lost his life to the system.

I took my last chug. The barrel stopped and I pushed it into the chamber as I placed the nose of the gun at the side of my head. My finger was on the trigger. The tears hadn't stopped. I was petrified of living.

My bedroom door flew open and so did my eyes. My mother was standing in the doorway with bloodshot eyes.

Over the years, I could tell that stress had taken a toll on her body. She was fragile, her hair was no longer there so she wore a wig, and at age forty-eight, she looked almost sixty-eight.

My hands were shaking but I'd come too far to turn back now.

"Mom, turn your head." Snot was running down into my mouth. "I don't want you to witness me take my life."

"Ricardo, please, don't!"

No more time to waste, I pulled the trigger.

***

I pulled the trigger, but nothing happened. I tapped the trigger again. Nothing. Before I could do it one more time, my mother snatched the gun out of my hand and… *Boom!*

My ears were ringing from the sound of the gun going off. She stood in front of me with a confused look on her face. The gun powder was so strong that I could taste it on my tongue. I quickly ran my hands over my body checking for any blood.

"Don't be scared now, you wanted to go out like a bitch, huh?" I could hear the damage that I'd created in her voice. "Huh?" She wailed the gun in the air.

"What's the fucking point of living? I've already committed the ultimate betrayal!"

I'm stood as she paced the room, gun still locked in her hand.

She knew that Rocket was coming for me and I was hoping he took her ass out, too. Fuck it.

Rocket needed to just sweep us all under a rug and live his life. The more I thought about how he grew up, it killed me. No love from his blood, but yet he still managed to stand strong.

"You might as well kill yourself, because if I make things right with my brother, I'm coming back to kill you!" She stopped dead in her tracks. "And my disloyal father, too."

It felt like a burden had been taken off my shoulders after I spoke my mind. My feet moved towards the door.

Click.

Click.

Click.

My mother, the woman that birthed me, had the gun aimed at my back and pulled the trigger. But I'd only had one bullet in the barrel.

Dumb bitch!

Chapter 37
JAE

The girls were having a great time with their father. Just seeing Rocket smiling made me happy. Those girls were his world. Every little girl deserved to have her father in her life. I felt like shit knowing that the man who took part in my creation wasn't there to raise me. Although my grandfather raised me, I didn't respect my father as a man. He didn't play his position as a father, a protector and as my first love, so fuck him.

MiMi's head was resting on Rocket's left shoulder as MooMoo was on the right side. We were watching reruns of The Cosby Show. Rocket's phone ringing lead to him removing himself from the living room with us. MiMi and MooMoo were cracking up at Rudy's silly performance.

"What's good son?" I heard him talking while going into our bedroom.

The girls would be spending the weekends starting every Friday evening until Monday mornings when we dropped them off at school. I couldn't wait to add to the bunch. Rocket had told me over and over how he wanted a Jr., and I couldn't wait to fulfill that wish of his. Our child will be beautiful and healthy but most of all, loved.

"Bae!" He yelled from the room and I got up. He was on the bed, still talking on the phone. The light from the TV gave me light to see.

"Aite. You know the Jamaican Golden Crust on Empire and Nostrand Ave.?" I opened the curtains allowing some sunlight into the room. "Aite, bet." He ended the call.

Looking at me, he asked, "You remember the nigga Rob I told you about from VA?"

"Yes." I didn't forget a name or face.

Rob was a nigga that he went to high school with, along with supplying him way back in the day. Nigga came home a few months ago from doing a Fed bid for distribution of crack and cocaine. Rob was born in Lynchburg, VA but moved to NY when he was twelve with his father. He ended up getting caught in VA, though.

"'The nigga had his sister hit me up a month ago with a number for me to reach him at."

I listened, but I wondered why Rob didn't reach out himself. One thing I knew, and that was Rocket better not be trying to hook up with a bitch under false pretenses.

"Word to the wise, don't make me be the cause of your eulogy," I warned.

He smiled but I was dead ass serious.

"I rather die a real man than live a lie, and if I expect you to honor me why wouldn't I honor you?"

He made sense but sometimes niggas let their dicks do the thinking for them.

"I hear you." I stood in front of him and I could smell my strawberry scent coming off of him from our love making this morning.

His hands hugged my hips.

"Believe me."

I could tell from looking into someone's eyes if they are telling the truth. My grandma told me, "Read the eyes, they'll never lie."

With him, he was speaking from his soul. I believed him.

I smiled, and his shoulders dropped. He was relaxed, so I waited on him to get back to the Rob subject.

"He knows the nigga, Wayne, real good," he started.

"Have you told Trap?"

"No. I want to have that nigga secure before I alert him."

"Do you trust Rob?"

Niggas couldn't be trusted, bitches either.

"Yea, dude is a real stand up nigga."

Real recognized real from a mile away so if he recognized the nigga as real, I could relax.

"We going to link up and he's going to take me around the hood and let me check things out." He released me from his grip and walked over to the left side of the bed and tucked the forty cal under the pillow.

"You're not taking it with you?"

"Naw, I'm going to walk to meet Rob and you know the police will search you while you taking a stroll, especially a hood nigga."

"Trrrue."

I closed my eyes for a few seconds as I said a quick prayer for my man's protection.

"If you need me, you know what to do."

"Already."

I watched from the kitchen as he kissed the girls on their foreheads before heading out the door. The girls were his soul but the streets were his true love. I knew he would never leave them alone, even though he'd told me different during his bid.

"Shorty, you're priceless! I don't want nothing or no one but you and our babies. If I had to do it all over again to end up with you at the end, I'll do it in a heartbeat. Bullet wounds, betrayals, the many lonely nights and days. Yea ma, I'd do it all to have you at the end. Even if I wasn't promised to survive that shot to the chest and although I was married to the streets, for you I will cheat on her, divorce the bitch and how I feel right now over you, I'd put the beam on her for you."

But I knew he would never pull the trigger on the hoe. The streets were home, so I resigned myself to just ride with him.

***

"Ready to go shopping?" I asked the girls. MooMoo was up off of the sofa first.

"Can we get our nails done, too?" MiMi asked taking her eyes off of the flat screen.

"Anything you want, you can get."

"Yea!" she cried out with excitement.

Chapter 38
ROCKET

Summer had felt better in NYC. I was free! I could hear and feel the vibration of the train running on its track underground.

The bus stops were packed with all age groups of people. The dollar vans and five-dollar cabs were still running and you could spot them from anywhere. Hardly any yellow cabs around here. Police officers patrolled the streets in a group on foot. This was the hood. The hood that helped raised me into who I was.

I answered my vibrating cell phone while crossing the street.

"My nigga, I'm right here, yo." Rob stayed in VA so much that his southern accent was deep and heavy.

"Ayo, that's you in the black BMW, son?" He laughed.

"Yea, that's me."

Son was parked in Bus 44's spot in front of the beef patty and coco bread joint. I swear them Jamaicans that ran that spot could cook. The smell of fresh baked bread was all over the block.

I couldn't see inside the ride because the tints were mad dark. I was glad I left the strap at the spot. Wouldn't want to get pulled over and have it.

I pulled the door handle. "Son." I greeted Rob as I entered. The nigga was skinny when we were going to high school but the bid he had pulled had him buff.

"My nigga, welcome home." We dapped each other up hood style. My eyes roamed around the inside of the car, it was just us.

I leaned back into the seat as he pulled out into traffic. Boosie's song *Windows of My Eyes* from his *Touch Down 2 Cause Hell* album was playing.

"Tryna holla at my kids, baby ma's never home, Serge and his boys got a problem 'cause I'm Boosie. Surrounded by rats so they can tell on me, cruel shit ... "

"That's some real deep true shit, right there," I acknowledged.

"Boosie did his thing on that album. He came home and gave the streets what they were missing. Him and Jeezy together, mane the South will never be the same without them."

I saluted the hustle with the mic, but that shit was not for me. Trapping in the streets was all I knew.

"Shit is not the same like it used to be when we were growing up. Niggas don't respect each other like they are supposed to. Kids tell on their parents, parents set their own kids up to get high. Friends ain't even friends when the money adding up." We were the same age and our morals were the same.

"Open the glove box, yo. There's an envelope in there." I did as he asked, and grabbed the brown manila envelope. "That's a little something for you."

I closed the glove box and opened the envelope. White faces looked up at me.

"I know it's not a lot, but it's something."

"Son, I'm straight," I said reaching to put it back where I got it from.

"My nigga, don't reject me like that. I didn't tell you no when you tried to help me."

Back in the day when we were in school, some niggas from Linden Blvd were trying to jump Rob in the hallway behind the gym in George Wingate High school. Trap, Tray and myself had just finished playing basketball when we ran into the little crowd. Rob was outnumbered eight to one.

"Take ya pussy ass back to the South." One of the Linden niggas demanded.

"Fool, I'm here and I'm not moving," Rob said with his fist balled up ready to strike. The nigga had heart so he never crumbled or dropped to his knees begging for mercy. We walked up on them clowns and stood at Rob's side.

"What's craccin'?" I asked.

"These pussies don't want no beef, Rocket," Tray answered for them.

"Hell no, triple threat, we good!"

Trap added his piece and we all busted out laughing in them fool's face. Those clowns backed the fuck back and that's how we met Rob.

I took the money out of the package and pushed it inside my front pocket. "Thanks."

"That's nothing," he replied.

We rode in silence for a minute before he spoke again.

"When I heard what that nigga Wayne did to your brother, I knew I had to get out and befriend that nigga. I fucks with you hard! What you, Trap and Tray did for me in high school will forever be in my heart." He fist-bumped his chest. I looked over at him, waiting on him to continue. "And because of that, I'm putting that nigga's life in your hands. What he did to Tray is unforgivable."

As we cruised down Nostrand Ave., Rob put me up on game with what he had being doing in the streets. He was still running back and forth to VA like he hadn't just done some years.

"The grind never stops! I have two boys to feed, my nigga."

He explained that he was getting a brick of powder for 26 stacks and selling it for $32,000, plus he was stepping on it, too.

"The only thing I hate is driving that bitch to the South. The interstate technology is stupid crazy these days, son."

"I know, but a nigga still has to live. Take me, what kind of job am I going to get with four felonies on my back?"

Homie couldn't even debate that; we both accepted we were married to the game. As he continued to talk about the new police technology, I listened intently, but Jae and my princesses were on my mind.

Chapter 39
JAE

We are on Flatbush Avenue, doing what most women wanted to do— blow money. I held onto MiMi's hands as MooMoo sashayed beside me. Rocket was going to have his hands full with these girls.

"Moo, you want to hit up Dr. Jays first?" I asked as we passed the store.

"Jae, are you going to get me the new Jordans?" MiMi inquired with her father's puppy eyes.

"We're only getting shoes from out of there, right?" Moo stopped and asked me. I smiled at MiMi first before I gave Moo my attention.

"Yea, because you made it clear to me that you want to go to 34th street and hit Macy's up."

"Daddy told me if I ball, I must ball hard."

"Well let's get going, Ms. Baller."

We turned around and entered Dr. Jays. Reggae music was blasting inside the store as people checked out the oldest and latest shoes on the racks on the walls.

"Ave yuh eva wonda wha mek a girl cum? A woman must be satisfied before yuh sey yuh dun. Yuh can't sey a ting if yuh end up a get bun," Tanya Stephens sung.

"Wah a gwan?" A male voice spoke in my language, telling me hello. I looked at him, realizing that he worked there from his name tag on his shirt— Melvin.

MooMoo and MiMi were checking the shoes out already.

"Nutin, mi deh ya a luk pan deh shoes em." My language slid off my tongue easily whenever I was talking to another Jamaican. With Rocket and my co-workers, I tried to speak proper English but when I got mad, fuck English, my Patwha was coming out.

"If yuh need help, find mi," he said with a smile. I didn't return a smile but I gave a nod as I walked off to see what the girls were looking at.

"Can I have this one, Jae?" MiMi quizzed, knowing I was not going to say no.

"If they have your size, you sure can."

I watched as Melvin helped MooMoo by removing a pair of J's off of the rack so she could get a better view.

"Can I get a six in boys in these three?" MooMoo requested.

"I'll be back," Melvin said as he wrote something on a piece of paper and disappeared.

I knew I was 'bout to spend some serious cash on these girl's feet.

My Gucci pocketbook was on my shoulders with about five thousand in cash along with other valuable items.

"Well damn!"

It can't be. Our eyes locked like chains and the hatred that I had for him was still there. We met at my job and exchanged our seven digits. I hit the nigga that same night and we linked up. We chilled that night but that was that. I thought I knew everything about Mac but I didn't. He was into the streets, hard. I can't even front, he was getting that money. I also thought that I was the only female in his life, but I wasn't. I didn't know until the night I was shot because he fucked up.

One of his side bitches that he was fucking with had a nigga in the Bronx that she was in a relationship with. Together they decided to set the Bronx nigga up. The bitch and Mac stole $150,000 from dude. Word got back to the Bronx nigga who had did the hit. I was Mac's main bitch so they paid me a visit and caught me slipping, hard. I was entering my apartment when four big ass niggas tackled me. They had guns all in my face asking me about Mac.

"I don't know where that nigga is," I spoke. I didn't give Mac up because that's just not me. Plus, I hadn't heard from the nigga in weeks.

"'The bitch that set ya' nigga up with the lick gave you up," one of the attackers said, "but I sent that bitch on her way after she gave me ya' name and address."

They searched the apartment and found a couple stacks that I had put away and took it, but before they bounced they made sure to leave a message.

"Tell that nigga, it is not over."

Boom! One of the niggas shot me in the right arm before they left my spot. My neighbor took me to the hospital, the police were called, but I came up with a lie that I was walking and some dudes started shooting and I ended up getting hit. I never told my neighbor or anyone what happened that night but Mac and Rocket.

I called Mac that night from the hospital and told him what had happened and the nigga told me.

"You knew the life that you was in." He changed his number and moved from his spot. This is my first time seeing him in five years. I observed him as he took several steps towards me. The buck fifty scar on his face was still there but no more long dreads. His style was still on point. I wanted this nigga dead so I could show up at his funeral and piss all over his grave.

"You look good, Jae." Standing in his presence had me feeling sick to my stomach. He was still ugly. "You know the love we had for each other will never die between us," he said.

The closer he got, the more I wished I had brought my gun with me. He's the reason why I have a registered pistol in my life. I couldn't shake Mac7. He would show up at my job, call me nonstop daily until I threatened to get my brothers involved. Eventually, he gave up.

I looked back at the girls and they were busy looking at shoes, still. People kept shopping and minding their own business.

"We can start all over." He stopped as he got within my arms reach.

"Yuh musa gan—"

That's all I got out before he smacked the fuck of out of me. I don't know if it was the blood on my tongue or the fact that I hated the nigga so much that made me kick him in his dick before I two pieced his ass. He curled over in pain. I'd gotten ass whoopings all my life from my grandparents and Rocket knocked me one time on my ass.

I slung my bag off my shoulder in the kids' direction. Moo had MiMi behind her as she watched in horror. By the time I turned back around Mac had me by my hair. We had drawn a crowd. I heard Melvin telling him to let me go but Mac wouldn't budge.

"Bitch, I will find you and finish what them clowns should have done," he whispered in my left ear.

"I'm not afraid to die, batty boy!"

He tried to push me to the ground but I caught my balance.

***

RO

As luck would have it, I had gone to Dr. Jays to pick up a chick, from work, who I had started fuckin' with, when I happened to find myself in the same store with Jae. Quickly, and with a thumping heart, I looked around for Rocket. Upon sight of him, I was going to dash out of there and get in the wind. But lo and behold, he was but with his bitch.

I watched with a huge smile on my face as a big, black goon smacked the shit out of Jae.

"Damn!" The little old lady beside me gasped.

Jae kneed the guy between the legs and hit him with several quick punches to the face. Whap! Whap!

I had seen her in action a few times. When bitches got slick with Rocket, Jae went to work with her knuckles and the outcome wasn't pretty.

***

The second Jae turned around from the nigga to toss her pocketbook, I knew she had fucked up. I figured whatever weapon she had on her was in that purse. Without a weapon, the man would eventually overpower her and beat her down.

The man snatched Jae by her ponytail and tried to sling her like a rag doll. Someone yelled for security and dude dashed out of the door before Jae hit the floor.

With a brilliant ulterior motive in mind, I tracked behind him. TaShonda, my boo, that worked there would just have to find a ride home.

Chapter 40
ROCKET

We were in Coney Island where Wayne rested his head. My breathing was heavy, not with fear 'cause no man put fear in my heart. I was anxious to see this nigga, so I could store his photo in my head because the next time I saw him, he would be on his way to visit the rest of his family that Trap and Jae murked.

"'The nigga runs that joint over there." Rob pointed to the car wash that's attached to a barber shop. A few men were posted in front of the building. "Over there on the left." I followed his finger. "He runs the entire apartment complex." I was soaking all the information up. Niggas were everywhere.

"He's there at the barber shop every day from six p.m. until midnight, him and some of his goons."

"How many?" I asked so I knew what I was facing.

"About five. His main crew is tight. He hands down the orders and his goons carry them out."

Cool, I lived for that shit. Nothing but God could keep me from smoking Wayne. "Circle the block, again."

"Bruh, we can't be doing that hot shit. These niggas will start shooting."

Understanding what he was saying, I told him to ride out. I would be back, though, and that's on my seeds. It must've been a sign from God because MooMoo was calling me.

"Hello."

"Daddy, someone just hit Jae in the face!" She was crying and I could hardly make out what she was saying.

"What?"

She repeated the message to me and I was heated as fuck. A muthafucka put hands on mine, oh I' was 'bout to turn the fuck up.

"Where you at?"

MooMoo disclosed the information as I relayed it to Rob. I inquired about MiMi and she was straight. Thank God.

"Daddy, hurry up and get here."

Hearing how terrified MooMoo was broke my heart but I knew for a fact that Jae would put her life on the table to protect my kids. Rob almost hit a car head on just to make a left.

Within minutes we were at Flatbush. MooMoo was still on the phone. I could hear a lot of noise in the background and the Jae I knew was not going down without a fight.

***

JAE

Deh ugly bloodclath really tink seh mi neva a guh it em back.

Pussyhole had mi ficked up. Nuh man a guh put em hand pan mi. Demya bloodclabh Yankee tink seh et cute fi beat up pan a woman. Weh mi cum from, et nuh guh suh.

No man was going to put his hands on me. Where I came from it didn't go like that.

MooMoo and MiMi were at my side. I was mad as fuck that I was ready to go after that nigga but I couldn't, because the girls were with me. I wiped the blood from my mouth with the back of my hand. It hurt but I sucked the pain up.

Two toy cops aka security guards briskly walked up to me. "Are you okay?" One had the nerve to ask.

A lady handed me a handful of tissue to help stop the bleeding from my lip. I was so embarrassed that I wanted to cry but I refused to shed a tear in public and in front of these girls. My pride wouldn't let me. I assured the play cops that I was good and they vanished.

I pinned my bun, as a few customers continued shopping while others just stared at me like I was a statue.

"You can always come back Jae." Melvin tried to smooth the situation over.

"No, I'll continue shopping." I didn't want to spoil the girls' day.

The total for all the shoes came up to $2,500. I could tell by the girls' unusual silence that thet were shaken up.

I pulled my phone out of my bag to call Rocket as I counted the money out to pay the cashier. But before I could finish the transaction, I heard my name being called.

"Jae!" No doubt it was my man.

MooMoo and MiMi turned around and ran to their daddy while I ended the call and collected the bags. I tipped Melvin a Franklin and headed towards my dude.

Once I told Rocket what happened, I knew all hell would break out. But that's exactly what the bitch nigga who hit me deserved.

***

ROCKET

I had told Rob I would link up with him later when he dropped me off in front of the store where my ladies were. The place was packed as fuck with people, but I spotted Jae and the kids at the counter.

My daughters dashed in my direction when I called Jae's name. MiMi wrapped her arms around my legs, MooMoo stood near me and explained the incident.

Jae didn't look unsteady or wobbly. It was like nothing happened but the closer she got to me, I could see that her lip was busted.

"You good?" I asked as she stood behind MooMoo. She nodded quickly before she gave MooMoo a bag to carry.

"Where did you park?"

"Down the block," she replied as she led the way.

I could tell she had a lot on her mind but we always said we would never discuss grown people business in front of the kids. I pulled my phone out of my pocket.

"Bruh, how long you think it will take you to get to me?"

"Son, I'm already in the city."

"You know where I lay my head?"

"You know Shotta keep me up to date on everything."

"Say no more. See you in a few." I ended the call with the girls in front of me.

Jae was quiet as a church mouse on the ride to the crib. The girls were talking about whose shoes looked better and how they couldn't wait to wear them to school.

I rubbed Jae's leg.

"I got you." She smiled. "You know my get down, no matter the cost or title. I vow to do my part and as the standup nigga I am, they will be laid to rest."

"Oh, I plan on it!"

I had never heard her talk with such venom in her voice before. Her eyes were bloodshot red and I knew she was mad as hell.

We arrived at the crib and the girls disappeared to their room. Me and Jae sat down on the sofa, and I immediately said, "Aite, give me the rundown."

Jae gave me the play by play with tears in her eyes. She was talking in Patwha, but thank God I understood her. I pulled her into my arms. It hurt me to my heart to know that the bitch ass nigga laid his hands on mine.

"Promise me, you'll let me handle this," she pleaded. I pulled back from her to see her face to make sure I was hearing her correct.

"You want me to let the shit go, so you can avenge it?"

"Yes!"

"What the fuck I look like to just let you handle that, Jae?"

"I just want to handle it, myself."

"How Jae? How?"

"I'll keep you up to date, I promise." Her accent was thick and firm.

My phone starts going off in my pocket. Sighing, I answered it. "Yeah?"

"Yo, I'm at the door."

"This conversation is not over," I told Jae as I released her to get the door.

I opened the door to find my nigga in a pizza outfit. I hadn't seen Trap in a few months. I wanted to laugh but I couldn't because I wanted to shed a tear. He moved past me like I was not standing in the way. I closed the door and looked my nigga up and down before I spoke.

"What's up with the outfit, son?"

"A camouflage, my nigga."

"You skinny as fuck." I embraced him.

"When you're on the run, the food is never good," he joked. "But you have enough muscles for the both of us, though." He patted my back as we let each other go.

Jae was talking in her language and I knew she was on her phone with her peoples. The girls were in their room so I decided to take our conversation into the basement.

"Nigga, where the fuck you been?"

"Mane, I knew you touched down today so I left the 'A' a day ago so I could be here, today."

"The A?" I was at the mini bar making us a drink.

"Mane, the Atlanta is where it's at, my nigga. Pound Cake got peoples up that joint."

"Copy that."

As we took a few shots of black Henny, I told my comrade exactly what I had found out about Wayne. He knew what the nigga looked like and that's all I needed.

"How are we going to come up with the burners?"

"Rocket, when do you know me to not have enough guns to go to war?"

I dropped the conversation but only to inform him about what had taken place today with Jae's ex, Mac. For the nigga to be on the run and in a different state, he knew what was going on in Brooklyn, still. He exposed a lot of information about Mac to me. The streets didn't have a clue to what was about to happen.

***

Hours later, the kids were in bed as I got myself ready for the ride. Jae was watching TV refusing to go to sleep without me.

"I'm not going to bed, Rocket."

Trap was dressed from head to toe in black, too. I tucked the loaded .45 in my waist as I checked the .9 millimeter out.

"You ready son?" I asked Trap as I kissed Jae on her lips.

"Ready as I will ever be."

Trap got us four guns apiece and a rental. It was almost 11pm when we hit the road.

"You ever heard of the nigga Kevin Gates?" Trap always listened to music when we were going on a mission. Tray would be smoking on some loud ass weed. Damn, I missed that nigga. Since Trap was the driver, I let him press play.

"Yea, I heard the nigga's album, *Islah*, when I was down and one of his other mixtapes."

"The nigga is the truth. I saw him perform in the A."

The dude Kevin Gates got my respect and props. The old head Killa, put me onto him a few years ago. Any man who claim he'll go to war with God for his wife or woman is a nigga who was crazy and in love for real.

Traffic was flowing as we zoned out to the music. It didn't take us long to reach Coney Island.

"You ready?" Trap asked as we parked a block away from the car wash.

"Most def. I'm hard-body. Brooklyn built, but Ford tough with a G5 price tag." I cocked the hammer back on the .40.

Chapter 41
JAE

A woman of my character only comes once in a lifetime and if a man ain't equipped emotionally and mentally to accept and appreciate me then it's going to take life to spank his ass. Or he just won't ever grow up.

I was cut from a cloth that has yet to be duplicated and for the nigga, Mac, to test my gangster. It let me know that he really didn't know who the fuck I was.

People viewed me as a pretty bitch with a nice smile, but they didn't know that I was as ugly as sin under the beauty. I held grudges bad and when a muhfucka pissed me off or tried to hurt me or the ones I loved, best believe I was planning revenge.

"It's an eye for an eye world, Jae," my grandfather told me growing up.

I made a very decisive phone call to Jamaica earlier, and within days my three oldest brothers would be in the states. I would have let Rocket handle the problem but my man had enough on his plate, so I decided I was going to let my blood help me take care of this nigga, Mac.

I truly didn't give a fuck if Mac's momma had to die for that nigga to show his head. I wasn't horrified or chilled to the bone at the thought of bodying a human. It would be no different to me than slaughtering an animal.

"Cut the main support line off, Jae," my g-pops displayed.

Growing up, he taught me how to kill with a machete and my grandma showed me how to shoot a rifle, but when I left Jamaica, I left that life behind. Now, thanks to Mac, I was 'bout to become a real bloodclath bitch!

That nigga was going to be practice for when me and Rocket caught up with Ro.

***

RO

To fully gain Rocket's trust back, I had a lot to prove. Thanks to this clown in front of me, I had a chance to save my own life. And I'd be damned if I fucked this move up.

This nigga must not have had the slightest clue who Rocket was for him to put his hands on his woman.

"Don't fuck with my family and my money," Rocket stayed preaching to the crew he had under him when we were on good terms.

Jae was his world besides his kids and even though I hated the bitch, I had to salute her. The bitch was a phenomenal woman. The way life was set up these days, I didn't know if there as many women that would put their life on hold for a nigga who was doing three years. She was definitely the last of a dying breed.

As for the clown who disrespected her, he was taking me on a tour around Brooklyn. My distance was far enough so he wouldn't suspect that I'm following him. Twenty minutes later and this fool hadn't stopped.

Ta'Shonda, the shorty I had gone to Dr. Jay's to pick up, had been calling me for the last hour straight and I knew she was mad as a bat in hell, but I couldn't answer her call. I sent her to voicemail once again. I had to keep my eyes on the prize ahead.

"Fuck Fuck! Fuck!" I punched the steering wheel. The last time my gas tank was empty, I got hit up by Rocket. I had about five more minutes to ride before the car cut off.

"Just go to ya' spot!" I was screaming at the top of my lungs, hoping the nigga would just park and get out so I could see where he rested his head. I couldn't let him out of my sight, this was my only chance to make things right with Rocket.

"Gotdamn, Ta'Shonda," I answered her call finally. "Why the fuck is there no gas in the car?"

"Nigga, I've been waiting on you for the last hour and you want to talk about gas not being in the car. Bring me my shit before I call the police."

"Bitch, call the police and see what I do to you." I knew she was mad and when that happened her mouth turned reckless. We had been messing around for two years. She knew nothing about Rocket or what I did to him, and I didn't plan on telling her. I ended the call in her ear. *Fuck her.*

Seconds later, the car cut completely off in the middle of the street. No one was behind me, so I steered the car out of the street with the help of my left foot.

"Fuck!" I punched the windshield in frustration when I parked. Blood leaked from my fist but I couldn't feel the pain that I had caused myself. The windshield cracked and, worse, the nigga was out of my vision.

I dropped my head in defeat

Bam! Bam!

The noise at my window brought me up off of the steering wheel. The nigga who smacked Jae was holding a gun in his hand. I jumped over into the passenger seat.

Boc! Boc! Boc!

Chapter 42
ROCKET

The extended clip in my .9 milli was fully loaded. Soon, there was going to be a lot of slow singing and flower bringing.

We had already mapped out how we would enter the building, through the front door, guns blazing.

I examined Trap for a second and I swear I was looking at Tray himself. Trap's dreads were tucked under a black Turban. No masks were on our faces because this was too personal for us to hide our identity.

There's wasn't even a shadow in front of the car wash, but I could hear The Notorious B.I.G's music blasting from inside. As we approached the entrance of the building, I tapped my left pants pocket to make sure I had the extra clips for the burner, which I did.

The glow from the car wash banner, 'One Stop' provided light as it flashed on and off.

"'Turn the knob." I motioned to Trap with my hand. And to our delight it wasn't locked. These niggas must have thought that they were untouchable to leave the door unlocked and it's not business hours.

Trap pushed the door open slowly. We were in the front office where people made appointments, no one was there so we made a left and spotted someone. He was slumped back on the sofa with a bottle of Royal Elite in his left hand, and his mouth wide open. A .45 rested on his lap; he must've been the watchdog.

Trap had a silencer on his joint so he did the welcoming. He pushed the hammer inside the fool's mouth and dude's eyes popped open but his reaction was sluggish. A millisecond after Trap squeezed the trigger, his head opened up just like his eyes.

Biggie give me one more chance. One more chance. Biggie give me one more chance.

The music was coming from the room behind the dead body. Trap had death in his eyes. I had never seen him like this in all the years I'd known him.

Although I was labeled in the streets as being unpredictable, a live wire and relentless, I still had feelings. Emotions were getting the best of me right then because this nigga Wayne took Tray away from us.

Trap turned the door handle just like the first one. Their backs were to us and the music was way too loud for them to hear us slide in. One man was sitting on a sofa with a female beside him as three niggas shot dice in front of them.

Trap fired and the bitch head exploded. The nigga shrieked like he had a pussy too, and then he quickly pushed her body off of him.

"None of y'all muthafuckas move!" Trap backed.

The nigga on the sofa didn't listen, he lunged for a gun that was on the table across the room, and I made that ass regret that dumb shit.

Boc! Boc! Boc!

His body dropped with a thud. The three dice shooters raised their hands in the air, begging us not to drop them next. I stood over the dead man and squeezed two more slugs off into his body.

"Wannabe-hero, look at you now!" I sneered.

The place smelled like straight loud pack when we first entered but not anymore. An explosive mixture of salt, pepper, Sulphur and charcoal was the new scent.

Trap laughed a devilish laugh and I had to glance at who he was staring at while laughing. He separated the trio by waving his gun at the target. One nigga was blinged the fuck out, even his pinky was glistening. *That must be Wayne*, I concluded.

***

TRAP

"Do you know who I am?" I questioned Wayne. The other two niggas' hands were shaking in the air like leaves on a tree. "Back the fuck up to the wall!" I directed them, while at my feet the bitch's body twitched and jerked before it went completely stiff.

"So, I guess it's fuck me, huh?" Silence. "I can dig that!" I answered my own question.

"ls this the nigga, bro?" Rocket asked.

"Yea, this the nigga who took our brother from us!"

"I don't know who y'all talkin' 'bout." Wayne dummied up.

"We'll let me remind you who I'm talking' bout." This was going to be my first time talking about Tray's death. "So, you kidnapped my Twin, beat and starved him for days because he wouldn't give up the location with the money. Then when you realize that he wasn't going to crumble you shot him in the head." I took a moment before I continued. "You see, he refused to give up the spot with the funds because he was a real nigga and our mother was the bank teller." I paused again for a second or more. "I rocked my brother's face on a tee shirt for months, every day!" No one knew that. I unzipped my black hoodie and there was Tray's face on my shirt. *Gone 2 Soon* was above his picture. *I Got U Bruh* was under it.

Wayne looked at his boys as if he sensed this would be his last day. He rested his eyes on Rocket, then back on me.

"You took my love ones, too, so we should be even." The nigga had the audacity to say.

Rocket shot the tallest nigga in front of him in his knee caps, out of rage. When he dropped, Rocket finished him off with two to the top.

The other clown started begging and pleading for his life. Disgust covered Wayne's face as if he detested his man's reaction.

Niggas not about this life when they're on the other side of the gun.

Me, I was a solidified goon. Whenever it was my time to go, I wasn't going to bitch up. I was going out like a G, standing on my feet, and talking mad shit to whoever caught me slippin'.

"Pussy ass nigga!" Rocket let the Nine talk this time to the nigga's dome. Wayne's face displayed no emotion from seeing his man's stretched out. I couldn't sense any fear coming from him at all. This nigga knew death was near, but yet he stood strong.

"You have anything else to say to this nigga?" Rocket wanted to know.

I shook my head *no*, and with that we both let our hammers do him ten times worse than he did my twin. By the time Wayne's body smacked the floor, both of our weapons were empty.

Chapter 43
RO

It was crazy how hours before, I was about to kill myself, now I was shot the fuck up by another nigga's bullets. I couldn't allow myself to just lay there and die, so, with all my strength, I lifted my body up with my right hand trying to locate my phone. My body was blazing hot from the slugs that the nigga pumped into me. I couldn't feel my legs and my left shoulder was losing feeling as time ticked away. *Fuck!*

That bitch ass nigga going to really wish he had aimed right and took me out. I was seeing little white spots in my vision and I know

I had to find my phone fast before I passed out and bled to death. My right hand hadn't stopped moving under my body.

"You can do this," I coached myself. "Lord, help me."

My body was getting weaker and weaker by the second but I couldn't give up. Sweat was pouring from my head onto my face and for the second time in my life, I was scared. I could feel death knocking for me to cross over.

I finally reached my phone under my leg. Pain was shooting through my entire body but I managed to pull the device out, though it was a struggle.

"911! What is your emergency?"

"I've been shot!"

"Where are you, sir?"

I could see Red's face. She was even more beautiful than before. She was not even fat anymore. Damn!

"Sir?"

I coughed and a wave of pain traveled over me. "In my car."

"Where, sir?"

I tried my hardest to focus on my breathing, but I couldn't.

This was it for me. I couldn't survive all these slugs to my body, from Rocket and now this nigga. I really wished I had a chance to tell Rocket, sorry.

"We have a location on the individual." I heard the dispatch say. "Sir, help is on the way."

Please God, let them hurry.

Chapter 44
ROCKET

Trap informed me that he was heading back to the A tonight after he pulled up at my spot. He's going to connect me with a plug so we can chop the streets down and outdo the next niggas, and live great.

"Bruh, you know I'll be in touch," he said as we fist bumped each other.

"Death before dishonor, bruh!"

"Already, tell Shotta hello for me and watch over Ma and the kids."

"Say no more!" I stepped out the car with a smile on my face as Trap pulled off. His blood was my blood and us finishing Wayne tonight, together, just made our bond rock steady.

Jae was up waiting on me in the living room with her burner on her lap, fully dressed in black.

"What you doing, boo?" I asked standing over her.

"Waiting on you."

"In all black, with a gun?"

She smiled but I knew her response before she said it.

"If you needed me, I was on my way."

I smiled back at her. My shotta had no equal. I picked her up and carried her to the bedroom, anxious to reward her with my love.

***

JAE

I'd never trusted love until I met Rocket, because of all the flaws that came with it. The pain it seemed to carry and the manipulation behind it. I've been told true love lasts forever by my grandparents. And ever since I've allowed that emotion to capture me, I only wanted it until my last breath.

Rocket's beauty was magnificent. He had a killer body that was tricked out with muscles. His lips were full and thick; just drop-dead gorgeous. Rocket's heart was what got me, because it was pure and real.

"Never judge a book by its cover, Jae," my grandma always told me. And if Rocket had looked like a baby Japanese monkey, I would still be with him and love him the same.

"Tonight, I want you to cum for me three times," Rocket told me as he got on top of me, "and you better not stop until you do!" I was already wet from his command.

He was between my legs as he pushed them high on his shoulders. His tongue was dancing in my mouth as he inserted his dick inside my pum pum. Rocket wasted no time pumping in and out of me, as he grinded on my clit. He slid out to the tip then slammed deep inside of me. My pussy made the splash sound because I was dumb wet. My fingernails clawed away at his back. I could feel myself building up to cum, so I met him at every thrust. Within minutes, I was releasing my first nut and he could feel it.

"I want you to hop on top and ride daddy with all of me tucked off inside of you."

On top, I was a beast, because I was in control. I kissed the head one good time before I jumped on the joystick. I moved my body up and down, side to side. He squeezed my nipples. I watched him bite down on his bottom lip and I knew he was enjoying the ride. I let my knees fall onto the bed. I arched my back, and bounced my ass up and down as my pussy held his wood in place. His hands were spreading my ass cheeks apart as I rested my hands on his chest for support.

Wham! He smacked my ass and it drove me to ride him faster. "Rocket," I mumbled not wanting to wake the kids up.

"Cum for me, baby." I dropped my head on his chest as I winded and grinded my hips to another orgasm.

"'That's two. I want you to bust before I do and cum hard, too, so I can see the cream on this dick each time I pull out," he whispered in my ear. He turned me over 'cause he knew this is was our favorite position. Face down, ass up. He slipped right in and pulled me back by my neck to suck on it. He was hitting my G spot and sucking my neck like a vampire.

It took no time for me to cum again. He put a finger in my ass and it drove me over the edge. I nutted so hard and long that he had nutted before I was finished. My body was his, so was my soul. I passed out with him pulling out of me.

Chapter 45
RO

"I need him hooked up, now!"

"Doctor, the operation table is ready in room four."

"Sir, can you hear me?"

My eyes flashed open but the bright lights caused me to shut them.

"He needs to be sedated."

Muthafucka's didn't know I was protected by the system. They would do anything to keep me alive. *With all the information I had given them, they better make sure I pull through this shit.*

Rocket was the first person that I told on but he hadn't been the last. Damn right I snitched on his plug, Cuba, but the information was no good. I didn't know the nigga's name or location so I had to tell on someone else to stay free.

Not only was I an informant, but they paid me to do it. Snitching had become my fulltime job. No need to push dope when I could just sit back and point a muthafucka out and collect the government's free money.

The last nigga I told on was from the Bronx. The feds paid me fifty thousand in cash and the nigga ended up with an life sentence because he took it to trial. The system was fucked up but so was life.

With all the snitching I'd done, the feds promised me protection for the rest of my life as long as I continued working for them. So, where the fuck were they when ugly filled me up with bullets?

After this Wayne case, I'm done, I promised myself. The feds mentioned that they wanted him off the streets, for good. I planned on asking them for two hundred and fifty thousand. Once everything was over, I was moving away. Fuck trying to make peace Rocket, that fool was unforgiving.

Hours later, I was patched up and medicated to the stars. I felt like I was floating on a cloud and couldn't be touched.

Dick Face Rider was sitting across from me while his partner, Chucc, was checking my wounds out.

"I'm glad that you are still alive," Chucc told me. "You're the hardest muthafucka to kill."

"Thank goodness for the tracking app we downloaded on your phone," Dick Rider chirped in with a smile on his face.

"I told you that was the best thing they created," Chucc added.

The hospital's room door snatched open and both of them crackers drew their weapons.

"Baby, oh my God! What happened?" Ta' Shonda screamed as she ran to my bed. Chucc stepped out of the way to let her through.

"Mr. Johnson, if you remember anything, please, call us. Any information is better than none," Rider sang out as they handed Ta'Shonda a card.

"Baby, I'm so sorry." She was crying but to hell with her tears. Her ass should've had the car full on fuel. "Ro, I love you."

I close my eyes and thought about how I was going to set Wayne up so I could bounce from New York before it was way too late.

Chapter 46
ROCKET

It was a Sunday, and I broke Jae off with a nice tap back out quickie before I left to hit the streets with Rob. Niggas really thought that I was not coming to get my respect and reclaim what was once mine. I'd be a bitch in a skirt before I let Crown Heights go.

"Yo, my nigga," Rob saluted me as I got in his ride in front of MS 61 Junior High School.

"Everything straight on this joint?" I touched the dash board. He wasn't driving the BMW but a brand-new cream 2016 Chevy Impala.

"Yea, this my baby ma's joint." He covered the mouth piece of his phone. "What!" He expressed on his phone as he pulled off.

I've got to let niggas know the Young King is back. The nigga Yellow Man is titled the boss of Bedford Stuyvesant Projects. The clown collected my money without my permission and built up his own operation. Son, didn't send me a dollar or word for me to link up with him when I came home. Nigga going to pay up and bow the fuck done. He doesn't get to pick.

"Yo," I looked at Rob as he ended his phone call.

"My people said that they found Wayne and four of his lieutenants, murked!"

I've never been a nigga to put on a show for another nigga so I listened as he repeated the information that's he's heard.

"Whoever did the wipe out didn't take shit from them niggas." I was staring ahead with my right hand on my hip. "Niggas are probably going crazy over there in Coney Island right now. They worship that nigga like he's God himself."

Niggas looking up to other men like they God and role models. I'll die before I worship another nigga that bleeds, eat, sleep and shit like me.

"So, he ran the whole Coney Island joint?" I asked.

"Hell yea, that nigga had that whole shit shut the fuck down. Muthafuckas fucked with him hard, so whoever did the nigga in, has it coming."

I didn't comment, there was no need to. Rob didn't know that I helped send the nigga over to the other side, and I damn sure wasn't going to volunteer any information. The first time I saw, sensed or slightly felt some crazy shit coming from Rob, I would squeeze before I ask, 'what's good'.

"So, what's up with Yellow Man?" I changed the subject about the dead.

"Oh yea, him and his brother, Mayo, has shit on lock. Them niggas eating real good."

It didn't surprise me that they did; I knew that nigga could hustle.

"I heard through the walls, that he had collected some nigga's bread and that's how he got on."

Shit spread faster through the prison system than it did on the streets.

"Word?" I'm like a dog. I never speak, but I understand.

"Yea. Now the nigga is the man."

I was silent because this nigga must have been boasting about what he had done.

"You want the nigga to put you on or what?" Rob asked.

"Naw, I'm good. I just have a message for him."

"Oh 'cuz it's like Fort Knox just to get up in this bitch." Rob pointed as we pulled up in front of Marcy Projects that Yellow Man is always at.

"No problem."

I hopped out the car. Little young niggas were posted up all over the block. Some selling dope, while others were watching out for the jakes. The game had changed. It was never like this when I was younger. I used to walk to the smoker's house to deliver what they wanted or they would come to me and I would serve them in an alley or inside their cars. Now the shit was wide open and the little ones didn't give a fuck because they'd just go to Juvie and then come back out.

"Yo, where Yellow Man at?" I asked a youngster nigga no older than fifteen.

"Fuck is you?" He barked back.

I whipped out my .45 and stuck it to his temple. Niggas were just looking, and I dared one of those little bastards to move.

"I'm Rocket!"

He was too young to know who I was, but my pistol had him shaking. "Aite, aite, let me pull my chirp out and hit him up for you."

"Any funny move and you know the rest."

He pulled the Boost Mobile joint out and did as he was told.

"Yo, Black, get boss."

"What?" the person on the other end responded loudly.

"I got a nigga out here with a joint in my face. He needs Yellow Man!"

The little one said all that shit in one breath. His comrades hadn't moved a muscle and Black hadn't hit back.

"Yo!" The little dude hit back, but no response. He was shaking so bad, but my .45 hadn't left his temple.

The building's front door flew open and there was Yellow Man with six goons behind him. He was surprised to see me and his face dropped the smile that was plastered across it. I removed the .45 from the little one's face and he took off running into the building faster than lightning.

"You counted me out, son?" I stepped to Yellow Man with my .45 still in my hand. He tried to dismiss his goons but I spoke up. "They need to hear how disloyal their boss is."

They stopped and I continued. "You collected bread from two of the projects and didn't send me a dime?" I was loud enough for his crew to hear me. Disloyal niggas needed to be exposed. "I see you eating good." I could tell from all the ice that he's rocking that his pockets are heavy.

"Rocket, it wasn't like that." His whole demeanor had changed.

"I need what you owe me by the end of the week," I demanded

"And how much is that?"

"You should know the amount and if that shit is not correct, you know how I get down."

I turned around and tucked the .45 back on my hip as I headed back to the car. Rob was posted up on the hood of his ride.

"You playing with the wrong nigga." Hearing that clown ass nigga's statement made me laugh. He got his balls back when I wasn't in his grill. Rob was pleading with me with his eyes not to react. I knew we were outnumbered but that was cool. I liked to strike when a muthafucka least expected it.

"If I wanted to play with something and get a reaction, I'd pull on my dick."

We pulled off on them pussy ass niggas still standing there looking stupid.

If a nigga ever came up in my space like that, his ass wouldn't be alive. I had a heart of a lion and my trigger finger was fearless.

Chapter 47
JAE

I was up and well rested, even though my body was sore from Rocket's love making. I reached over and grabbed my phone off of the nightstand and sent Rocket a long text.

Thank you for allowing me to be a part of your existence and for opening up to me. For trusting me and letting the emotion, love, become the substance to our future. Thank you for giving me this opportunity to finally experience what I've both feared and craved at the same time. God answered my prayers. I love you!

I got out of bed to put my robe on so I could wake the girls up. We were hitting 134th and 142nd Street to do some heavy shopping. I decided not to drive because it was hard to find a parking spot in the city. The train would be our transportation.

The girls were up the moment I mentioned going shopping. MiMi was a diva in the making. Her fashion screamed, 'Yes, I'm that girl.'

MooMoo on the other hand was very colorful, mix matched colors were her thing. Rocket's hands were full to the top with these two.

I was back in my room, ready to hit the shower so I could get Rocket's cream off of me, when I heard my phone going off. It was a text back from my man. I raced to read the text.

I vowed to never keep a secret from you. Before we met, I too found myself praying to the heaven above for someone real. One night, I got on my knees and poured my heart out, asking for a woman who can see past the shine and genuinely want a nigga who they can love and be loved by. I prayed for a woman who, like me, was fed up with the games. Now I find myself thanking God, 'cause this is real. Like you, I needed this! I love you more.

Tears ran from my eyes reading Rocket's words, because I was finally happy.

No matter what happened in life, I could dwell on the fact that we'd created something just like my grandparents.

"Not even death can separate us!" I said like Rocket was beside me. "Not even death, babi."

***

ROCKET

Jae's text message made my heart glow, but when I'm was in the streets, love didn't cover my back, so I put her on the backburner so I could concentrate on the streets.

"My nigga, you is crazy!" Rob told me when we were a few blocks away from Yellow Man's spot.

"How you figure?"

"You were outnumbered and talking mad shit to a nigga that has goons that will bust at his command."

"And if they had a heart like mine, it would've been a bloody mess back there!"

Niggas were scared to die, but not me. When it's my time to go, God is going to be at the gate with his hands wide open, telling me, *'Job well done, son.'* I'm 'bout that life. Fuck all that talking shit!"

Rob shook his head at my come back. Niggas knew I was in the position to take the Heights over before I was sent away. Now that I was back, they had to bow down and crown me King, or the murder rate would reach an unprecedented high.

"Where we heading to?" I asked, leaning my seat back.

"Mac's crib."

I didn't know how Rob knew all these niggas' business and location, but I was glad he did, especially with Trap out of town.

Mac was Jae's ex, the nigga that slapped her the other day. The nigga was probably thinking shit was gravy, but he was living on borrowed time. I knew Jae had called her peoples from Jamaica to come handle the nigga, so the least I could do was give them the location.

I tried to talk her into letting me take care of it but she refused to let me get involved. "Fuck!"

Rob hit the brake. I was sitting straight up with my strap in my hand and my finger on the trigger, ready to blast a sucka for the day. Police cars were all over the street in front of us.

"Reverse this bitch!" I told Rob but he already had the Impala in reverse. We had just turned on the block so it wasn't hard for us to back up.

"Yo, that shit was live" Rob said as we were back on the main road. I knew within an hour that if I was still with Rob, he would have the word on what had taken place.

"Swing through President Street." I directed him.

***

"I'll be right back. Keep the engine running." I told Rob as he parked. He pulled his phone out from the console as I exited the car.

My .45 was stuck to my hip like I was born with it. Mufuckas counted a nigga all the way out, but it's all good. I was 'bout to let them know I'm back and heartless.

I rang the bell like they were expecting me. The bitch opened the door, but after seeing my face, she tried to shut it back but my foot stopped it. Wrinkles had taken over her forehead like a note book page. She looked bad.

"Draymond," she called me by my first name.

"You was never there for me, so fuck addressing me by that name. I've put up with a lot dealing with you. From the abuse, to that abusive ass husband, and the abandonment so you could be with him. Add on the weeks and months of not knowing what would happen. I know hunger because you decided to put a man in front of your child. I know what it's like to not have Christmas, or the only gift at birthdays is just the blessing of being here on earth, alive."

Tears were flowing from her eyes. I took a long wind before I continued.

"Think before you act in public." I could hear Killa's words in the back of my head. My .45 was ready to be used.

"I was forced to hit the block and pick up the biggest gun I could find." I tapped my side. "I was forced to adopt the mentality that it's kill or be killed. I didn't have anyone to teach me how to be a man, that shit came naturally. I didn't know normalcy until I lived with Ms. Judith and her boys but by then I knew how to trust in me. I felt if the woman who gave birth to me could leave me then it wouldn't be hard for anyone else to, but Jae's love shut all that shit you've done to me out."

Her tears hadn't stopped running, but I wasn't moved by them.

"Let ya' snitching ass son and husband know I'm back in full goon mode."

I pulled my .45 out and placed it on my heart to let her know I meant business before I walked back to the car. *God bless these niggas' souls, 'cause I'm out here!*

Chapter 48
RO

As soon as Shonda left, I called my police partners up and delivered ugly on a gold plate to them. They got the video footage from the store where him and Jae got into it at and they ran his name through the police data system.

Hours later, when I called Chucc back, he told me that they had found enough drugs and guns in Markeese 'Mac' Edwards' crib to send him away for life, but he started talking so damn good that they were just going to charge him with malicious wounding.

"How much time does that carry?" I asked over the hospital phone as the nurse changed my bandages.

"We're not sure as of yet, Ro." Chucc informed me.

"What the fuck you mean?" Pain shot through my body when I tried to sit up.

"The way he talking, he might just do a year."

"A year!" I shouted in the phone. Dude must have told on El Chapo. The nurse never stopped doing her job as I listened to Chucc tell me that the information that Mac had given up was that damn good.

I got tired of talking to Chucc so I told him to put Rider on the phone.

Rider was the more understanding and the more open one between the two. I understood him better, and we tended to be on the same page most of the time.

"Ro, Mac's information is great, don't get me wrong. But you just have to go harder than him when you get better."

I shook my head wishing I never started snitching, 'cause that shit was getting way out of hand. No matter how many niggas I had turned in, it wasn't enough.

"Yea, I hear you." I was tired of being the government's pawn. Just when I was about to hang up, I heard Rider hit me with another bomb.

"Oh, you know the dude, Wayne, from Coney Island that you're supposed to set up?"

"Yea, what's up?"

"Well they found him and five people dead this morning."

Well there goes my money. Damn! I sighed.

Not in the mood to hear shit else, I dropped the phone on its base and told the nurse to get the fuck out. I needed to get my thoughts together. Who the fuck was I going to tell on now? My thoughts were quickly interrupted by my mother's voice.

"Ro," I closed my eyes pretending to be asleep. I was not in the right frame of mind to go back and forth with her especially when she just pulled the trigger days ago.

I could feel her presence over me. Goose bumps covered my body.

"Ro," she touched my face. "Ricardo, if you can hear me know that I love you and I'm sorry you're going through all this bullshit in life." My vital machine continued to beep.

"I wish I could change the way things are, but I can't. I'll stand by you through the obstacles that you are facing."

My father must've whooped her ass, so now she was back to her senses, again. I truly believed she loved my father more than herself and me.

"Rocket showed up at the house," she blurted.

It took everything in me not to open up my eyes. My heart was beating fast, as I waited for her to go on.

"He was mad." She removed her hand from my face. "And he made it clear that he was back to finish what he started."

I opened my eyes to see tears streaming down her face.

"But I'm standing by you and your father. It's us against, Rocket."

Fear caused a bolt of fresh pain to surge through my body. My muscles tensed and my mouth felt dry. All I could do was pray that God would protect me against my brother's ire.

Chapter 49
ROCKET

A few more stops and I would be done for the day. Rob delivered the information to me about the road block that we missed.

"Mac's house got raided and now the FEDS are involved. My people believe that nigga going to sing like a humming bird," he kept talking.

Niggas fool themselves but the facts always come out. They the first to testify to the alphabet boys.

"They said that the nigga's plug from The Land."

I can see the nigga telling because his plug is all the way in Cleveland, Ohio. I'll never sell my soul! I'll do life plus whatever before I set up or tell on the next mufucka.

"Mac was the nigga to call when you was waiting on ya' plug or shipment to come through. His main nigga was a cat named Felipe. He runs the Red Hook Projects."

Snitches spare no one, and if Mac started talking, then Felipe could hang the game up.

"This shit is not made for everybody, son. Niggas catch cases every day, and claim they're so real but when they realize what they are facing, they snitch on their own blood, their momma if they get to walk free."

"That shit is crazy, but it's the truth," Rob said as we headed back to my side of town.

I had to visit this old head that's been running the whole Crown Heights since I've been gone. I got word from him to link up with him when I came home, through pen and paper.

Old niggas can't be slept on so my .45 traveled with me to the visit. Rob dropped me off at the entrance of Prospect Park.

"Yo, if you find out anything that I need to know, hit my line, B."

"Bet."

My phone went off and it's Ms. Judith. I've been home for days and she was just now hitting me up.

"Ma, what's up?"

"Rocket, how are you doing, son?" I could hear the love she had for me in her voice.

We talked as I walked to the old head's crib. She'd been out of town spending time with her sister in New Jersey.

"Trap took lil man back to the 'A' with him. He's getting older so he needs a man constantly in his life."

Our conversation lasted all the way to Gotti's house. There was a tall white gate with cameras on it. I hit the intercom as I admired how big the fucking house was.

"Aite, Ma, I love you." I ended the call.

The grass was well kept. High quality cars were on display in the front of the house.

"Hello." A female voice blared through the speaker.

"I'm here to see Gotti."

"Who are you?"

"Rocket!"

A few seconds passed and the gate opened. I walked through with my hands at my side. There was a statue of a naked black woman that was spitting water into a fountain. I took in the beauty of the house and the cars. Mufucka was really eating. The walk to the front door was about thirty seconds.

Standing in the doorway was an older man with a Kangaroo hat on. It was tilted to the left side. He was rocking an Armani shirt with a pair of slacks with house shoes on his feet. There was no hair on his face except his low trimmed mustache and eyebrows.

"Son, you look just like ya' damn hard head father," he said as he extended his hand out to me. "Welcome home."

I shook his hand. "Thank you."

"Hope the walk wasn't that bad?"

I was wondering how the fuck he knew that I walked and didn't drive.

"I have my eyes on Crown Heights," he said as he let my hand go and gestured for me to come in.

To say the inside of the house is was would be an understatement. The ceiling was so high up that I couldn't stop staring, plus I was looking dead at the clouds. Cameras were in every corner of the room.

"Take a seat. Would you like something to drink?" he offered.

"Water."

"Good choice. Your father's favorite thing to drink is water," he disclosed as he disappeared into another section of the house while I took in the pictures on the wall.

I was looking at an older version of myself with Gotti standing in front of Junior's Cheese Cake on Fulton Street. It was my father, Draymond Sr. aka OX. They looked like young pimps back in the day.

"That picture was back in the 80's. You weren't born yet." He caught me staring hard at the photo as he handed me a tall crystal glass of water.

"Thank you."

"Me and your father was raised in Crown Heights. I was his right-hand man and a best friend and still am to this day." I took my eyes off the pic. "We ran the streets together, hard."

I was at a loss for words.

"Your father's legacy made it hard for anyone to take control over the Heights." I listened closely to the new information about my pops. "When he got sentenced, he handed the title over to me but I refused to go as hard as he did. Look at the time he doing."

"When your pops heard that you entered the game, he was crushed, but he understood that his blood was running through your veins, so he had me watch you, daily."

How the fuck I miss this nigga on my back and didn't notice.

"So, I talked to your father, today."

I took a sip of water as he took a seat across from me.

"What he had to say?" I placed the glass of water on the table beside me and got comfortable.

"He said that he wanted me to give the game up and let you take over."

He didn't stop me when I got with Cuba, he sat back and watched.

"Ms. Judith was one of the many women that he had, so when he got the news with how you were being treated, he moved Ms. Judith and her boys down the street from where you lived."

All this information was mind blowing to me, I took another sip of water.

"Ox showed Ms. Judith mad love when she was homeless."

My father was the man, and from the way Ms. Judith treated me, I could tell that she loved my father.

"So, what's the point of this meeting," I cut to the chase.

"I'm going to do as I'm told. I have a great feeling that you'll be a great leader of Crown Heights." He crossed his legs as he pressed on. "You don't need a connect or workers, everything is already in motion for you."

"How can I trust these people that don't know me?"

"They all know about you from years ago, they just been waiting for you to arrive, Rocket." He stopped and took a sip out of his glass. "Plus, I've watched you trap with the Twins for years."

I took in what he was saying. "We push heroin, crack, cocaine, weed and pills through this operation." This was the muthafuckin' big boy league for real.

"You don't need to travel to get ya supply, it comes straight to a building downtown on a tractor trailer that delivers import cars. You have killers in your possession, so there's no need to get your hands dirty."

"I agreed on everything, except for the killers. I can do my own touching and I'd rather it stay that way."

I could tell he wanted to know why because of his hand movements.

"No one will know when I strike. I don't run my mouth so it would be hard to stick a body on me."

***

We visited every project in Crown Heights that was under Gotti's hands as he introduced me to each soldier in charge of each housing building. Niggas showed me mad love when he told them that I was taking over.

"Your father will contact the plug and they will get things rolling." Gotti told me as he showed me the building where the drugs were dropped off. "You can change the prices on the products if you like."

Niggas better respect my take over.

"You have clients in seven states."

"Gotdamn! I've got to let Trap know all this shit. I trust that nigga with my life."

"The connect you had, you need to cancel him!"

"Say no more!"

Gotti pulled up in front of my house and I didn't even give him the address.

"After you drop the kids off at school and check in with your P.O. you need to show ya' face to the projects," he said as he unlocked the door from his side.

It was 8PM when I walked in my house.

Chapter 50
JAE

We bossed up in the city today. We bought everything designer. We took a tour around Time Square snapping pictures. We visited where the old Twin Towers were, even though security was extra tight. On the subway ride back, I made sure to get the girls a seat together while I stood over them. I could tell that all the shopping and walking had them drained.

I hated taking the train because there was hardly any space or room for me to breath or stand with the amount of people on each cart. Then burns that walk through each cart smelling like garbage begging for money, food, whatever you can give them. Then there's the hustlers, the ones that be rapping, singing, dancing or playing an instrument for money. It's all about a dollar.

When we got off the train on Sterling Street, we took a five-dollar cab and got off two blocks before our house. I didn't know who the driver was or who he knew so to be on the safe side, we walked home. The girls were exhausted, so I told them to take their bags to their rooms and take a shower as I prepared dinner. I hit the shower and headed to the kitchen to cook. Fried snapper fish, steamed cabbage and baked potatoes had us full. The girls ate and left me in the kitchen so they could watch music videos. I called Jamaica to see if things were okay with my grandparents, and as always, they were straight.

As soon as I joined the girls, Rocket walked through the front door.

"Dad," MooMoo acknowledged him.

"Daddy," MiMi said, never taking her eyes off the TV.

I smiled up at my king as he kissed the girls on their foreheads. He signaled with his head for me to get up.

"Tomorrow is school, so no late party, tonight."

"Okay," they both said in unison.

Rocket's swagger had my pum pum beating its own reggae beat.

Soon as we closed the bedroom door, I attacked my man with my hands and lips in a sexual way. I had to have him at that moment.

"Damn," he mumbled with my lips on his mouth. I pulled away to comment.

"I missed you all, day." I was undressing him while I stroked his dick. It didn't take more than a few seconds for his dick to be standing straight up. All I needed was a quickie to quench my thirst.

I held onto the bed and bent over so he could hit it from the back.

"Gotdamn!" he said as he entered me. I looked back and motioned with my finger on my lips for him to be quiet. I. didn't want the girls hearing us having sex. He pulled my hair so hard that my body arched. He knew my spots and he knew them well as he placed kisses on the back of my neck. I bit my bottom lip to hold in my moans.

"Rocket," I whispered and he dug deeper. "Rocket." I called out again as I grabbed his head with both of my hands. His dick game was on point, but if he got a little drink in his system it was a wrap. He put a black eye on the pussy.

"Cum for me."

My man didn't have to tell me twice to cum. I relaxed my body while he held onto me. His strokes got longer and deeper and I knew at any minute his seeds would be flying up inside of me.

"Jae, I fuckin' love you." I could feel his dick exploding in me. I clinched my inner muscles, sucking him for every drop.

"Rocket, I love you, too."

My heart, my body and my soul was his. We cleaned each other up before we headed into the kitchen so he could out some food in his stomach. We checked on the girls and they were watching Beyoncé perform.

"Today's been a crazy ass day," Rocket expressed as he took a seat at the kitchen table. "But tell me how your day was."

I love that no matter what's happening out in the streets, he still makes it his business to see how my day was. I told him everything we did as I sat his food in front of him.

"Which news you want first, bad or good?" he asked as I put the extra food away.

"It don't matter."

It really didn't matter what news I got first. He was mad hungry, so he didn't look up from the plate for a minute or so. I ran the dish water as I waited on him to talk.

"The feds." My eyes got big as a lightbulb. I turned around and waited for him to continue, but his mouth was full of food.

"The feds what, Rocket?" He took a sip of water before he answered me.

"They arrested Mac, today."

"Huh?"

He spilled the news before he took another bite.

"Damn!" I said reaching for my phone on the table. "Eat ya' food while I call Jamaica to inform my brothers about the news."

I was mad that Mac got picked up because I wanted him dead. Fuck the feds for taking his freedom when I was starving for his life.

"Mail nuh badda cum up yah, babiland ave ern."

I listened to my brother telling me to let him know if things changed.

"Yea mon, mi. weh calliyuh." I ended the call letting him know that I will call him.

Rocket told me how he had seen some of what happened to Mac but he didn't know who he was watching until Rob told him.

"And I visited my mom, today."

"And?"

"To let her know I'm back and I am gunning for her bitch ass son and husband."

I knew this day was coming and I knew he'd never harm a female, so I'd take that life for him if he wanted me to. Fuck that bitch.

"Fuck all that though. I linked up with dad's right-hand man and best friend. He gave me the key to open up Crown Heights however I want to."

I could see the excitement, the love and hunger for the streets in his eyes. That bitch would always be his first love.

***

ROCKET

We dropped the girls off at their schools early so I could get to my probation officer on time. That shit didn't last long either.

Ms. Walker asked if anything had changed and I told her no.

"Have you seen your brother?" She asked me as she took her glasses off of her face.

"No, I haven't seen him."

"Good. And if you do?"

"I must be five hundred feet away from him." I said what she wanted to hear.

"Great I'll see you next week, Mr. Wallace." And I was out the door.

Jae was in the car listening to reggae music when I returned. I couldn't understand shit that was coming out the speakers because it was way too fast. She switched genres on her iPhone to trap music for me. Jeezy's *In the Air* song came on as she pulled out of the parking lot. I turned the volume down so I could talk to her about my plans. "Trap should be here in a couple of days to help me take the Heights back over."

"But in the meantime." She knew me like the back of her hands. She was waiting on me to keep going.

"But in the meantime, Jae, I need you by my side twenty-four-seven." She nodded. What's understood didn't need to be explained.

There were nine projects in Crown Heights that I had to run and manage. Our first stop was Sterling Place Rehabs on Sterling Place. I had told all the soldiers in charge that we would be stopping through around eight thirty and they needed to have every member present, no excuse even if I was late.

The guy in charge over there was named Beam. I hit his phone up when I was parked outside the building.

"Yo, I'm here."

"Aite," he said.

Jae cut the engine off. "Do I need to bring this?" She pulled the .9 millimeter from between her legs.

"You feel safe with it?"

"Always!"

"Well, bring it."

Beam was standing in the building's doorway.

"Let's go, boss lady."

I exited the car first, then Jae followed. She was rocking fitted jeans and hoodie that showed her waist and ass off good. The 9-millimeter was tucked, but it could be seen.

Beam dapped me up as we entered the building. Jae stood back checking the building's lobby. It was early so there was no traffic or noise, that's why I planned the meetings early.

He led the way to an apartment on the first floor. Niggas was sitting at desks like a classroom. There was a chalk board on the wall in front of them with names and numbers, but all these goons' eyes were looking past me at Jae, thirsty-like.

Jae going to have all these niggas leaking.

I stood directly in front of the board. Jae stood still by the closed door with her hand on her hip. Beam was by the window sitting in what looked like a teacher's chair. I loved the set up. I counted the niggas, quick. Twenty-five to be exact.

"As you already heard, I'm the new boss in charge." All their eyes were now on me. A nigga to the left sat back in the desk. "A title means nothing to me, but loyalty means everything. I ask that you live by that at all times, no matter what. And if you don't know, you fucking with a nigga that will definitely get you eternal sleep. I don't just spit shit because I'm bored. I live, eat, sleep, shit and death before dishonor." I paused for a second to look each nigga in the eye before I continue. "I'm bout business and money, if you want to eat, this is the team for you, if not, you can bounce." I waited to see if anyone disagreed, but not a soul moved. "Beam, make sure each person gets a five-thousand-dollar bonus." He nodded as I looked at the smiles on their faces.

"Oh yea, one more thing before I ask if there's any question. I don't rock with any other projects in Brooklyn. It's all about Crown

Heights, so if you are tied in with another project, take ya' self away or you will be wiped away. The choice is yours."

Niggas heads were moving up and down. They understood my get down.

"Questions?"

Heads motioned no.

"Well, Beam, holla at me later so we can chop business up."

"Say no more."

I headed towards the door. Jae opened it for me and I exited, only to turn around to find every pair of eyes on Jae's ass. I reached back and smacked her ass as we headed out.

Out of all the nine spots, Kingsborough Extension Projects had four members missing. "Where the niggas at?" I asked J-Money, their leader.

"Boss, I don't know."

"That's cool. When they show up, cancel them. I told him in front of everyone present. Niggas got the game fucked all the way up."

I gave the same speech that I gave to Beam's crew to each project, before I headed to meet Gotti at the drop off building.

"You are going to need just more than Trap's eyes, Rocket." Jae spat some real shit. "And you just can't pick anyone to watch over ya back, either."

I'd never ever brush her feelings, thoughts or opinions off. I needed her to feel comfortable expressing herself to me.

The ringing of my phone fucked up our conversation. It was a number I didn't recognize.

"Como esta mi amigo?"

"I'm good and you?"

"We need to talk!"

I disclosed the location for us to meet.

"Babe, stop at Popeye's over there by Junior's Cheesecake."

"Okay."

***

I spotted Cuba's army before Jae parked. Those clowns were everywhere, but that was nothing to a lion. I feared no human being. Jae followed my eyes with hers.

"You ready?" she asked me as she stepped out the Audi with her baby, still showing.

Cuba was sitting at the window by himself. He stared straight ahead as I opened the door for Jae. She went to the front to order some chicken as I took the open seat in front of Cuba.

"Welcome home." His English wasn't that good but I understood him enough.

"Thank you."

He wasted no time. "So, when do you want to start back doing business?"

I leaned back in the chair and glanced out the window before I turned my attention back to the subject at the table.

"I no longer need to do business with you." I watched how his cool, calm, demeanor stayed the same. Real recognized fakeness, all the time. Jae was sitting down, waiting on her order to get done.

"After all that I've done for you." His voice was low, but it spoke volumes.

"I made you millions and I mean muthafuckin' millions," I countered.

Wetback ass muthafucka never gave me shit. I had to grind my ass off just to prove to him that I was hungry, and he still didn't drop the prices or make a way for me to get the product. I was the one making trips back and forth. It was all about the money with him, when I looked back on it.

Muthafucka never reached out and handed Jae shit or showed my niggas love when I got jammed up. Not that I needed it, but it's the principle.

"And you made millions, too, Rocket."

"I made a million and nothing more because you were taxing me hard, but I never complained 'cause I got all yours to you."

He looked over at Jae and smiled. "Your brother told on me." His eyes came back to me.

"You not locked up, is you?"

He moved his hand. I was pretty sure that it was to signal his goons.

I knew when to play with fire, and the difference between him and me was that he had people to kill for him. With me, I laid a nigga down myself.

"And I know that nigga told on you. He will get his because he's a snitch, you can bet that."

Jae picked up her order.

"So, that's that, Rocket?"

"That's that, Cuba!" I said, getting up from the table to follow my woman out the door.

I knew I was going to have to body the head so the arms would fall, or else my ass would be six feet under.

Chapter 51
RO

I was cooped up in my parents' house for four days again on prescription medication. The Percocet had me feeling so damn good, but after the pills wore off, it was hell. I popped three or four at a time just so I couldn't feel any pain.

My mom had been hella nice to me since I was released from the hospital. TaShonda was over every day after work, blowing my high, talking about me coming to stay at her apartment in Crown Heights. My father claimed he stopped drinking the day he heard I got shot the fuck up, again. I could tell because he didn't smell, or stagger, or stutter when he was around me.

"You going to stay with me or not, Ro?" Shonda asked me while she changed the bandage on my shoulder.

"When I'm better, I'll stay with you."

"Now was that hard?"

Not in the mood to argue with her, I pretended to fall asleep so the bitch could leave me the fuck alone and go home. Gotdamn, I was just tired of the hoe.

"I love you, Ro," she said, kissing my lips.

I just laid there, thinking about what me and my mom had talked about until I drifted off to sleep for real, and the nightmare of Rocket coming after me resurfaced.

Chapter 52
ROCKET

I had just gotten off the phone with MooMoo when it rang in my hand. "Yo."

"What's good, son?"

"Yo, this nigga out here at the Forty-Forty spot, claiming that he fuckin' ya' baby mama and how he checked you when you was behind bars on the phone."

"What?"

"Yea, the nigga said he ran up on you and you pulled the white flag, wanting peace."

"What?"

"My nigga, I'm looking at the nigga right now, B."

"Aite, hold that nigga there. I'm on my way."

"Bet."

"Babe, get up." I wake Jae up. "Get dressed."

"What's the occasion?" She asked, putting her panties on. "You already know."

***

It took us less than twenty minutes to get to Jay-Z's club. A nigga was tryin' to degrade my character and thought he was going to walk free. *Fuck outta here*. "Yo, I'm outside in the parking lot." I hit Rob up. "I'm around the back of the building, son."

"Aite, don't get me dirty." He laughed before he ended the call.

Shooting a nigga in the back was not my style. I let a pussy know what he had done to bring death upon himself while I pulled the trigger, face to face, man to man.

I was in front of the club, waiting on Rob to escort this cold pussy out to me. I warned the nigga not to put his hands on my baby mama, but MiMi told me she got home from school that Monday that her mom's arm was in a sling. The pussy, woman-beater, pulled her arm out of the socket. Now he was trying to downgrade me.

I watched Rob and the nigga exit the building. "Park right here, babe, and flick ya' lights."

Rob spotted me and walked towards the rental that I got to travel around in instead of the Audi. My window was cracked just a little. I could hear the nigga that clowned me that night on the phone, clear as day.

"Fuck all these niggas, son!" He was spitting mad smoke.

"When I get out the car, hit the trunk button."

I jumped out of the car and walked towards the niggas. My fitted covered my eyes but I could see where I was going. I bumped dead into the sucka with my pistol in his stomach. "Act a fool and watch me work."

I checked his pockets for his phone. Rob disappeared. The parking lot was crowded with drunk people. I found the phone in his back pocket. "Walk to the car." My gun was in his back as I directed him to the car.

"My nigga!" he screamed out to Rob.

"Shut the fuck up, bitch!" I jammed the burner deeper in his back. "Another word from you and it's a wrap." He didn't know who the fuck I was. "Naw, son, you taking a ride in the trunk."

"Mane, my nigga, whatever you want, I can get it to you."

He climbed in the trunk and I slammed it shut. Jae pulled off when I got inside.

"Where to, babi?"

"I don't know, just drive."

She pulled out of the parking lot with the nigga screaming and banging away. She turned the volume up to the music and hit the highway back to Crown Heights.

***

"Pullover right here."

She unlocked the trunk while I was standing over it.

"Let's go!"

I didn't have on my hat anymore, plus the street lights gave him the right amount of light to see my face. When he looked up at me, I saw the terror in his eyes. "Man, I'm sorry, yo!" He begged with his hands up.

"Fuck your apology and get the fuck up!"

Jae was standing beside me, looking at the fake gangsta pleading for his life.

The nigga didn't move.

"Don't let me tell you again! Get the fuck up!"

He swung his legs over the edge and sat up, bumping his head against the door. "My nigga—"

"We ain't cool. Stop adressin' me as your nigga."

"I'm sorry! I'm sorry, yo!" He started crying.

"I'm a real nigga, and real niggas do real things, so I'm gonna let you know you striked the fuck out, face to face."

He begged again. "Yo, I'm sorry."

"You tested my gangsta over the phone the day I called home to talk to my seed. I warned you not to put ya' hands on my daughter's mama, but you did it anyway. Then, you had the nerve to downplay me to niggas that I know, tryin' to fuck up my reputation?"

"Rocket, it wasn't like that!"

I shoved him on the curb of the street with the pistol. Death waited for no man. I finger-fucked the trigger as his body leaned from side to side before it finally hit the pavement, hard. I dumped four more slugs in him just for GP.

Jae hopped in the car and started it. She pulled off like normal as I leaned back in my seat. "Niggas better respect ya' name and your demands or their asses gonna bow the fuck down." Jae said on the way home.

"And they better respect yours, too!"

***

JAE

Seeing Rocket slaughter with the pistol like that had me feeling safe and untouchable. I knew he had it in him, but witnessing him fuck the trigger had me nutting on myself every time I thought about it.

"Mane, that nigga Rob said that Mac was out on bond and staying with his mom."

Never let a man belittle you and get away with it, Jae. My grandma's words rang over in my head.

"You want the nigga to vanish, right?" Rocket questioned me.

"You already know, babi."

***

We were camped out at Mac's mother's house, waiting on Rob to pull up with the nigga. They were out having a few drinks, Rob told Rocket.

"You ready for this, Jae?" Rocket asked me for the tenth time within that hour.

"I was born ready, babi."

"Well, here they come."

I watched the lights in the rearview mirror. Rocket had got me a .40 earlier in the day to handle this situation. Rob pulled right in front of the two cars ahead of us and parked.

We were dressed in all black with blue bandanas covering our face. Just in case that snitching ass nigga might've had extra eyes.

My door was already open. We had taken the interior lights out. Both Rocket and I hopped out the car at the same time. I walked to the passenger side with my gun in front of me and tapped the window with my black gloves covering my hands. I watched Rob hit the button to let down the window. Mac's face was priceless when he saw the gun aimed at him.

"Bloodclath pussyhole, tek dis!" He knew my voice. I shot the nigga dead in his mouth. His hands reached up as his head hit the head rest.

"This wasn't the plan!" Rob yelled, but I pulled the trigger again, hitting Mac in the hand that he smacked me with, before I finished him off with two to the dome.

Boc! Boc!

"Dat's fi mi am, pussy!" *That's for my arm that the Bronx nigga shot me in.* I pulled my bandana down as the nigga's eyes rolled in the back of his head.

I wanted him to see my face before he crossed over. When his body stopped moving, I pulled the flag back up on my face and walked back to the car.

Boom! Boom! Boom!

I turned around to see fireworks going off in the car on the driver's side.

"You killed, Rob?" I inquired as we pulled off.

"You know I did. Son, knew way too much."

His answer was good enough for me.

"Let me find out you a killa, and didn't tell me?"

"I Was born to kill, like I was born to die," I told Rocket. Then, I took the black gloves off my hands.

Chapter 53
ROCKET
Two Weeks Later

The first week with Crown Heights under my command, the team pulled in almost a million dollars. That was the most Gotti and OX ever made in a week. "Son, I am so fucking proud of you," my father called and let me know how he was feeling.

The murder rate went down by twenty percent. Shit was looking good in The Heights because everyone was eating and not starving.

"I know you had something to do with Knight getting killed!" Ashanti acted a fool when I went to pick MiMi up. MiMi was in the car with Jae and MooMoo when she started going off.

"You the dumbest hoe I ever met!" She'd rather have a nigga in her life that beat her ass and let her child witness it. "Fuck you!" I cussed the bitch out and walked off on her stupid ass.

***

Cuba hadn't reached out to me, but I knew he was somewhere plotting my death. I saw it in his eyes the day I turned him down.

Trap was in town, on the low, in the cut. He'd left Trap Jr. in the A with Pound Cake who he'd being fucking with. He had to be feeling the bitch 'cause the nigga didn't just allow anyone to watch his seed.

The girls were at my house every weekend. I showed up to see my P.O. faithfully and on time. I hadn't seen Ro, his father or my mother, but they were on my To-Do list, for sure.

***

Yellow Man's time had expired. I wouldn't be me if I didn't address the bone of contention. I was a man of my word and I'd targe rather die before I changed who I was.

Me, Jae, and Trap were dressed for a war. Jae had on a vest with two Glock .40's in her hands. Trap was loaded from the waist down to his ankles, like a soldier. I had a brand-new AR-15 that I was packing with my Mac 11.

Rob told me before I killed him, "Marcy Projects is not ya' average projects. Kids die every day more than adults do over there, because they want a name for themselves. They want to be remembered as a G when they go, so they'll do anything to make that happen. Even if it means killing their brother, mother, or father, so when you go to tackle that nigga, Yellow Man, you go correct. His little niggas are fearless warriors." Rob showed me where the nigga lived.

"I heard the nigga's got a few shooters livin' with him just in case he needs extra ammo." I told Jae and Trap what I had learned. "Babe, can you just stay right here."

Trap laughed at my comment 'cause he knew Jae wasn't going for that shit.

"Yuh a joke, right?" Her Patwha came out with a serious look on her face. "You know I am! The extra eyes won't hurt."

We checked our weapons one last time before we moved out.

"This shit gotta be quick!" I told my woman and brother.

"Leave no hearts beating," said Trap as he closed the car door.

The house was on a dead end on Linden by itself. A few feet from the door, a light turned on downstairs. We stopped to see what happened next.

"They have a sensor out this bitch, bruh." Trap relayed to me.

"I see." I whispered as a little nigga opened the front door.

Killing kids is not my style, but these little mufuckas are savages. They are trained to kill.

Boc! Boc! Boc! Boc! Boc!

The Mac 11 ripped his body apart.

I was scared as a mufucka for Jae. I wouldn't be able to live with myself in something happened to her.

A little nigga put his head out, and *BAM!* I watched Jae blow it off like it was nothing. Trapped looked at me and smiled. Her fucking aim was perfect. *Damn!*

We waited a few seconds to see if anyone was brave enough to come out, but nothing happened. I moved my hand up, signaling that we were going in blazing. I let the AR-15 rip and direct traffic for me.

Boc! Boc! Boc!

A little ugly mufucka ran down the steps leading to the upstairs area, busting his joint, he didn't get midway before his body rolled down the steps, headless, thanks to my aim. *These little bastards got heart.*

Blood paved the way as we stepped over his body. Trap kicked the body down the stairs when we climbed up. Jae was walking up the stairs backwards. Shorty was official with this murder shit. I was glad that she was on this trip with me now.

A bitch screamed and it caused us to stop. I moved my head to the left, letting Trap know that I was going that way, where I heard the noise. Jae was on my heels.

"Search the rest of the rooms up here, babe."

I kicked the door open to find a Spanish looking bitch sitting on the bed with her back against the headboard, holding a pillow between her legs at her chest. I'd seen the bitch before but I couldn't remember where.

"Please don't kill me!" She cried.

"Where the fuck is Yellow Man?"

"I don't know!"

I fired the Mac 11 up toward the ceiling, above her head. Her screams got ten times worse. "Where the fuck is that, nigga?" I asked again.

Her cries stopped as she lifted her head up, dusting the debris off of her.

"Nigga, I'm right here!" I felt the cold steel at the back of my head. "Drop the heat."

Fuck! I turned around with the pistol in my face to look the nigga dead in his eyes. "I came to collect mine, son."

"Drop them muthafuckas, B." He wanted me to release the guns from my hands. "I told you I wasn't the same nigga that you left out here."

I dropped the guns and smiled. "Show me then, pussy!" I pushed my forehead on the nose of his pistol.

Chapter 54
JAE

I searched all the rooms upstairs, finding nothing. I hadn't heard any more gunfire and I was wondering if Rocket killed the bitch.

"Fuck!"

I tiptoed out the room, wondering where the fuck was Yellow Man. That nigga hadn't showed his face, yet. I saw Trap from the balcony, downstairs, searching all the other rooms.

"Show me then, pussy!" I heard Rocket's voice. The door was open, so the second I turned the corner, I saw Yellow Man with a pistol in my man's face. "Nigga, you gonna pull the trigger or not, son!" Rocket barked as he looked past Yellow man.

I winked. "Pussyhole, put deh gun dun!" I said, putting both .40's at his head on my tiptoes.

"You heard the lady, B." Rocket smacked the gun away that Yellow Man had aimed at his forehead.

"Drop the gun, my youth!"

The nigga dropped the banger from his hand and I kicked it away as Rocket picked up his machines.

I saw a figure behind Rocket, crawling off the bed towards the gun, and my finger fucked the trigger.

Boc! Boc! Boc! Boc!

Two shots to the body before I hit her with two to the chest.

***

ROCKET

Seeing Jae behind Yellow Man had my adrenaline pumped up. My bitch was always on time.

"Son, I gave you enough time to pay up, now I'm here to collect."

Jae stepped from beside the nigga and took a spot beside me.

"Bruh, where was the nigga?" Trap asked as he joined the party.

"In this bitch, hiding somewhere."

"Ain't that Cuba's daughter on the bed?"

I heard Trap's words but it was too late; the bitch was dead.

"Oh well, 'em can get touch too." Jae said with a smile on her face.

"You have the money that you owe me, son?"

"I'd rather die than pay you shit!" Yellow Man said.

"Well, bow down then, nigga!" Jae's .40 spat, hitting the nigga in his ankles.

"Argggggh!" He screamed as he fell at my feet on his knees.

"Your choice!" I pulled the trigger on the Mac 11 and his body tore into pieces. Niggas wanted to act hard, so I let them bow.

We searched the closets and found a few duffle bags full of money.

***

I gave Trap a bag of money when we dropped him off at his hide out with the guns, and changed our clothes.

"Hit me first thing, bruh."

"Aite, son. Love you."

"Love you, too, nigga."

The ride home between me and Jae was silent. We knew a war was about to take place with Cuba's daughter's death.

Jae dashed out the car and into the house before I could cut the car off.

I ran in behind her, slamming the door behind me. "What's wrong?"

She hugged the toilet, throwing up. "I don't know."

"You scared?"

She picked her head up and rolled her eyes at me.

I laughed and let her handle her business. "I gotta go get my phone from the car!" I yelled as I headed out the front door.

I heard the tires screeching, but it was too late for me. I tried to turn back around and run, but a bullet caught me in my leg and slowed my movement. My body dropped as another bullet pierced my side, then my shoulder.

"Fuck!" I screamed from the pain. I was trying my hardest to pull myself to the door, when another bullet hit me in my chest, but I refused to just give up. I turned the door knob and then everything turned black.

Chapter 55
JAE

I hadn't had my period since Rocket came home, so I had to make sure I wasn't pregnant. I pulled the EPT pregnancy test from under the sink and I pissed on it. I watched the urine run and then the words appeared.

The sound of gunshots had me up and off the toilet. I dashed towards the front door, screaming Rocket's name. I turned the knob, but it was already open.

The sight in front of me had me on my knees. Blood was everywhere. I pulled Rocket's bloody body in the house as tears poured from my eyes.

"Babe," he coughed, and blood flew from his mouth.

"Shhh, babi, don't die on us."

His eyes popped open wider and I placed his bloody hand on my stomach. "I'm pregnant and you can't do this to me!"

I watched his eyes close, but I wasn't about to sit there and give up. I laid his body down and ran for my phone. "Rocket, please!" I begged when I was back at his side.

"911, what's your emergency?"

"My boyfriend has been shot! Please get, here!" I gave her the address as I held onto my man. I added pressure onto his chest with my spare hand. "Don't do this to us."

He opened his eyes.

"I love you."

"I love you, Jae." And then his eyes closed.

"Pray!" I heard my grandma's voice like she was standing beside me, and that's what I did.

Dear Father...

To Be Continued...

Blood Stains of a Shotta 2

Coming Soon

Coming Soon from Lock Down Publications/Ca$h Presents

BOW DOWN TO MY GANGSTA

By **Ca$h**

TORN BETWEEN TWO

By **Coffee**

BLOOD STAINS OF A SHOTTA **II**

By **Jamaica**

WHEN THE STREETS CLAP BACK

By **Jibril Williams**

STEADY MOBBIN

By **Marcellus Allen**

BLOOD OF A BOSS **V**

By **Askari**

BRIDE OF A HUSTLA **III**

By **Destiny Skai**

WHEN A GOOD GIRL GOES BAD **II**

By **Adrienne**

LOVE & CHASIN' PAPER **II**

By **Qay Crockett**

THE HEART OF A GANGSTA **III**

By **Jerry Jackson**

LOYAL TO THE GAME **IV**

By **T.J. & Jelissa**

A DOPEBOY'S PRAYER **II**

By **Eddie "Wolf" Lee**

IF LOVING YOU IS WRONG… **III**

By **Jelissa**

BLOODY COMMAS **III**

SKI MASK CARTEL

By **T.J. Edwards**

BLAST FOR ME **II**

By **Ghost**

A DISTINGUISHED THUG STOLE MY HEART **III**

By **Meesha**

ADDICTIED TO THE DRAMA **II**

By **Jamila Mathis**

LIPSTICK KILLAH

By **Mimi**

Available Now

RESTRAINING ORDER **I & II**

By **CA$H & Coffee**

LOVE KNOWS NO BOUNDARIES **I II & III**

By **Coffee**

RAISED AS A GOON I, II & III

By **Ghost**

LAY IT DOWN **I & II**

LAST OF A DYING BREED

By **Jamaica**

LOYAL TO THE GAME

LOYAL TO THE GAME II

LOYAL TO THE GAME III

By **TJ & Jelissa**

BLOODY COMMAS I & II

By **T.J. Edwards**

IF LOVING HIM IS WRONG…I & II

By **Jelissa**

A DISTINGUISHED THUG STOLE MY HEART I & II

By **Meesha**

PUSH IT TO THE LIMIT

By **Bre' Hayes**

BLOOD OF A BOSS **I, II, III & IV**

By **Askari**

THE STREETS BLEED MURDER **I, II & III**

THE HEART OF A GANGSTA I & II

By **Jerry Jackson**

CUM FOR ME

CUM FOR ME 2

CUM FOR ME 3

An **LDP Erotica Collaboration**

BRIDE OF A HUSTLA **I & II**

<u>THE FETTI GIRLS **I, II& III**</u>

By **Destiny Skai**

<u>WHEN A GOOD GIRL GOES BAD</u>

By **Adrienne**

<u>A GANGSTER'S REVENGE **I II III & IV**</u>

<u>THE BOSS MAN'S DAUGHTERS</u>

<u>THE BOSS MAN'S DAUGHTERS II</u>

<u>A SAVAGE LOVE **I & II**</u>

<u>BAE BELONGS TO ME</u>

<u>A HUSTLER'S DECEIT I, II</u>

By **Aryanna**

<u>A KINGPIN'S AMBITON</u>

<u>A KINGPIN'S AMBITION **II**</u>

<u>I MURDER FOR THE DOUGH</u>

By **Ambitious**

<u>TRUE SAVAGE</u>

<u>TRUE SAVAGE II</u>

<u>TRUE SAVAGE **III**</u>

By **Chris Green**

<u>A DOPEBOY'S PRAYER</u>

By **Eddie "Wolf" Lee**

<u>WHAT ABOUT US **I & II**</u>

<u>NEVER LOVE AGAIN</u>

<u>THUG ADDICTION</u>

By **Kim Kaye**

THE KING CARTEL **I, II & III**

By **Frank Gresham**

THESE NIGGAS AIN'T LOYAL **I, II & III**

By **Nikki Tee**

GANGSTA SHYT **I II &III**

By **CATO**

THE ULTIMATE BETRAYAL

By **Phoenix**

BOSS'N UP **I , II & III**

By **Royal Nicole**

I LOVE YOU TO DEATH

By Destiny J

I RIDE FOR MY HITTA

I STILL RIDE FOR MY HITTA

By **Misty Holt**

LOVE & CHASIN' PAPER

By **Qay Crockett**

TO DIE IN VAIN

By **ASAD**

BROOKLYN HUSTLAZ

By **Boogsy Morina**

BROOKLYN ON LOCK I & II

By **Sonovia**

GANGSTA CITY

By **Teddy Duke**

BOOKS BY LDP'S CEO, CA$H

TRUST IN NO MAN

TRUST IN NO MAN 2

TRUST IN NO MAN 3

BONDED BY BLOOD

SHORTY GOT A THUG

THUGS CRY

THUGS CRY 2

THUGS CRY 3

TRUST NO BITCH

TRUST NO BITCH 2

TRUST NO BITCH 3

TIL MY CASKET DROPS

RESTRAINING ORDER

RESTRAINING ORDER 2

IN LOVE WITH A CONVICT

Coming Soon

BONDED BY BLOOD 2

BOW DOWN TO MY GANGSTA

DEDICATIONS

Oswald- Papa, your unconditional love, support and presence have made me feel safe even in here. You are always there to support me with advice. I have not told you often enough how much I love you. I LOVE YOU.

Wilber- Whenever I talk to you, I feel protected and safe. You are my support. You are the joy of my life. It gives me a wonderful warm feeling to know that you love me no matter what. I LOVE YOU and thanks, daddy.

Tamaine Jr., son, I miss your warmth. You are the one that makes my life complete and who I count on to place a smile on my face during my sad days. I can't wait to be with you again. I LOVE YOU and I MISS YOU, know that.

Ca$h, you always find a solution for every obstacle that appears on the path of life. Your thoughtfulness is an inspiration to everyone around you. YOU are one in a million. Thank you for all you've done for me and mine. I LOVE YOU.
#DEATHB4DISHONOR#

ACKNOWLEDGMENTS

Lord, thank you. Thank you for your grace, your mercy, unconditional love and blessings. You're my light and salvation, so who shall I fear? NOBODY. This trip right here ain't nothing but a minor setback and even though I'm on it, I'm still standing with my toes flat and head above water because of YOU. Thank YOU. Protect me in your blood from my so-called friends, my enemies are light weight. I know how to handle them. Bless those that I carry close to my heart daily and abundantly. Artist: Boosie... Song: God Wants Me to Ball

Oswald James, when I was born, you took me under your wing, you loved me like you gave birth to me. Papa, I love you with all of my heart. You showed me how to kill my first animal, I'll never forget. I remember grandma saying, "Oswald, deh babi nuh need fi duh dat," lol. You brushed grandma words off because you wanted to learn firsthand and I DID. You've been my superman since I opened my eyes and you still are. I'm who I am because of YOU. I love you with every fiber in me, always and forever. Artist: Jeezy... Song: Forgive Me

Wilber James, daddy hearing you crying on the phone broke my heart into a million pieces. I know you're hurting because I'm locked up but don't worry. I'm way stronger than you know. I was born a gangsta from the sack, believe that. I'll never allow this journey to get me down. I am a James breed for life, so this isn't nothing to a G. I love you. Artist: Boosie & Jeezy... Song: Better Believe It

Tamaine Jr., son, I'm poooooo sorry that I'm not there to raise you, to see you off to school or kiss you good night. I am so sorry, you just don't even know. I love you, know that. I am proud of the little man that you're growing up to be. I can't wait to get home to you, but in the meantime, I want you to know that I carry you every day in my heart. I love you from my heart to the stars and back to my heart. Artist: Boosie... Song: I'm Sorry

Ca$h, I salute you for what you stand for, real talk. You are one of the realest nigga alive and in my life. No lie. You give me the truth, real and uncut all the time. Sometimes I wonder what planet you came from, LOL, but I am dead ass serious. You stay pushing me to the limit in everything that I do. I thank God for you every day, 'cause you know my struggle, you can relate to my pain and you see where I am trying to get to. If it wasn't for you, I wouldn't be able to feed my kids like I do and for that alone, I owe you nothing but LOYALTY until my casket drops. I love you. I get real emotional when it comes to the ones that I love and care for. You said it yourself, THUGS CRY 2. I'm telling you now, I'll go to war with you and for you. Artist: Jeezy... Song: Let Em Know

Cortez, I wish I could take all your troubles and turn them into confetti, then toss them so high into the air so they would fall back to earth on you as blessings. Hold ya head, ya pops got you, I know that. I'm riding with you too. I put that on my life and everything that I love. Artist: Jeezy... Song: Soul Survivor

A-Town, bruh, I know them succa ass niggaz happy that you're off the streets but what they don't realize is that they can't hold you forever. You know I'm trappin' with you no matter the time or the location. Only death can stop me. Keep ya head up and only down to pray. Your loyalty is that and for that I ask God to have mercy on ya. I love you, know that. Artist: Boosie ft Jeezy... Song: Mercy on My Soul

Terrell, Rex, what's good with you? I know it ain't easy, but you make it look easy. You are so positive and I admire that about you. Now let me get on ya back. I need you to get motivate and get that book complete, real talk. You've got ppl in ya corner that want nothing but the best for you and I'm one of them. I know you've heard it all before, but I'm riding this wave with you. Artist: Boosie... Song: My Struggle

AD, nigga I should be cussing you the hell out but I ain't gonna go there, not yet anyway. You know I'm the realest bitch to ever enter the game, what's understood doesn't need to be explain. You seen it first hand, the streets of Lynchburg had a hella hold on me, I couldn't shake it. I thought I was Lil Mizz Jeezy (LOL) but truth be told, I'm still Lil Mizz Jeezy but smarter. Hold ya head. Artist: Jeezy ft Jay Z...Song: Seen It All

Jamauri, Gotti Montana, you at the door now. By the time this book hit the stores, you'll have a month left. I heard everything that you said but with me action speaks for itself. Artist: Gotti... Song: Different

Jeremiah, Mr. Lynchburg(I hate that name, lol) no matter what I'm going to show you some love cuz you are a real nigga. Nobody can take that from you. You know me well, so you already know that them digits that they dumped on you ain't nothing to me. I'm going to ride with you, so tell ya ducks to stay in their lanes. Hold ya head and stay the HELL out of trouble. Artist: Boosie... Song: Wipe Me Down (Ya favorite)

Brad, I remember when I first touched the Burg, ya name was the name and it still is in my ears. I remember when I heard all that time that you got, it crushed me cause you had just had a seed. I didn't have to know you like that to know that you was going to stand firm. Judge tossed all that time at you and you didn't crumble. I remember that shit like it yesterday. I fucks with you the long way, know that. Hold ya head and if I touch before you, you'll see that loyalty is a must for me. Artist: Gotti... Song: I Remember

Nutz, who's city is it? Lol... You're a legend. I know that time is crazy but you making the best of it. Keep writing, that shit gonna pay off, trust me. Stay focus, stay strong. I ain't gotta tell you to stay real, you bleed that shit. Hold ya head and when I touch you'll see that there is still a real bitch alive. Artist: Jeezy... Song: J.E.E.Z.Y

Maurice, damn! What the hell. That shit is crazy, but hold ya head. Stay strong and real no matter what. Artist: Jeezy... Song: Who Dat

Antonio, Dee, whenever I think about ya time I get sad. I feel like WTF. Keep ya spirit up, you're a real nigga. I told you from day 1 only death can stop me from riding with you. Artist: Jeezy... Song: Trapped

Oshay and Dominique, I pray that everything works out for y'all in court. This ain't nothing but a minor set back for a major come back. VA, stand UP. Artist: Gotti... Song: Pay The Price

Marcus Miller, hold ya head my nigga. Real Recognize Real from a mile away. I'ma stay screaming ya name, till they free you. Artist: Jeezy... Song: Bottom Of The Map

Roderick aka Smells, you've got so much time in and you still the same-Real. I salute you. Hold ya head, they can't hold you forever. Artist: Boosie... Song: Get Em Boosie

Donald aka D'Mac, I pray that you'll learn from this journey and put ya skills to work. I'm not a fan of R&B, but I'll listen to yours. Keep ya head up. Artist: Boosie... Song: Heart Of A Lion

Cuben, hold ya head up, don't let this drag you down. Stay strong and prayed up. You're in my prayers. Artist: Boosie... Song: On Deck

Benny, hahaha, I bet you didn't think I was going to show you some love, my word is all I have my nigga. I live what I preach, you see it. You don't have that much longer to go. Stay strong, duck them haters and keep pushing. Artist: Jeezy... Song: Amazin'

Timothy aka CAKE, mane you've shown me that death before dishonor is real. Thank you. It doesn't mater what's going on with you or around you, you still show me and my two love. I recalled ya words from day one, "Loyalty is me" and I see and feel it with you. I can ask you for anything, you might scream for a second but before that minute is up, you giving me what I asked for. Yo, real talk, thank YOU. It ain't nothing but love and loyalty. Artist: Jeezy... Song: Never Settle

To all the dudes on the GREATEST label ever, LDP:

Ca$h, you know you ain't had to do the THUGS CRY series like that! I stayed up all damn night reading slow not wanting part 3 to end. Mon yuh a beast with dat ink. Yuh kill dat, Shotta!
Askari, them BLOOD OF A BOSS series had me up all night. I can't wait for part 4 to touch my hands. I know it's gonna be fya.
Aryanna, mane them HUSTLER'S DECEIT ain't nothing but the truth.
Asad, TO DIE IN VAIN had me in my feeling.
TJ Edwards, BLOODY COMMAS, mane you smoked that- Real talk.
Jerry Jackson, I truly enjoyed THE HEART OF A GANGSTA.
Eddie "Wolf" Lee, you definitely did ya thing with A DOPEBOY'S PRAYER.
Ghost, Yo them RAISED AS A GOON--- SPEECHLESS!
Frank Gresham, I loved the King Cartel.
Cato, I'm waiting for something else from you, but the GANGSTA SHYT series was dat.
Chris Green, you said it right: TRUE SAVAGE, that's your pen.
Bryan Ambitious, I love your flow.
Marcellus Allen, Jibril Williams and any other newcomers to the team. I know if Ca$I signed you, your game is official.
To the many QUEENS of LDP, the next one will me yours. I haven't forgotten you.
LOCK DOWN PUBLICATIONS and CA$H PRESENTS the REALEST!!! Artist: Jeezy... Song: By The Way

To my personal assistant Jessica, thank YOU. Anything you need done from behind the wall, they can do it for you and I mean anything, they 1hunnid. www.textingforyou.com ain't just a company, they are the truth. Add them to ya corrlinks---txt4unow@gmail.com and let them handle all your needs. Real talk, they are that!

To my FANS (Free and Caged up) without y'all, I just don't know. Thanks for the love and support. I promise that I'll never let y'all down. Without y'all there is no me. I LOVE Y'ALL, know and believe that...

To my favorite Rappers EVER, JEEZY and BOOSIE... I'ma add Yo Gotti too...

They gonna hate me for this: #WARRIORS... #NEW ENGLAND PATRIOTS...

To my sperm donor,
I've been waiting on this for some time. Now that it's here, I am gonna let you know how much of a bitch you are. You took me to the gates of hell with Tameia but you dragged me through hell with Tamaine Jr. Not once did I call the boyz or fold on you. You fought me in public, state pressed charges on you, but I lied just to save you. I wanted you to see the real in flesh plus that snitching shit ain't in my blood. I kept that shit so gutta with you on the strength of my kids. Rode every bid with you, sent green like it was growing on trees. That's not even the half, every morning at 8am without a license, I was in the parking lot outside Blue Ridge so you could see the kids from ya cell. Took pics of the kids, accepted every phone call like a phone company so you could talk to yours and the crazy part is, NOW you trying to stunt on my kids and those that care for them. I get it, fuck me, but when you screaming fuck my two, bitch, we have a problem. When my seeds cry 'cause you don't remember their birthdays or pay a visit or show them some love, nigga, we beefing. I'ma make you feel every tear drop that they shed. Take it how you wanna take it, when it comes to mine, you should already know. You call yaself a gangsta, you might wanna reconsider 'cause they can't hold me forever. I'ma show you first-hand that I might be a female but there's no bitch in my blood. Artist: Jeezy... Song: Get Ya Mind Right

Rest in Peace: SK1P, QUELL, JUSTIN, CHRIS AUSTIN, CHIEF, SWERVE, DRE, CLYDE, FIDGET, WHYTE MIKE, 50. If I missed a name, don't charge it to my heart... Gone but never FORGOTTEN

Feel Free to reach out to me and know that I'll hit you back.

Julian James #16692-084
Po Box A-B1
Alderson, WV, 24910

#FreeDaReal

Made in the USA
Middletown, DE
25 May 2018